VEILED SECRETS
Copyright © 2017 by Jodi Vaughn

Printed in the USA.

Interior Format

VEILED SECRETS

JODI VAUGHN

Madison,
There's a little Celeste in all of us!

CHAPTER ONE

Present Day
Atlanta, Georgia

CELESTE HART STARED UP AT the palatial mansion in front of her and fought back a sinister shiver that nearly stole her breath. Once she stepped inside there was no going back.

The mansion was bigger than any home she'd ever been in. Manicured shrubs and extensive flowers beds wound around the stone and brick building and the front doors were made of wrought iron and glass. Darkness had long descended on the Atlanta suburb and despite the streetlights, it was unusually dark. The darkness went deeper than just lack of stars and moonlight. The darkness seemed to be trying to settle across her flesh, seep into her skin, and soak into her very soul.

She couldn't help but think that once she dug out one secret, several more were bound to tumble out like an avalanche. Was she really prepared for the consequences of what she would discover tonight?

"I can't go inside wearing this. I look like a hooker," Celeste muttered to herself and tugged at the hem of her short red dress in a vain attempt to make it longer.

Should have known better than to buy something without trying it on. She hated shopping, much less trying something on to make sure it fit. Or in this case, didn't make her look like she'd just stepped off a back-alley street corner.

She didn't fit in here. The second she stepped through that door, everyone would know she didn't belong.

She gazed up at the huge mansion and shivered again, stunned and terrified by how closely the details of the house in front of her matched the details of the house in her dreams.

I need to find out what I am. I need to know the truth.

Ever since she'd been a little girl, she'd had dreams with visions of the future. It had been a dream that had led her here tonight. To this very house. She knew deep in her gut that the answers she'd sought all her life lay behind those heavy mansion doors.

According to her dream, somewhere within the mansion, there was a book that would explain, once and for all, *what* she truly was.

The time had come to find out. Whether she was good, bad, or evil.

"Just don't let me be evil." Her words melted into the dark night, and her chest tightened.

A gust of cool March wind licked across her bare skin. Her snug red dress and sky-high heels did nothing to guard against the spring breeze. In the distance she swore she heard the howl of a wolf.

She shook her head and looped the strap of her

clutch over her wrist. Rubbing her hands up and down her arms, reminding herself that no wolves lived in the city.

She looked around in the dark at all the parked BMWs, Audis, and Mercedes. The other guests had long since arrived and were inside enjoying the party. She, however, was late.

"It's now or never." Before she could change her mind, she reached out and pressed the doorbell. A melodious chime bellowed behind the massive wood and wrought-iron doors. Her heart raced inside her chest. There was no turning back now.

The large doors swung open without a sound.

Her gaze drifted up to meet the intense glare of a large bald man dressed in black with the word "Security" stamped in white across the front of his skin-tight shirt. In his enormous hand he held a clipboard.

"Invitation," he barked.

She blinked. Her body froze, unable to follow the simple command.

"I need to see your invitation," he reiterated.

"Yes, of course." She opened her clutch and fished out a crisp linen invitation for his inspection.

His pinched gaze studied the invitation before he glanced back at her.

"Your name, please."

Her stomach plummeted.

He wouldn't find her name on the guest list. The invitation had been placed in her box at work by mistake.

She was caught, like a rat in a trap. If she left now, her boss would find out that she'd tried to crash the party. He was probably filming her right now with some sort of satellite imaging. Lord knew, the Nordstroms were among the world's richest families.

"Celeste Hart." She smoothed her hand across her dress. Her words sounded hollow between her ears. Not at all confident like she wanted them to sound.

His gaze scanned his clipboard before he lifted his eyes back to her.

"Your name is not on the guest list. This party is for employees of Cryptic only." His brows furrowed, and he took a step toward her.

"I *am* an employee. I work in development, specializing in operating systems." That much was true. She fumbled with her sequined clutch, and dug out her badge.

He leaned forward as he studied the laminated name badge and then glanced back at her.

"This party is only for employees who have been with the company for at least a year."

"I've been with the company right at a year last month. My manager said they were adding me to the list." She forced a smile, hoping he would buy the lie, hook, line and sinker.

She cleared her throat. Several seconds of silence seemed to stretch out on a thin thread, a thread that threatened to snap any second.

He stepped back and waved her inside with the clipboard.

She blinked.

"Well, are you coming in or not?" He cocked his head as if he was considering retracting the offer.

She forced her feet across the threshold before he could change his mind.

Two steps inside, she froze. The click of her red stiletto heels silenced against the luxurious marble floor.

Her stomach quivered.

The enormous ballroom had walls of rich maple paneling and beautiful marble floors. The coffered ceilings were detailed white inlay, and several large crystal chandeliers cast the room in a magical glow. The tables were decorated with white linen tablecloths, matching white candles, and lush floral center pieces.

The room looked exactly like the one in her dream.

She pressed her hand to her quivering stomach and took a deep breath to steady her nerves.

In that moment, she knew she was meant to be there. It was the confirmation she needed.

The strains of a slow song drifted through the room from the band playing in the corner. Lavish decorations in neutral tones carried the theme of elegance through the room. Even the beautiful couples seemed to be part of the flawless landscape. It was apparent that no expense had been spared for the party.

Despite the impeccable beauty, an undercurrent of the macabre enveloped her.

I need to find that book. She needed to know she wasn't some kind of evil freak. And if she was, well, she'd have to deal with that too.

Her gaze sifted through men in crisp black tuxes and women in dazzling gowns, laughing and eating and dancing like they didn't have a care in the world.

Were they like her?

She shivered and clenched her sweaty palms.

She scanned the crowd again and frowned. Odd. There wasn't a single familiar face from work.

Then again, it was a big company, and she wasn't exactly a social butterfly. For once, not having a lot of friends would work in her favor.

If no one from work recognized her, then no one would realize she didn't belong.

A large door across the hall drew her attention. A tall, elegant floral arrangement rested in front of it, an obvious sign the room was off-limits to visitors.

A perfect place to hide the book.

"You look very beautiful, my dear."

Celeste turned toward the matronly voice dripping with a Southern smile.

An older woman was dressed in a silver gown and had perfectly styled white hair. Shimmering diamonds dripped from her neck, wrists, and fingers.

"Thank you." Celeste glanced down at her dress and clutched her purse to her chest. "It was on sale."

The woman's smile fell. Something flashed across the woman's face, something wrong.

"If you'll excuse me." Celeste turned to make her escape, but the woman's bony hand caught her elbow.

"Listen and listen well." The woman's eyes narrowed and her fingers tightened around Celeste's arm.

"You're hurting me." Fear slithered up Celeste's spine and settled at the base of her neck.

This was all wrong. She hadn't seen this. This hadn't happened in her dream.

The woman leaned closer, her withered lips twisted in a sneer. "Celeste Hart, you shall know the bite of betrayal and your heart will splinter within your chest. There shall be no respite from your loneliness and no end to your heartache. You shall watch as your blood gushes like a red stream upon the altar until the grave claims your body."

Images of every horror movie she'd ever watched flashed through her head.

"Let go of me." She tried to yank her arm free, but the woman's grip was steel-like.

Shaking with fear, she looked up into the woman's face.

CHAPTER TWO

THE OLD WOMAN'S EYES FLASHED from gray to white like lightning. Her teeth changed and lengthened, protruding from her mouth like a shark's. The diamonds around her neck turned to spiky barbed wire and punctured her wrinkled flesh. Blood oozed and trailed down, staining the front of her dress.

"You, Celeste Hart, are marked for death." Her lips curled back over her disgusting teeth in a predatory smile.

Celeste's heart raced and she frantically glanced around, but no one looked in their direction. No one seemed to be paying attention to them.

How could no one else see the monster in the room?

Adrenaline pulsed through her body and flooded her veins. She twisted her body and brought her heel down on the old bat's peep-toe shoe.

The woman howled in pain and released her hold.

Celeste bolted toward the hallway, determined to put distance between her and the crazed lady.

Sucking in quick breaths, she glanced over her shoulder to make sure the woman wasn't following her.

Distracted, she slammed into something hard and unmoving. Thrown off-balance, she threw out her hands, groping for something to steady her. Two strong arms wrapped around her and pulled her into a wall of compressed muscle.

She looked up.

Eyes the color of the Mediterranean Sea stared back at her.

Eric Nordstrom.

The CEO of Cryptic, notorious womanizer, and, most importantly, her boss.

Her heart sputtered. She could feel the heat crawling into her face.

Getting thrown out of the party didn't seem like a bad idea anymore.

"Are you okay, Celeste?" His warm hands slid from her back down her arms, sending a thrum, palpable and strong, through her body.

She sucked in a breath, shocked that her body reacted from his simple touch. She'd never felt such a strong reaction before.

"I'm fine." She stepped out of his embrace and pressed a hand to her stomach. "How do you know my name?"

People didn't notice her. They never did. It was how life had always been. Never seen, never acknowledged.

"I asked my uncle who you were." His blue eyes narrowed. "Are you sure you're okay? You look a little flushed."

"I'm fine. It's just a little stuffy in here." She took

in his intimidating frame and gave him a sheepish smile.

His concern expression relaxed and shifted. A slow smirk played at the corners of his beautiful lips. "It does seem to have gotten quite…warm."

His deep seductive voice sent her heart careening out of control.

What the hell was wrong with her? She was here on a mission to find that book. She wasn't here to flirt. She didn't even know how to flirt.

She brushed a nervous hand across her plunging neckline. Her fingertips skimmed bare skin. She hadn't thought the dress too sexy when she'd bought it, but the way his eyes slid over her body made her wish she'd worn something more modest.

Again, one more reason to try the stupid dress on before buying it.

She brushed her long blond hair forward, attempting to cover her bare skin from his penetrating gaze.

"Are you enjoying yourself?" His eyes sparkled as he kept his gaze locked on hers.

She glanced over her shoulder for the old woman but she was gone. Maybe she had imagined the whole thing. Maybe the stress of crashing a party had made her hallucinate.

"Yes, I am. It's a lovely party." She looked back at him and felt heat rise in her cheeks.

"Very lovely, indeed." His eyes lingered a little too long on her mouth.

Why was he looking at her mouth? Did she have something on her lips?

She wanted to sink into the floor. She never

should have eaten that cookie in the car. Damn her emotional eating. She dipped her tongue to the corners of her lips, trying to subtly retrieve any cookie crumbs, but she didn't feel any…

His nostrils flared and he lifted his gaze from her lips. "Are you here alone?" His voice was harsh and gruff.

"Yes."

"You don't have a date? I find that hard to believe."

Her lungs squeezed tight. Was he on to her? Was everyone required to bring a date?

She should have paid more attention to the details on the invitation instead of worrying about if they would let her in.

A waiter with a platter full of champagne paused in front of her. "Champagne?"

"Thank you." She selected a crystal flute and lifted it to her lips, thankful for the interruption. The sensation of cold bubbles burst on her tongue and tickled her dry throat. She closed her eyes. It might not be a cookie, but she would take what she could get to calm her nerves.

She opened her eyes and her smile slipped.

"Were you expecting me to be gone?" He flashed a quick grin, one of those grins that turned women into gooey puddles on the floor. It was a grin that no man had ever used on her.

"Yes." She winced. His mocking tone had somehow pulled the truth out of her. "I mean, I know you have a lot of people to speak to, since it's your party."

"This is my uncle's home, technically it's his party." He tilted his head. "He should be the one making the rounds."

"Oh." She glanced around, her gaze settling once again on the closed door. There was no way she was getting into that room with him standing here. The longer he stayed, the more he distracted her. It was a feeling she wasn't used to.

"I didn't realize you were still in Atlanta. I thought you just came in for the board meeting." She took another sip of champagne.

"My uncle invited me to stay a few days before I return to Vermont. He's the only family I have, so I agreed." He shrugged. "Plus it gives me the opportunity to see how this office is performing." He leaned in and the scent of his sandalwood and ocean cologne wrapped her in a sensual kiss. "If you have any complaints about my Uncle Stephen, feel free to let me know."

"I really like my job." She cleared her throat and tried to concentrate. "You won't hear me complaining."

The corners of his sensual lips lifted toward the ceiling.

Her stomach warmed.

How can one man be so gorgeous?

She tucked a strand of hair behind her ear and tried to think of something witty to say. "I hear New England is very beautiful in the fall." Perfect. She was engaging in conversation about the weather.

"It is. I don't know how you Southerners manage to make it through winter without a white Christmas." He sighed as if he were remembering holidays. "It would drive me insane not to have snow every year."

Nervous laughter bubbled passed her lips.

His smile grew.

Okay, it was official. He thought she was an idiot.

"Have you ever been to New England?"

"No, I haven't." She studied her high heels before looking back at him. She'd never been outside Georgia.

"You must visit sometime."

Surprised by the sincerity in his voice, she faltered, unsure of what to say.

"You really didn't bring a date?" He looked over her shoulder, scanning the room.

She followed his gaze to see who he was looking at. Not seeing anyone, she turned back to him. "No. Did you?"

"I didn't bring a date either." His gaze rested on hers.

"Right. The CEO without a date?" She snickered.

"Baffling, isn't it?" He cocked his head and let a smile play at the corners of his lips.

"I'm sorry, I shouldn't have said that." She grimaced. Why didn't he just leave her alone? God knew what was going to come out of her mouth next.

"Why don't I give you a tour of my uncle's home?" He held out his arm.

She glanced down at his offered elbow. Excitement, unease, and anxiety filled her chest and tumbled her thoughts.

"Unless you're afraid to be alone with me."

Her face heated with embarrassment.

His smile faltered. "I've heard the rumors,

Celeste, and I promise I won't bite. Don't believe everything you hear."

CHAPTER THREE

HER BREATH QUICKENED. A TINGLE of excitement shot through her stomach like a current of electricity.

"I really shouldn't. It's not appropriate." She was here to find that book, not to flirt with the sexiest man alive.

"I understand." Hurt flashed through his eyes before he shuttered his expression. "I hope you enjoy the rest of your evening." He nodded, gave her a polite smile, and turned to leave.

What if she went off alone and ran into the crazy lady again? He knew this place better than she did. He might even lead her to the book.

"On second thought, I would love a tour."

He smiled and offered his arm. She rested her hand in the crook of his arm. What could possibly happen?

The instant she touched him thrumming heat shot through her body. She gasped. The strange thrumming intensified, like gentle electricity flooding every cell of her system with desire.

Their gazes met. Something flickered in his eyes

and she wondered if he felt it to

She took a deep breath and tried to calm her racing heart, but it was impossible with his cologne coiling around her like satin ribbon.

His scent made her want to do wicked things, things she had never done before. It made her want to do things like lick his neck.

Was he even aware how irresistible he smelled? Of course he was. It was probably European cologne containing some kind of panty-dropping pheromone to make even the most intelligent women lose their heads. And their underwear.

He lifted another glass of champagne from a passing waiter and changed out her empty flute.

"Thank you." She took a sip before he escorted her out of the room and into the hallway.

She stopped at the closed door.

"Is something wrong?" His brow creased and he looked down at her.

"Are we not going in there?" She waved her hand toward the closed door.

"It's just the library."

Exactly where the book would most likely be kept.

"I thought you were going to give me the full tour." She blinked.

"I will. But there is something I want you to see first." His eyes twinkled as a devilish grin played at the corners of his beautiful mouth.

"Okay." No need to make him suspicious by pressing the issue.

Eric led her down a long hallway filled with portraits of the Nordstrom family. Each of the aristocratic males had the same blond hair and icy blue eyes that seemed to follow her and bore into her soul.

He stopped at a set of large French doors leading outside.

"Let's start the tour here." He flung open the doors and stepped aside to allow her through.

She stepped into the brisk Southern night and fought a shiver.

The entire backyard - trees, shrubbery, and statues - were wrapped in white fairy lights and dangling clear crystals. The enormous kidney shaped pool glittered like jewels under the colored lights and gentle splash of the waterfall. The three outdoor living areas were adorned with white candles that cast a mystical and enchanting glow.

"It's breathtaking." While the inside of the house had an elegant but oppressive air, the ambience outside was light, cozy and inviting.

"I had a feeling you'd like it." He stepped behind her, his hot breath grazed her shoulder.

She felt the heat radiate off his body and burn into her back. Her breathing increased.

He was much too close.

The echo of approaching footsteps made her take a quick step away. She pressed her hand to her neck and tried to calm her fast beating heart and restrain her emotions. She needed to remain in control and stay on task.

"Sir. This is from the lady inside." A waiter carrying a silver tray with a single glass of scotch stopped in front of them. A thin line of perspiration glistened on the top of his lip and his Adam's apple bobbed while he swallowed.

The disappointed breath slid out of her lungs.

From under her lashes, she noticed Eric level a glare at the waiter before lifting the drink from the tray. The intimidated waiter scurried into the mansion like a rat racing for cover.

"It sounds like someone's looking for you. Maybe you should go back inside." She lifted her chin and tried to sound confident. She should have known there would be other woman seeking out his attention. Someone more elegant, who truly fit in here.

"I'm enjoying the company out here." He shoved a hand into his pants pocket and lifted the glass to his lips. He took a sip, his gaze never leaving hers.

She nodded at his scotch and changed the subject. "I don't know how you drink that stuff. It doesn't look very appealing." She shuddered. But she wasn't much of a drinker at all. Her two glasses of champagne was a new record.

"It's an acquired taste." He set his glass on a nearby table. "Let me show you the pool house. It's the most recent addition." He held out his hand.

She pressed her lips together, willing her voice into a nonchalance she didn't feel. "And then will you show me the library?"

"Why are you intent on seeing the library? It's the most boring room in the house." His eyes narrowed as he studied her.

Now she'd done it. Her insistence obviously made him suspicious.

She cleared her dry throat.

"I'm a voracious reader. Always have been. A library is my most favorite room in a house." That much was true. Books had been her friend all through her childhood and on into adulthood.

"Pool house first and then I will show you the blasted library." He laughed.

She smiled and placed her hand in his hand. The second they touched, the thrum was back, like a slow and sensual burn.

He opened the door to the pool house and waved her inside.

An ornate four poster bed sat in the middle of the living area.

Her mouth dropped and she let go of his hand.

"I think you've gotten the wrong idea about me." She shot him a glare.

"It was my uncle's idea." He held his hands up and chuckled. "He wanted a bed in the middle of the room, so guests could see the waterfall as they drifted off to sleep. I have no hidden agenda, I swear."

She turned and looked out the glass doors. He was right. It provided a perfect view of the waterfall.

"I wanted to show you the art, not the bed, Celeste. I swear." His voice matched the sincerity in his expression.

She glanced around the room. Her gaze locked on famous painting consisting of blues and purples and greens. One that was obviously not a copy. "Is that a Monet?"

"Yes."

"Is it real?" She looked from the painting back to him.

"Yes."

Her mouth dropped open.

"You should see the Van Gogh in his bedroom." Eric stepped closer. Heat radiated from his hard body and seared into her back. She squeezed her eyes shut and tried to fight the hot flames of desire licking the pit of her stomach.

"You know your art." His breath was but a caress on her shoulder. "I'm impressed."

"I minored in art in college." She needed to leave, to turn around and walk out the door before something happened. "I didn't want to be a starving artist, so I majored in computers."

"Smart girl."

Something in his gaze held her rooted to the floor and made her warm all over.

"Would you like to dance?"

Her stomach quivered. Dancing would be good. Dancing would happen inside with the other guests. Dancing would be safe.

"Sure." She moved toward the door but his hand caught her arm. He spun her around in his arms and held her tight.

"Not inside. Dance with me here."

CHAPTER FOUR

THE THRUM FROM HIS TOUCH rushed through her body, like a heated wave, pulling her under and making her want something more. The undeniable pull toward him was something she couldn't explain. From his heated gaze, she knew he felt it too.

She relaxed in his strong embrace, letting herself rest in his confident strength. Slowly they began to move, swaying to the music spilling out from the party into the backyard.

"You look beautiful." His warm breath sent goose bumps skipping across her skin like a rock across a lake's surface.

He nudged her chin up with his fingertips, his thumb grazing her bottom lip. Her heart fluttered against her ribs.

Seconds ticked away into eternity and the air grew too thick to breathe.

He lowered his head. His lips covered hers in a soft caress of a kiss. A gentle kiss that left her yearning.

She melted as intense pleasure rippled through

her, heating her body to a thousand degrees. Her palms slid up his chest and she tightened her fingers in the lapels of his tux.

"Eric," she moaned against his mouth.

He groaned at the sound of his name and deepened the kiss. He slipped his tongue between her lips, tasting and teasing and tempting.

Somewhere in the deep recesses of her mind, a tiny voice whispered for her to stop, that this was a huge mistake. But as she pressed herself against him and slipped her arms around his neck, those whispers faded like wisps of smoke into the night.

Without breaking the kiss, he lifted her off her feet and walked over to the door. The audible click of the lock tumbled into place followed by the rustle of the shades being lowered, quickened her heart beat. The only sound in the room, their breathing.

His hand slid down her back, pressing her farther into his hard chest and modeling her body against his.

Her nipples pebbled at the heat of his body.

He moved his mouth from hers and trailed hot kisses down to her neck, murmuring sweet words between flicks of his tongue across her fevered skin.

She arched against him, needing to be closer, needing something more.

The soft sound of metal teeth separating, the sound of a zipper, her zipper, seemed loud in the small room.

Good girls don't do this, her mother's voice echoed in her head.

Maybe she wasn't a good girl. Maybe she was a bad girl. A really, really, really bad girl.

Right now, she really didn't care.

He cupped her face between his hands and pressed his forehead against hers. His hot breath caressed her face and his heated gaze bore straight into her.

"Celeste, if you don't want this, tell me now." His gravely words made her heart tumble faster while his gaze searched her face for any doubts.

"I don't usually do this. I mean I never do this." She licked her dry lips. "I don't know what's gotten into me."

"I've never wanted a woman as bad as I want you." He breathed.

His smoldering gaze made her feel something she had never experienced before. The way his gaze consumed her made her desired, made her feel seen.

"Just tell me what you want and I'll do it." Desire burned in his gaze and saturated his voice, making him even more beautiful.

"Don't stop. I don't want you to stop," she whispered.

His eyes flashed and he brought his mouth down across hers, kissing her hard and deep.

Desire, swift and forceful, flooded her veins, and she ground her pelvis against his erection.

He groaned and swept his hand across her shoulders down to her back. Fingertips trailed downward to her hips. The swishing sound of material pooling on the floor made her catch her breath. He stepped back and ran his gaze down her body.

"God, you're beautiful." His dilated gaze swept across her nearly naked body.

He swung her up in his arms, she tightened her

arms around his neck, never wanting to let go. He carried her to the bed and gently laid her down.

She couldn't take her eyes off him as he tugged off his clothes in a rush. Seconds later he stood before her naked.

Her chest squeezed with desire and fear.

He was like nothing she'd ever seen before. From his broad shoulders to his flat, defined stomach, he looked like a male model. She dropped her gaze lower and her breath caught in her chest.

Oh, god. Were all men this big?

"I won't hurt you." He settled his knee on the bed and crawled toward her, like a lion stalking its prey until he hoovered over her body.

Lust so intense shot through her and spread to a dull ache between her legs. He had awakened something in her she didn't think she could ever tame.

She opened her mouth under his kiss letting his tongue slide against hers. He tasted hot and spicy and domineering. All things she didn't like, but suddenly found herself drawn to.

He found her bra clasp. A few seconds later he threw the bra over his shoulder. He released her lips and sat back and hooked his thumbs in the sides of her panties and pulled. They joined the bra on the floor.

He slid his hand from her knees across hers legs up between her thighs and cupped her wet heat. His fingers teased with soft caresses building her pleasure with each torturous stroke.

"Don't stop." She grabbed his wrist and held it against her.

"You feel so good, Celeste." His dilated gaze

stared down at her while he teased her with his talented fingers.

She moaned and arched off the bed. Pleasure roared through her as fierce and out of control as any wildfire. She squirmed beneath him. What was happening to her? She didn't crave . . . didn't need to be so close.

When their gazes met her heart almost stopped at the intensity in his eyes. He covered her body with his, and their lips met in a fiery kiss. She slid her hands across his shoulders, her nails digging into his flesh as he settled between her thighs.

"I need to tell you something." She whispered as his mouth found her nipple. She moaned as his tongue flicked over the taut peak sending her thoughts careening.

"You taste so sweet." He pushed her legs wider while his lips brushed across her nipple.

Without warning he entered her in one swift motion.

Pain sliced between her legs, every muscle in her body rebelled against the invasion.

He froze above her. His wide-eyed gaze bore into hers. "You're . . ."

"A virgin." She slammed her eyes shut and swallowed the pain. She shifted to ease the sting.

"God, no. Don't move," he hissed. A single bead of sweat dripped from his temple and rolled between her breasts.

The pain ebbed away while another sensation began to grow. Hot thick pleasure rippled between her legs and spread through her body.

"I'll go." Eric stared down at her, his jaw clenched.

Celeste hooked her ankles around his legs and

pulled him closer. The friction of skin against skin intensified her pleasure. "No. Don't go."

"Are you sure?" His body trembled. The strain in his voice reached his eyes.

"God, yes. This feels incredible." She pulled his mouth down to hers.

He kissed her long and deep, their tongues caressing in a wicked dance.

He thrust inside her slow and deliberate.

"I'm not hurting you, am I?"

"No. Don't stop."

He pulled out and then thrust deeper. His tongue mimicked the movement, leaving her breathless and wanting something more.

His tongue licked and nibbled her neck until she clawed at his back like a feral cat.

His hips thrust faster and deeper. She arched up, meeting his thrust for thrust.

Pleasure built between her legs, something delicious and powerful. She ground her hips against his. Liquid pleasure spread through her, like melted caramel, as she exploded into her first orgasm.

Eric shuddered, held her close, and plunged inside her one last time, finding his own release.

Why had she waited this long to have sex? If she had known it would feel this good, she would have cashed in her V card years ago.

When he rolled to his side her gaze traveled down the length of his muscular body. Her insides throbbed, craved and needed more. She lowered her gaze down further.

Her heart dropped like a stone in a river. Fantasy quickly faded like early morning mist, leaving behind the clear dread of reality.

Oh, god, what had she just done?

CHAPTER FIVE

Eight weeks later...

"WHY ARE YOU BRINGING UP Celeste Hart again? I thought after the first fifty conversations on this topic we were done." Eric narrowed his eyes at his Uncle Stephen as he spat out the words. God knows he was done talking about it.

"You can have any woman you want, but you go and screw an employee. What the hell were you thinking?" Stephen thundered. He stuck his finger in his collar and worried his tie with his fingers until it hung loose around his neck like a noose.

Eric shifted in the leather chair and glanced around his uncle's library refusing to take blame for something that was consensual. His gaze locked on a family portrait hanging on a nearby wall. His parents' gaze stared back at him with harsh condemnation.

If they had survived the car crash, he was sure his father would remind him what a fucked up son he turned out to be.

He swallowed, remembering the stench of gasoline and the pain that had bolted through his body before he'd kicked open the door and crawled out of the wreckage, leaving his parents trapped in the twisted metal. Desperate to get them out of the wreck he'd grabbed the side of the car, rolled and righted it.

How he'd accomplished such a feat still mystified him.

He touched his face, remembering the intense heat and the pain of being knocked backward as the car exploded into a fiery mass.

All his physical scars had healed. The scars on his soul still hurt.

For the millionth time he wished his parents had lived and he had died.

He looked away and caught his uncle's last few words.

"Is that what she's saying, that I sexually harassed her?" How could he explain that his attraction to Celeste Hart had been addictive, that he could feel her, hell, he could hear her blood pulsing in his own veins? The pull of wanting her had intensified after they had stepped outside, like some kind of sexual magnet.

His uncle sighed and steeple his hands together on the desk. "I've not talked to her. Not since I found you two in the pool house. She's not been back to work either. She used up all her vacation time and is now using her sick time as well."

"Maybe she's just embarrassed. She's probably waiting until I go back to Vermont before she comes back to work." He ran his hand through his hair. The morning after the party he had planned to get on his jet and fly home, not get involved in the acquisition of another company that had needed his attention and presence in Atlanta for the last eight weeks.

His uncle rubbed the back of his neck and looked away.

"Uncle Stephen, what are you not telling me?" Unease curled in his gut.

"You're not going to like it." Stephen pressed his palms onto the ornate desk and eased back in his chair.

"I don't like any of it. Now spit it out." Eric leaned forward.

"The board decided to keep you on suspension for another month." Stephen sighed.

"What?" Anger exploded like a gasoline fire through his veins.

"They want to make sure there are no more," Stephen cleared his throat and leveled a hard gaze at Eric. "Indiscretions."

Eric stood. His fists met the solid desk in an ear-splitting echo. "It's my fucking company."

"It was your father's company. You put that in jeopardy when you tangled with that oil baron's daughter."

Nausea rose in the back of his throat at the reminder. He prayed that his situation with Celeste didn't turn into another Elizabeth Humphries nightmare. His one-night stand with Elizabeth had ended with her falsely accusing him of rape.

The board had placed him on suspension while they and the police conducted a thorough investigation. They'd tried to keep it out of the papers but to no avail. Then in no uncertain terms they informed him that if he were found guilty he would lose his position as CEO.

After three months of pure hell, he had been found innocent.

Apparently, in the eyes of the board members he was still a liability.

If they ever found out about Celeste, if she ever went public, he'd lose his company, this time for good.

Uncle Stephen cleared his throat. "There's more."

"Of course there is." Eric crossed his arms over his chest.

"Celeste's parents contacted me. They asked to meet with you."

CELESTE FOLLOWED THE STOIC BUTLER down the hall to the library. Her ballerina style shoes cast no echo on the marble floor. Her footsteps, like her, were invisible.

She cast a warning glance at her parents who walked silently behind her.

Stephen Nordstrom's library. The one room she had desperately tried to get into the night of the party, was now the last place she wanted to be.

Eric would be in there waiting for this meeting. She'd wanted to speak with him alone, but her overbearing parents insisted being present.

The truth was they didn't think she could handle it by herself. And in the end, she had been too emotionally drained to fight them.

Nausea, swift and bitter, rolled across her stomach as she entered the room and spotted Eric. He turned from where he was standing at the window.

His emotionless gaze met hers for a brief second before he turned away.

Pain lanced across her heart at his quick dismissal. Old childhood wounds broke open.

Once again, she was discarded.

She was the girl no one picked at recess. She was the girl never voted anything in high school. She was the girl no one remembered.

She grimaced as she caught a glimpse of her reflection in a large gilded mirror. The makeup didn't conceal the dark circles under her eyes. She had spent the last few weeks in restless sleep dreaming of horrible creatures. Since the night they'd made love, she couldn't stop dreaming.

And lately her dreams were all nightmares.

"Please sit." Stephen Nordstrom motioned to three leather chairs on one side of a large expensive desk. She eased into the middle chair and clasped her hands together while keeping her gaze ahead.

Blaring silence filled the room and she was sure they could hear her heartbeat drumming in her chest.

She shouldn't have let her parents come with her. She should have made them stay out of her business. She didn't have it in her to hurt their feelings and some part of her knew they only wanted to protect her.

But now, sitting here, she didn't feel protected. Instead she found it suffocating.

She fought every instinct in her body that told her to bolt. She had been a fool to think their one night together had actually meant something to him.

She inhaled and focused on the task at hand. She

would tell Eric the truth.

After that, she was sure he'd never want to see her again.

CHAPTER SIX

ERIC KEPT HIS EXPRESSION NEUTRAL despite the restlessness gnawing in his gut while Stephen made the formal introductions of Celeste's parents, Ben and Sarah Hart. Like all his enemies, he needed to study them to see what he was up against.

Sarah Hart was a slightly older version of Celeste, blond and beautiful with those same stunning green eyes that her daughter possessed. Ben Hart was tall, ruggedly handsome with brown eyes and matching hair. Both parents greeted him with looks of repugnance and offense.

He eased into a chair, lifted his chin and crossed his arms over his chest He needed to keep his anger in check and keep his wits about him.

If they were here to blackmail him, they were in for a big surprise. There was no way in hell he was losing his company.

Unable to resist, his gaze flickered over at Celeste. He felt her parents' glare but he couldn't look away. Not yet.

She didn't attempt to make eye contact with him,

except for the brief moment when she entered the room. Instead, she sat with her hands in her lap and looked straight ahead.

It startled him how pale she appeared. Dark circles marred the delicate skin under her eyes and her lips were white. She had even lost weight, making her slim body appear fragile.

For someone trying to blackmail him, she sure wasn't presenting a confident front.

Ben Hart dropped a brown folder on the office desk and sat across from him.

"What's this?" Every muscle in his body tensed. His mind raced, imagining the extravagant amount of money they would be demanding.

"Before you look at what's in that file, Mr. Nordstrom, let me just say that we are seeking what is best for Celeste." Ben Hart sat forward in the chair, his gaze razor sharp and hard.

Eric held the man's stare, refusing to look away.

"Of course, Mr. Hart, I certainly understand. I've no children of my own, but . . ." His Uncle Stephen, ever the peacemaker, gave the family a contrite smile.

"We are not here for you to blow smoke up our asses," Ben Hart snarled.

Celeste visibly paled and lowered her gaze.

Eric clenched his jaw. He knew it. The Harts had probably Googled him to find out his net worth.

"Nordstrom. That's a Finnish name, isn't it?" Ben's voice dripped with obvious distaste.

"No, it's Scandinavian."

"The Vikings. How appropriate. Descended from barbarians, I see." Ben scorched him with a glare of pure unfiltered hatred.

He sucked in a deep breath to calm his anger. "Mr. Hart, I'm sure you didn't request a meeting to discuss my genealogy. We are here to deal with a situation."

"We wouldn't have a situation if you would've kept your hands off my daughter."

His thin thread of restraint snapped and anger exploded in his chest. "I don't know what she's told you but your daughter was just as willing. I didn't force her to do a damn thing. In fact, you should have seen the scratches she left on my back."

"You son of a bitch!" Ben jumped to his feet, sending his chair tumbling onto the Persian rug.

Eric pierced Celeste with a glare, waiting for her to deny everything.

Instead she buried her face in her hands.

Guilt gnawed at his gut. Why didn't she say something? Try to deny it? It would make hating her much easier.

"You will regret what you've done." Ben leaned over the desk and jabbed his finger at him.

Eric stood and faced the father. "Let's cut right to it, shall we? How much money do you want? Isn't that what's in the folder? Your asking price?"

"Money? Money means nothing to me." Ben's eyes widened and he lifted his chin. "People like you always try to escape the consequences of their actions. Sorry to tell you Viking, but there are always consequences."

"Let's just calm down, shall we?" Stephen cleared his throat and rested a restraining hand on Eric's shoulder.

"Stop it. Both of you." Celeste stood and faced her father.

All eyes fell on her and the room went quiet.

Celeste faced him, sadness etched into the corners of her eyes. "I'm pregnant."

No one moved. No one said a thing.

"And before you ask, yes, it's yours." Her voice faltered but her gaze never wavered from his.

Blood rushed from his face and pooled into a nauseating puddle in his stomach. His legs threatened to buckle.

Pregnant? That couldn't be possible.

"But don't worry. It's not your money I'm after." She lifted her chin.

"Then what's in the folder?" He glanced down at the envelope and frowned. He didn't trust a thing she was saying.

"It's the legal paperwork for you to sign forfeiting all parental rights. By signing those papers, you agree never to see or contact my child, or me, again."

The weight of all their stares bore down on him, waiting for him to speak.

"Celeste has come here for one reason only. To tell Eric." Sarah stood. "She's said what she had to say. There is nothing more to discuss." She put a possessive arm around her daughter's shoulder. "I think it's time for us to leave."

Both women exit the room as quietly as ghosts with the father walking behind.

At the door Ben turned and looked at him with vitriol in his eyes. "I'll expect you to damn well sign those papers, Viking."

ALONE IN HIS UNCLE'S LIBRARY, Eric stared at the lab results.

Positive.

Celeste was pregnant.

With his child.

He had been with numerous women and never once gotten one of them knocked up. Of course he had been careful and practiced safe sex religiously.

He'd slipped up one time.

With Celeste, he had lost his head and apparently his condom.

The physical pull, the thrum he felt when he'd touched her was unlike anything he'd ever felt with anyone else.

He had been unable to resist her.

He peered out the window at Stephen's well-manicured lawn.

Surprisingly, everything on the outside looked normal. The spring flowers were in full bloom, the grass had turned green awaking from the winter's brown, and the wind rustled new leaves in the tree tops. But he knew better.

From this moment on life would never be the same again.

He should be relieved at her ultimatum. Even Stephen had mentioned that after they were gone.

She wanted nothing from him. He wouldn't have to be saddled with scandal or be obligated to pay them any money. All he had to do was sign the papers and his life would return to normal.

Or would it?

In life things were never this easy.

He opened the folder and quickly located an address. The address listed was her parents' house, not her apartment in Atlanta.

He needed answers that only she could give him.

If she thought she could hide behind her parents she had it all wrong.

CHAPTER SEVEN

ACCORDING TO HIS GPS, THE Harts lived two hours outside of Atlanta, in the middle of nowhere. After the navigation system on his Mercedes hadn't recognized the address, he had been forced to stop at a gas station and ask for directions.

What should have been a two hour trip had turned into a three hour drive.

"Shit." His tire hit a rut in the winding gravel road and he tightened his grip on the steering wheel. Even though he'd slowed his speed considerably, he couldn't help but wonder at the damage being done to the undercarriage of his car.

Three miles down the narrow road lined with barbed wire fencing, the trees became sparse and he spotted a red mailbox. He checked the address on the mailbox with the address in the file before turning off the road and pulling into the driveway.

He soon saw a large white farmhouse with a wrap-around porch. The flower bed around the house burst with colorful blooms of spring and the large oak tree in the front yard had a tire swing hanging from a limb. Behind the house was a red barn with horses poking their long faces out of the windows.

"It looks like a fucking Norman Rockwell painting." He groused.

He pulled up in the driveway and killed the engine. He gathered the folder and slid out of the car. He stood and his foot sank into something soft. Grimacing, he looked down.

His right foot was firmly planted in a pile of crap. His new Prada loafers were ruined.

"*Honk!*"

He looked up and glared at the black and white feathers waddling toward him.

"Of course it had to be goose shit." He dragged the sole of his foot across the grass while showering the goose with profanities. The goose changed its trajectory and waddled toward the barn.

He tossed another glare at the bird before heading toward the house. He hurried up the steps and rang the doorbell.

Sarah Hart opened the door on the first ring, wearing a cheery yellow apron over her jeans and white blouse. Her welcoming smile slid off her face when she saw him standing on her porch.

"Hello, Mrs. Hart." He gave her a polite smile.

"Eric, I wasn't expecting to see you so soon." She smiled tightly and moved aside for him to enter. "Please, come in."

"Thank you." The aroma of cinnamon and sugar clung to her as he walked past.

He said nothing but followed her into the open living room. He was surprised that the décor was fairly modern. He had expected dated wall paper and antique furniture but he got neutral painted walls and sleek leather seating. It didn't fit the exterior of the house.

"Have a seat." She motioned toward the leather sofa. "Would you like something to drink? I just took some oatmeal cookies out of the oven. Would you care for one?"

"No, thank you, Mrs. Hart, but I would like to talk to Celeste."

The smack of a screen door made him clench his jaw.

"Honey, have you seen . . ." Ben Hart stopped in his tracks, his eyes narrowing on him.

He stood and held her father's gaze.

"Nordstrom. Didn't take you long to sign away your responsibilities, I see." Ben lifted his chin.

"I haven't signed anything yet." Eric kept his voice even and calm. He wasn't going to let Ben Hart get another reaction out of him. He was better than that.

"Then what the hell are you doing here?" The older man clenched his hands at his sides.

"I am here to talk to Celeste."

"The hell you are!" Ben roared and took a step toward him.

"Ben, please." Sarah spoke softly and put a hand on her husband's arm. "Let him talk to her. It will probably be the last time he'll ever see her."

Eric cut his eyes at her. "What do you mean?"

"We're moving." She gave him a smile that didn't reach her eyes.

"Moving? Where?"

"Iowa."

"Why?"

"We live in a small town, Eric. Celeste had a hard

time trying to fit in here while she was growing up." Sarah said.

"Jealously is what it was. Those rich girls were jealous of my girl's beauty." Ben sneered.

"Even though it's common enough today, being pregnant and unwed will cause a lot of people to talk and I can't bear to watch her go through that. Not again. Moving away will give her a fresh start." Sarah nodded as if she were trying to convince herself.

Celeste was leaving.

His gut twisted. Why did it matter to him if she were moving? It wasn't like he was going to be sticking around, either.

"Celeste is out by the lake, if you want to talk to her." Sarah nodded toward the window.

"Thank you." He hurried out the back door before Ben could stop him.

☾

PUSHING THE CURTAIN ASIDE, SARAH watched Eric walking toward the lake. "I don't think he knows."

"Knows what Celeste is?" Ben snorted. "Of course he doesn't. He's too busy thinking with his dick."

"Ben." Sarah narrowed her eyes.

"I don't like him." Ben crossed his arms over his chest.

"Spoken like an overprotective father."

"Apparently not protective enough." Ben sank into his favorite leather chair and rubbed a hand across his face. "She's too young, Sarah. She's not ready to be a mother. And she sure isn't ready to find out what she is."

"I know." She swallowed the fear that kept building inside. The instinct to protect her only child caused an ache deep in her chest that grew worse with each passing day. "The prophecy is clear. The child born from the linage of Naddoddr will die. And according to the research you did, Eric is from that linage. The only hope to save the child is for the mother and father to work together to find a way to save the baby before it's too late." She turned toward the window before Ben could notice the tear slipping down her cheek. She swiped it away with her finger. "He won't admit it, but he's drawn to her. I feel it."

"He doesn't know that the pull he feels for her is because they are destined to be mates." His voice dripped with distain. "I doubt he even knows what he's feeling."

"Men rarely do, dear. You certainly didn't know I was your mate." Sarah turned and faced him. "Your plan could backfire. What if he signs the papers?"

"He won't."

"How can you be sure?"

Ben stood and took her hand. "Because Eric Nordstrom is not the type of man to agree to another man's terms. He'll not sign those papers, if for no other reason than spite. He'll want to see Celeste again. By threatening to take her away, he made sure he'd find a way to make her stay." Ben shook his head. "The only obstacle is our daughter."

"What do you mean?"

"She wants nothing to do with him. Look how she avoids him. Hell, she might be the one to run away. Not him." Ben shook his head.

Sarah stepped into the comfort of his embrace and laid her head on his chest. "She needs to know the truth. She needs to know what she is."

"I know, I know. But not today, okay? I doubt she would even believe us. Remember, fairies aren't supposed to exist outside of fairytales."

CHAPTER EIGHT

ERIC HURRIED TOWARD THE LAKE while keeping an eye on where he was planting his feet. The last thing he needed was to slip in goose shit and land on his ass.

Celeste was leaving.

The thought of never seeing her again unsettled him. And he didn't know why.

He looked up and his gaze landed on Celeste strolling along the bank of the water, clutching a bouquet of wildflowers.

He froze.

A gentle breeze played with the hem of her white halter dress as she walked. She lifted the material to step over a log, exposing long slender legs.

Air whooshed out of his lungs and his chest ached like it had when he'd had pneumonia as a kid.

His gaze stayed fixed on the long slender leg peeking out from her dress. That same leg that had wrapped around his waist as he'd pounded into her tight body.

His body heated and ached with need.

"Stop thinking with your dick." He shook his head. "That's what got you into this mess in the first place."

He gritted his teeth and forced his feet to continue along the uneven ground.

Her movements were slow, deliberate, like she was perfectly present in that very moment, and wanted to savor every detail. It was something he'd never learned to do, to stay in the moment. There were too many things that needed to be dealt with on a daily basis, too many decisions that needed to be made.

She knelt and plucked a purple wild flower.

"Celeste."

She clambered to her feet, the flowers slipping from her fingers and landing on the ground in ribbons of color.

"Sorry. I didn't mean to frighten you." He bent and gathered the flowers.

"You didn't frighten me. You surprised me, that's all." She eyed him with suspicion and stepped back. Her deep green eyes flickered to the folder in his hand. "You've signed the papers?"

"I haven't." He stood and handed her the bouquet.

"Why not?" She took the flowers and wrapped her arms tight around herself, squishing her forgotten bouquet.

"I wanted to talk to you first." He made sure to keep his tone easy and light. He wanted her guard down to get to the truth. He needed truth.

"We have nothing more to say." She shook her head and looked away.

Well, that was new. When did a woman not want to

talk?

"We can't change what we did or what resulted from it. Meaning, there's nothing else for us to talk about."

"I need to know." He stepped closer and frowned.

"About what?" She looked down at the flowers and uncrossed her arms.

"What you plan to do about the baby." The odd words drifted out and hung in the air like a balloon. "Will you keep the . . .your . . . our baby?"

"Yes." She lifted her chin.

"Why?" He narrowed his eyes. "You don't even like me. Why would you want a reminder of me? Is it because of your parents? They can't force you to do anything you don't want to do."

"It has nothing to do with my parents." She gaped.

"Then why are you having the baby?" It didn't make sense to him. She didn't make sense to him.

"You don't get it, do you?" She shook her head and turned to walk away.

He caught her arm. "Answer my question, Celeste. Why have my baby when I know you think what happened between us was a mistake?"

"A mistake." She pressed her lips together and looked up at him. "Is that what you think?"

"Yes."

She flinched as if he had slapped her.

Damn.

"Eric, I can give you a hundred reasons for not keeping this pregnancy. And only one reason to keep him. And that one reason outweighs all the others." She touched her stomach. "This baby is a result of our actions. It's here because of us.

It shouldn't have to pay the price of our consequences."

Up until that point he had believed that her parents were forcing her to keep the child. Now he knew the decision had been hers.

Celeste might not need him, hell she probably hated him. But the baby needed him. He had a decision to make and he had to make it quick.

"I'm not signing the papers." He turned and started toward the house.

☾

BY THE TIME CELESTE MADE it back to the house, Eric was sitting on the leather sofa. She had been so stunned by his words, she hadn't been able to move.

"What do you mean, you won't sign the papers?" She rested her hands on her hips, and pierced him with a glare.

"There are some things I need to discuss with your father." He gave her a cool look and rested his arm on the back of the sofa like he belonged there.

"My father? This is between us." The blood rushed into her face. She fisted her hands to keep from smacking the smirk off his handsome face.

He shrugged. "But you brought him with you to tell me about the baby. You have already involved him in our situation."

"I didn't invite him. He insisted on coming." Her voice rose with each word.

Her mother walked in from the kitchen and rested her arm across her shoulder. "Come on, dear. Let Eric and your daddy have some time alone."

"But …"

"It's okay, honey. Go on upstairs." Her Daddy walked in from the kitchen, gave her a smile and then shot Eric a glare.

"Fine." If anyone could put Mr. CEO in his place it would be her father.

☾

"CELESTE." AFTER WHAT SEEMED LIKE an eternity her father called her downstairs.

She entered the living room. Her mother was sitting on the couch and her father standing by the window. Eric was nowhere to be found.

"Honey, sit down." Her father's voice was soft and gentle.

"Is everything okay?" She eased into the leather chair, her stomach twisting into a knot.

"Eric and I have reached a compromise." Her father turned and faced her. Her mother stood and reached for her father's hand.

Something told her this was not good.

"Compromise?"

"He refuses to forfeit his parental rights." Her father said.

"He wants to share custody?" She frowned. She hadn't expected that. Not from him.

"Not exactly." Her father looked at her mother and then back at her. "Eric wants full custody."

Her blood ran cold. She jumped up from her seat. "He can't have my baby. I won't allow it."

Her father nodded. "I told him you wouldn't part with your child."

Relief rolled over her and she pressed her hand to her heart and nodded. Thankfully, her parents had stood their ground with him.

That was good. That was real good.

"Eric wants to marry you."

"I'm sorry, what did you say?" She blinked as the words muddled in her head. It didn't compute. She must have heard them wrong.

"Eric asked for your hand in marriage." Her father's voice was firm, his expression stoic.

She blinked and waited to hear the punch line.

Her father held her gaze, sadness pulling at the corners of his eyes.

"And I gave my consent."

Her head began to spin and she tried to remember how to breathe. Her vision narrowed, and grew dark until there was nothing but blackness.

CHAPTER NINE

CELESTE HEARD A FAINT MALE voice calling her name. The voice, hollow and empty, reminded her of when she'd visited a cave when she was a little girl.

She blinked back the cobwebs and forced her eyes open. Her vision cleared and she saw Eric hoovering over her.

"What happened?" She tried to push herself up, but her arms refused to cooperate.

He wrapped his arm around her back and helped her to a sitting position. Purple dots swirled in front of her eyes. She squeezed them shut to clear her vision.

"You fainted." His voice, low and deep, sent shivers racing across her skin. He was much too close for her comfort.

She cracked open an eye. No more spots danced in front of her eyes, but now she was uncomfortably warm.

She opened both eyes. She was sitting in Eric's lap.

No wonder her body felt like it was on fire.

She tried to scramble away, but he tightened his hold around her waist.

"Let go of me." She hissed.

"Not until I'm sure you won't faint again."

She shook her head and pushed her hands against his immovable chest. The man was built like steel.

"I'm fine."

He relaxed his grip. She took advantage and scampered out of his lap and onto the love seat.

"I thought you left." She glared at him, irritated at her body's reaction to him.

"I stepped outside for your father to break the news to you. I assume you were not fainting with joy at becoming my wife?" A slow grin stretched across his ridiculously handsome face.

"How could you say that to my parents? They really thought you were serious." She pressed her fingers to her temples and studied the floor. This was worse than telling them she was pregnant.

"I am serious." He had the audacity to look offended. "I've decided that I want to keep my child. I've no heirs and I need someone to carry on my legacy."

There was the truth of it. He didn't really want to marry her.

He just wanted his child.

"You can have a relationship with your child without having to marry me."

His expression hardened like petrified wood. "I won't have my son growing up in a broken home. He deserves better than that. Plus, this way I can make sure you don't change your mind and blackmail me."

"Blackmail you? With what?" She dropped her

hands and looked up at him with wide eyes. "I want nothing to do with you. That's the whole point behind the contract."

"That document proves I'm the father. Signing it would give you all the control and that is something I can't allow."

Anger boiled beneath her skin and she curled her fingers into fists. The urge to slap him was insane.

"What makes you think I would ever agree to marry you?" She narrowed her eyes. She wasn't going to be forced into doing something she didn't want to do.

"If you refuse, I'll just get full custody after he's born and then you'll be the one who won't have any rights. I have the power and money to make that happen. We both know that." He sat on the coffee table and faced her.

What the hell had she been thinking, sleeping with such a jerk? She'd lost her virginity to this asshole.

"You wouldn't do that. You couldn't possibly be that cruel." Her heart picked up speed and her lungs constricted.

He leaned closer. "You have a choice. You can agree to this and make everyone happy, including your parents, or you can fight me and end up losing everything."

She opened her mouth to tell him just where he could shove his proposal.

Her parents rushed into the room. "Oh, honey, are you okay? I just telephoned the doctor. He wanted to know if you ate today." Her mother's cool hands cupped her face, her worried eyes searching for any distress.

She pulled away.

"I'm fine. I just skipped lunch." She had been too upset about the meeting with Eric to even think about keeping something down.

"I'll go fix you a snack." Her mother stopped in the doorway, looked back and smiled at Eric. "She never has eaten much, but now she's going to have to start thinking about eating for two."

"Then we need to make sure she's taking care of herself." He returned her mother's smile and stood.

What the hell was that about?

Her mom hated Eric. Why was she even being nice to him?

Her dad shot Eric a glare before following her mother into the kitchen.

"Celeste?"

She'd been so bewildered by her parents that she hadn't notice he had sat down beside her. Her stomach warmed. Despite her hatred, he still physically affected her.

Must be that damn cologne.

"I need to go outside for some fresh air." She jumped to her feet.

"Do you want me to go with you?" He stood.

"No, No. I'm fine. I just need some time to myself." She flung open the door and hurried out before he could follow.

She rushed out into the yard and settled into the weathered tire.

She rested her cheek against the warmed cracked rubber, finding it oddly comforting.

She had been in denial after she'd taken the first pregnancy test. By the time she had taken the tenth one she had been devastated.

Pregnant. From a one-night stand.

"And here I thought having visions was my only problem." After all she'd gone through she still didn't have the book.

The front door smacked shut. She pushed herself behind the tree, hiding from Eric. She wasn't ready to face him.

"Ben, where are you going?" Her mother's voice carried across the yard.

"I'm going to the barn. I'd rather look at a horse's ass out there, than the one that's sitting in the house."

She snorted and slapped her hand across her mouth.

"Ben, I know you don't like him." She could hear the weariness in his mother's normally upbeat voice.

"You think?"

"He's the father. He does have rights. Besides, if Celeste marries him, we won't have to move. I know how much you love our farm."

The rest of the conversation became nothing more than a mumble of words as her parents made their way into the barn.

Her heart tumbled in the emptiness of her chest.

They were moving? They'd not said anything to her about moving.

She should have known. Her father's pride wouldn't allow him to stay in a small town where the rumormongers would go wild at the fact that she was pregnant and unwed. It didn't matter that this was the twenty-first century and she didn't even live at home anymore. Her parents would bear the brunt of her mistake.

If she refused to marry Eric she didn't doubt that he would do everything in his power to make good on his intent of gaining full custody. He had the money and the power to make it happen.

She pressed her hand across her flat stomach.

Would her baby be like her? Had she somehow passed on this curse of seeing the future onto her unborn child?

She shivered.

If that were true, what would Eric do then? Would he still want the child once he knew the truth? Or would he have the child committed to an institution, hidden away from the world?

She gasped, her heart aching for her unborn baby. She couldn't let that happen. She wouldn't.

She made her way into the house.

He stood as she walked into the living room.

"I won't be married to a man I don't love. But I can enter a marriage where I know there's a way out."

He narrowed his eyes. "What do you mean?"

She swallowed. "The only way I will marry you is if you agree to a divorce six months after the baby is born. And we share custody."

He shook his head. "I told you I don't want my child growing up in a broken home."

"Would you rather it grow up in a home where the parents can't stand each other?"

He stared at her for the longest time, and she begin to doubt he was going to agree.

"An amicable divorce, shared custody, and you agree not to leave the state of Vermont." He crossed his arms.

She gritted her teeth.

"That way, the child will always have both of us near. If you move out of state then the agreement will be null and void."

"I'll need to find work and Cryptic is the only place I've ever been employed at." She stated.

"I'm sure you will be able to get by on alimony. Money will be no issue." He snorted.

"I don't want alimony. I want my own job." She glared.

Surprise swept across his expression.

"I don't need your money. I can support myself."

He cocked his head and studied her. "The main offices of Cryptic are based in Vermont. I can guarantee you a job there."

"I don't think working for you is a good idea."

"If you are worried about me interfering into your personal life, don't. I promise that after we divorce your private life will not cross my mind."

She lifted her chin despite the sting to her ego. "A no fault divorce six months after the birth. I agree to stay in Vermont, and we share custody."

"Plus I'll give you a job referral if you don't want to work at Cryptic. How's that?"

She knew she was entering a deal with the devil, but it was the only way to satisfy both her parents and Eric. In the end it would guarantee her a way out, an escape.

"I accept your proposal."

CHAPTER TEN

AFTER PUTTING ON A BRAVE face Celeste told her parents she'd agreed to marry Eric. She wasn't expecting to see the joyous reaction from her mother. Her father glared at Eric and looked like he was ready to skin him alive. His reaction did manage to cheer her some.

"If you'll excuse me, I think I'll go lie down." Celeste hoped Eric would get the hint and leave.

He didn't move from his seated position on the couch.

She ignored him and walked out of the living room. Let her mother, who seemed to adore him now, entertain him.

She climbed the creaky stairs to her childhood bedroom and shut the door.

She glanced around the pink and white décor, her gaze flittering to the 4H ribbons she'd won showing sheep.

She seemed to get along better with animals than the kids in her class, especially the girls.

She fell back on the white ruffled twin bed and

closed her eyes, hoping that when she opened them she would wake from this nightmare.

Her mind raced.

Surely Eric intended this to be a marriage in name only. He wouldn't dare ask her to share his bed as well. Or would he?

Panic pressed against her heart, the force threatening to suffocate her. Bolting up from the bed, she raced to the window, flung it open and stuck her head out. Crisp night air stung her lungs as she sucked in a deep breath.

"Celeste?"

She straightened and bumped her head on the windowsill.

"I came to see how you were feeling." Eric stared at her from the doorway.

"I'm fine." She scowled and massaged her scalp, feeling for a bump.

"Here, let me see." He crossed the room and gently pulled her head down. The motion made her a little dizzy. Or was it him?

"It's nothing." She pulled out of his hands and walked over to her desk. "So, you're leaving?"

"Yes. I'll be back tomorrow for the wedding."

"Tomorrow? The wedding is tomorrow?" Those damn purple spots were back and dancing before her eyes. She shook her head. Surely he couldn't be serious.

"That's too soon." Her voice quavered.

"I have to get back to Vermont. I want this taken care of before I leave."

Her heart pounded in her chest. "Eric what if . . ."

"What if what?" His intense blue eyes bore into

hers.

"What's going to happen after we are married?" Her face heated. She probably looked as red as a radish right now. "What exactly are your expectations? From me?"

"In what sense?" A slow smile tugged at his lips.

"You know what sense I'm talking about." She glared. He obviously enjoyed making her uncomfortable.

"I do, but I find it incredibly amusing that you can't even talk about sex without blushing."

She swallowed and pressed her hand to her throat.

"Exactly the way you're blushing now." His smile grew.

"Forgive me for having morals. I'm sure I'm not your type of woman. I don't jump into bed with everyone I meet." She crossed her arms and lifted her chin.

"That was made crystal clear when I discovered you were a virgin." His smirk grew.

She turned away and faced the window, her hands fisting at her sides. Why did he have to mock her?

"Celeste, I'm not a rapist." He stepped behind her and brushed her hair away from her neck. "No matter what you've heard."

She froze.

He was referring to Elizabeth Humphries and how she had accused him of rape. Cryptic had tried to keep it quiet but the word got around. She made a point of never listening to gossip. It usually wasn't true and always ended up hurting someone. She knew from experience. She'd been on the receiving end too many times growing up.

"Sex with me is always consensual. When you

are ready for me to give you another orgasm . . . or three, just let me know."

She spun around and glared. "You're such a jackass."

His lips twitched with amusement.

"This is serious." She shook her head. "What's going to happen when you find someone, someone you love, someone you trulywant to marry?"

"I don't believe in love." He curled his lip.

His words struck her in the chest. "Everyone believes in love. Or at least the possibility of love."

"Not everyone. Sure as hell not me." He headed for the door and looked over his shoulder. "I'll see you tomorrow for the wedding."

He shut the door behind him leaving her stunned and trying to figure a way out of their agreement.

☾

CELESTE SCREAMED INTO THE DARKNESS. She froze, every muscle in her body turning to ice. White-hot pain tore through her stomach. She curled into a ball and clutched her belly. Her stomach was wet.

Warm sticky liquid coated her fingertips. Another violent seizure of pain spread through her abdomen. She screamed, her throat raw and burning.

Her dark surroundings began to burn away into light. Long pointy teeth in a monstrous face hovered inches from her face. Slimy saliva dripped from its open mouth and onto her chest. She opened her mouth to scream but another spasm of pain tore through her stomach. The creature slammed a claw-like hand across her mouth and leaned in.

"You can't hide, Celeste. I'll find you. I'll always

find you." It hissed.

She jerked upright in bed, gasping for air. Her heart thwacked against her rib cage. She gripped her sweat soaked sheets and looked around at the pink curtains and awards sitting on the small dresser.

She was at her parents' house. She was safe. It was only a dream, one of many she'd had during the night.

She eased back down on the bed.

She had been too afraid to sleep, and when she finally drifted off she had horrible nightmares. Nightmares of evil creatures, clawing and biting and cutting her flesh.

Monsters didn't really exist. They only existed in fairytales and legends. Why was she dreaming about monsters if she only had visions of the future?

She glanced at the light coming through the window. Today was a new day.

Today was her wedding day.

Her stomach clenched. She had awakened from one nightmare only to step into another.

She flung off the covers and tugged on her pink chenille robe before heading downstairs.

She couldn't go through with this. She'd just tell her parents she couldn't marry Eric. Surely they would understand.

The sound of laughter and the scent of food greeted her at the bottom step.

She entered the kitchen and faltered.

A dozen aunts, uncles and cousins were squeezed into the kitchen, each working on various decorations and food. For the wedding.

Her wedding.

The hard shell of desperation clung to her heart like a varnish, hard, unmovable and suffocating.

"What's everyone doing here?" Her voice cracked as she looked around the room.

It was a stupid question. She already knew the answer.

Her extended family stopped their tasks and descended on her with squeals of congratulations and warm wishes. She tried her best to appear happy but her paper smile was about to tear.

"You know how our family is about weddings and birthdays. They drove all night, to witness you and Eric take your vows." Her mother pressed her cheek against hers and gave her a hug.

Her family expected her to marry a man she hardly knew. He was a known womanizer and didn't have a clue how to be faithful. And on top of that, he didn't believe in love.

What had she agreed to?

She tried to swallow but her throat had turned to ash.

Her mother looked at her and smiled. Guilt shot through Celeste's heart like an arrow.

The expectation and happiness evident in her mother's eyes killed any hope of telling her mother she couldn't marry Eric.

She'd made her bed and now she was going to have to lie in it, with someone she didn't love.

She needed something to occupy herself before she jumped out of her skin. She grabbed a coffee cup out of the cabinet.

She scooted the heavy platters of appetizers to the side and reached for the coffeepot.

Arrangements of purple hydrangeas, pink roses

and white lilies were sat on the kitchen counter, while miniature toile bags of birdseed tied with pink silk ribbon sat in a large white wicker basket.

She opened the refrigerator to get the creamer.

Her heart nearly dropped to the floor.

All the racks had been removed to accommodate the height of a white wedding cake. It had three fat tiers and was covered in elegant silver scroll and flowers, a matching silver Celtic knot topping the ornate cake.

"Do you like it?" Her mother's unsure tone tugged at Celeste's heart.

"It's beautiful. Did you make it?" Her eyes burned with unshed tears.

"Yes."

"You made this last night? You must not have slept at all." Another pang of guilt hit her square in the chest.

"I can sleep later. This is a special day after all. My daughter only gets married once."

She wouldn't count on it.

"It's beautiful. I didn't expect this. I didn't expect any of this." She forced her lips into a smile.

"I know this is all happening too fast, but things always work out for the best." Her mother squeezed her hand. "Just remember a little patience and understanding goes a long way in a marriage."

She looked away. Her heart ached as she thought of the one attribute her marriage would never have.

Love.

CHAPTER ELEVEN

"I WISH I'D WORN A TUX, Eric." Stephen leaned forward and straightened his tie in the visor mirror. "At least you should have. It doesn't seem right for you to be getting married in a suit."

"This is a very simple ceremony and it does not call for a tux." Eric wished his uncle would give him a break and let him have some peace and quiet. Stephen had not stopped talking since they left Atlanta.

"But it's not going to look right if she's in her wedding gown and you're in a suit. Just think about the wedding portrait."

"Portrait?" He snorted. "There's not going to be wedding photos."

"What do you mean no wedding pictures?" Stephen's eyebrows shot up and he twisted his Rolex on his wrist. "There's always wedding pictures."

"This is going to be a short ceremony, presided over by a justice of the peace."

Though he didn't think it was possible, but his uncle's eyes got bigger.

"A justice of the peace? You actually hired a justice of the peace?" He stopped fiddling with his watch and shook his head.

"Not me, her father did. He said he would make the necessary arrangements since everything was short notice. Besides, we've got to leave soon so I can make it to the board meeting tonight."

"I still can't believe you are doing this." His uncle's heavy voice matched the heavy mood in the car.

"After all those years of nagging me to settle down, I thought you would be pleased." He swerved, but not soon enough. His tire slammed in a pothole.

If he never saw a gravel road again it would be too soon.

"It's one thing to marry for love, and quite another to marry out of obligation." Stephen looked out the window. "You're not thinking about your future."

"Future?"

"What if you meet someone you fall in love with?"

"Celeste already asked me that question." The muscles in his cheek twitched, irritated with the direction of the conversation.

"Really? Well at least someone is thinking." Stephen narrowed his gaze. "Although, I am a little concerned why she agreed to marry you so quickly."

"I told her if she refused, I would seek full custody of the baby."

"You what?" Stephen's jaw dropped, dangerously close to hitting the floorboard. "Eric, you blackmailed her."

"Celeste and I made an arrangement." He shrugged. "Business will take me away the majority of the time, it's not like we'll be together twenty-four hours a day. Our arrangement will be mutually beneficial. She will have a life of privilege and I will have an heir to carry on my name."

"This doesn't have anything to do with ensuring your position as CEO, does it?"

He strangled the steering wheel in a white-knuckled grip. "It's more than that. I don't want my son growing up thinking his father didn't want him, thinking he was a mistake." The words spilled over his tongue making his throat ache.

"I know John wasn't a very good . . ."

"A very good what? Father? Husband? Human being?" He couldn't believe he still felt so strongly for a man who'd neglected him these many years.

Stephen laid a gentle hand on his shoulder. "Your father was a hard man. But he loved you."

Eric's stomach turned cold, bits of icicles breaking off and shards stinging his gut. "Right. He used to tell me I couldn't do anything right."

"He was wrong. You're one of the most talented and dedicated businessmen I know." Stephen's grip tightened on his shoulder. "And if this marriage is what you really want, then I'll stand by your decision." His voice grew husky. "And for what it's worth, this kid is lucky as hell to have you as his father. Don't ever forget that."

"Thanks, Uncle Stephen. That means a lot." He swallowed the ache in his throat.

"Even if you aren't getting married in a tux." Stephen added.

"It will be a short ceremony with me in my suit

and Celeste in her dress." He laughed.

"Dress? You mean no wedding gown, either?" Stephen gulped.

"No wedding gown, Stephen. Probably something simple." He gave his uncle a thoughtful look. "In fact I might be overdressed. Maybe I need to leave my jacket in the car."

"Overdressed?" Stephen opened his mouth then apparently thought better of it and closed it.

"Ah, here we are." The picturesque white farmhouse came into view. It looked exactly as he remembered. Except for the twenty vehicles parked off to the side in a neat row.

His internal radar went off. What the hell were all these cars doing here?

"I thought you said this was going to be a small ceremony." He didn't miss the amusement in his uncle's voice.

"It is. I need to find out what's going on." He killed the engine, and scrambled out of the car. On the fourth step his foot sank into a familiar soft mass. "Shit."

"What's wrong?" Stephen stopped beside him.

"I stepped in goose shit." He leveled a look at his uncle and pointed to the greasy pile of crap on the bottom of his shoe.

Stephen wrinkled his nose and carefully picked up and examined his own feet. He sighed. "Whew. I'm good."

He took a step to the right and slid his expensive loafers along the tuft of green grass. "Fucking geese."

"Eric, thank god. I was beginning to get worried." Sarah Hart called out across the yard.

He froze in mid-scrape.

Sarah Hart crossed the yard holding up the hem of a shimmery green gown to keep it from dragging the ground. Her shoes sparkled in the same dark hue.

"Ah, she doesn't look like she's wearing her Sunday church clothes, Eric." Stephen mumbled.

Stephen was right. Sarah Hart looked like she'd stepped out of a mother of the bride catalogue.

Sarah stopped in front of him, smiled, and pulled him into a hug. "Don't you look handsome?"

He stiffened under her touch. It had been so long since he had been shown any maternal signs of affection, that the gesture was awkward.

Not wanting to appear rude, he forced his arms to move, embracing her small frame. The subtle scent of her perfume brought back a bittersweet memory of his own mother.

He cleared his throat and stepped back. "Mrs. Hart . . ."

She swatted his arm. "We are almost family. Please call me Sarah." She turned toward Stephen and smiled. "Oh, Mr. Nordstrom, I'm so glad you came."

"Call me Stephen. As you said, we are almost family." He took her hand and held it between his palms. "And may I say you look enchanting, Sarah."

"Thank you." She blushed at the compliment as her smile grew.

"I am afraid we are a bit underdressed." His uncle sent him a glare.

"I know we had to throw everything together on such short notice, and I wasn't sure if you would be wearing a tux, so Ben picked up an extra one for you, Eric. And if it doesn't fit we have Aunt Agatha who is an excellent seamstress. She can have it tailored to fit you within an hour."

He frowned and shook his head. He didn't have time for that. He needed to leave in an hour. "Mrs. Hart …"

"Sarah." She reminded.

"Sarah, I don't think there is enough time for all that. I've got a very important meeting tonight in Vermont."

"But you're the CEO, aren't you?"

"Yes, of course."

"You're the boss, just move it to tomorrow."

He opened his mouth to argue, but Sarah grabbed his hand and pulled him toward the house. "Let's get you fitted."

Sarah stopped and turned. "I'm sorry, Stephen. If I'd known you were coming I would have gotten you a tux as well."

Stephen smiled. "Don't worry yourself, my dear. As long as the bride and groom are dressed for the occasion that's all that matters."

"You're absolutely right. Can you imagine what their wedding portrait would look like?"

☾

CELESTE SCRAPED HER THUMB ACROSS the flaking paint on the porch railing and fidgeted with her bouquet of white lilies and baby's breath. Everyone told her she looked like a princess.

She felt more like a death-row prisoner waiting to walk her last mile of freedom.

She ran a clammy hand across the front of her

mother's wedding dress.

Her wedding dress now.

Made of champagne brocade and shantung, the sleeveless gown had a fully boned corset and was trimmed in pearls. The mermaid-style skirt was fitted at the knees then flared out to the ground.

She strangled the bouquet and bit her lip.

There would be no escaping, not now.

She froze at the sound of footsteps.

Her father rounded the counter and she relaxed. His gaze met hers and a gentle smile spread across his face.

"You look beautiful, honey." His voice was soft and full of emotion.

She gave him a smile and pressed her lips to his warm cheek, trying to force back the tears stinging her eyes.

"Now, now, don't cry." His calloused thumb captured an escaped tear before it could find its path down her cheek. He pulled a handkerchief out of his pocket.

She accepted it and dabbed the corner of her eyes. "Sorry, I guess I'm just hormonal." She swallowed the thick emotion in her throat. "Is it time?"

"Yes, honey. It's time." Her father tucked her arm in his, and together they walked down the porch steps. His steps faltered. "I wish we had more time, you know, to talk."

"Talk about what?" She tilted her head back and looked up at him.

He glanced away and shook his head. When he looked back he gave her a thin smile and patted her arm. "Some other time, I promise. But not on your wedding day."

CHAPTER TWELVE

"DAMN." ERIC FLINCHED AND DREW back his wrist from the needle prick courtesy of Aunt Agatha.

"Oops. Maybe I shouldn't have had that last glass of elderberry wine." Aunt Agatha stopped her hemming on his tuxedo sleeve and gave him an apologetic smile.

"I've never had a tuxedo fitted in such a short period of time. It usually takes weeks." He arched his eyebrow and prayed he wouldn't need a blood transfusion after she was done with him. It was the third time she'd stuck him.

"I have a gift, or so they tell me." She continued sewing. "Although I wished I had been blessed in another area."

"Oh, yeah. Like what?" He glanced down at his Rolex and grimaced at the time.

"I don't know." She deftly worked the needle through the material in a swift motion. "I think I would like the gift of invisibility."

"Excuse me?" He jerked his gaze back to the older woman.

"Invisibility. I wish I'd been born with the gift of invisibility." Aunt Agatha stopped her sewing and narrowed her gaze. "What gift do you have?"

Was she serious?

"The gift of making money, I suppose." He spoke slowly, keeping his eyes on the old woman's hand holding the needle. No doubt about it. Celeste's family was weird. Hopefully that gene wouldn't get passed onto his child.

"That's not a gift. But soon you're going to need your gift, you better find out what it is."

"Why is that?"

She leaned in and lowered her voice. "If you wed when April flowers bloom, joy and sorrow you'll both know soon."

"Aunt Agatha, you're scaring Eric." Sarah Hart hurried into the room. She wrapped her arms around the old lady's shoulders and gave him a tight smile. "I apologize. She must have had too much elderberry wine."

"I didn't have *that* much." Agatha lifted her chin. "Besides, it's good for my heart. It's medicinal."

"No matter. It's almost time for the ceremony." Sarah straightened his lapels and smiled up at him. "Come on and let's get you in place."

She led him into the backyard under a tree filled with fragrant pink blooms. The pink canopy sheltered the guests in white chairs lined up in rows. He tapped his foot while waiting for the incessant chatter to die down and the ceremony to begin.

The sooner they got on with it, the sooner they could leave.

Not only had he endured having to be introduced to all of Celeste's extended family, he'd been bossed around by her father, who insisted they use the family wedding bands encrusted with tiny stones versus the expensive rings he had purchased and flown in from New York yesterday.

He was losing his patience with these people.

Standing in front of the priest, he patted the pocket of his tux, feeling the hard outline of the wedding bands. Something sharp poked his finger and he jerked his hand away. An angry scratch ran down the side of his finger. Whoever thought of putting a holly leaf in a boutonniere was crazy.

Hell, maybe the whole family was crazy. Aunt Agatha certainly fit the bill.

The musical chords from the harp broke through the buzz of voices and everyone quieted and stood.

He turned his attention down the aisle to the elaborate arbor decorated in greenery.

Celeste stepped into his line of sight.

His lungs constricted. He forced himself to take a deep breath.

Long blond hair hung in loose waves across slender shoulders framing her beautiful face. Her green eyes darted from one side of the aisle to the other and she smiled at each of her relatives.

Her wedding gown hugged her slender body, accentuating her small waist and long legs. The gentle swell of her small breasts stretched against the fitted bodice with every breath she took.

She was absolutely stunning.

He kept his gaze on her as she walked toward him. Time seemed to stop, come to a screeching standstill, with each step she took.

She finally stopped in front of him and the music faded into silence. The only noise he heard was the beating of his own heart.

He accepted her hand from her father who shot Eric one last glare before easing away.

Her cold hand trembled in his. He closed his fingers around her hers and looked down into her face. He waited for her to meet his gaze but she kept her eyes on the ground.

"Let us pray." The priest in a black robe bowed his head and launched into a lengthy prayer, none of which Eric heard. The beating of his heart drown out any words the priest had to offer.

Then came the vows.

He repeated the vows, his voice strong and confident

When it was her turn, she surprised him and repeated the vows without a tremor in her voice, despite the tremor in her hand.

Tension slid from his shoulders, knowing the end of the ceremony was near.

"And now for the traditional Celtic vows." The priest smiled, reaching within the folds of his black robe and pulled out a scroll.

"What's this? No one said anything about Celtic vows." He narrowed his eyes and refused to take the scroll the priest held out to him. He'd had enough of these people pushing their demands on him.

"It is our Irish tradition, part of our heritage." The priest held out the paper scroll and smiled.

"Eric, you don't have to read that." Celeste gazed up at him, eyes wide and fearful.

"We can't stop. Not now. The ceremony is not complete." The priest took a step in and looked between them nervously.

"It's not fair to expect him to read something

he doesn't mean." Celeste looked from him to the priest.

"Doesn't mean?" The priest glared at him. "You two are getting married. Of course he means every word."

He kept his eyes on her, took the scroll out of the priest's hands and unrolled it. He needed to know what was in the scroll that had made her nervous. His gaze drifted across the words and then he realized. It wasn't fear he saw in her face.

It was embarrassment.

He glanced out across the audience of wedding guests. If he refused to recite the words, it would no doubt cause suspicion as to validity of their marriage.

"Are you ready, then?" the priest whispered.

"Yes." He cleared his throat and began to recite the words.

"*I enter this marriage of my own free will.*

I pledge myself to be faithfully yours and no other's.

I pledge to share my body with you and no other. He met her gaze and smirked.

I pledge to give my love to you and no other.

I pledge to protect you from danger, both visible and invisible, and I will be a shield for you in difficult times.

I shall stand by your side as your mate as long as I draw breath."

Her face was flushed. The priest handed her the scroll and after a few uncomfortable seconds, she softly said the same words back to him.

"Let us now pray." The priest bowed his head for what Eric hoped was the final prayer.

The priest concluded the prayer with an "amen" and nodded. "You may now kiss your bride."

Eric captured her face between his hands and looked down into her startled green eyes.

He needed to know that the strange attraction was gone, that he had gotten her out of his system and gotten himself under control. He needed this kiss.

His lips brushed against her soft mouth. Hot thick pleasure coursed through his body like raging fire.

Once again he was sucked under her seductive spell unable to break the kiss.

He flicked his tongue in her sweet mouth. Her body tensed, her palms trapped against his chest. Any second now she would be pushing against him away. Any second now . . .

The priest cleared his throat.

Eric pulled back, disappointed in his discipline and self-control.

He hadn't intended to kiss her for long and certainly not like that, but the minute he'd tasted her he couldn't stop.

"It is my pleasure to introduce Mr. and Mrs. Eric Nordstrom." The priest announced.

Taking her hand, they turned and faced the applause of the guests.

He met Uncle Stephen's gaze as he walked up to them.

"Celeste, I've never seen a more beautiful bride." Stephen took her hands between his and smiled.

"Thank you, Mr. Nordstrom." Her eyes widened and a pretty shade of pink tinged her high cheekbones.

"Call me Stephen, dear. Or Uncle Stephen. Eric does."

Maybe he should have filled his uncle in on their little arrangement. She didn't need to get too comfortable with his family, since this marriage would be dissolved soon after the birth.

"And you don't look half bad either." Stephen slapped him on the back. "With a mother and father as good looking as you two, this kid is going to be gorgeous."

"Thanks." His gaze landed on Sarah Hart, who was making a beeline for them.

He had a feeling he should have headed straight for the car instead of mulling about.

Sarah enveloped Celeste in her arms. "The photographer wants to get some photos before you two cut the cake."

Photographer and cake. He'd forgotten about the photographer and hadn't been told about the cake. He rubbed the back of his neck and tried to bite his tongue.

The next minutes stretched into mindless poses with and without her family. After numerous photos they were herded toward the front of the house.

Tables positioned underneath the massive oak trees were draped with white tablecloths and laden with food. An elaborate white wedding cake sat in the middle of the middle of the table. Smaller tables with white tablecloths and chairs for the guests were arranged on either side of the tree. Each table held floral center pieces and tiny candles.

A wave of panic seized his lungs.

How had he lost control over his life so quickly?

More importantly, how had he let a woman disrupt his life forever?

CHAPTER THIRTEEN

"WOULD IT KILL YOU TO smile?" Celeste forced her lips into a smile and held it for the photographer. She held her hand over Eric's as they clutched the knife over the wedding cake.

Throughout the entire day, Eric hadn't even attempted to act civil to her family. He'd made it perfectly clear this whole day was an inconvenience of his precious time.

Had he even thought about the fact that her parents had made all the arrangements, stayed up late decorating, and paid for everything? He thought of no one but himself.

"You're one to talk." He snorted.

"Me?" She jerked her head up to meet his gaze. "At least I'm acting like this is the happiest day of my life."

"And I'm not?" He smirked.

"Looking constipated isn't the same thing as looking happy." She lowered her voice.

"Excuse me?" His mouth dropped open.

She bit back a smile. She bet no one had ever dared tell him that to his face before.

He dropped the knife and wrapped his arm around her waist and pulled her against him before she could blink. His pelvis pressed against hers. Even through the thick material of the wedding dress, she could feel his passion.

"What are you doing?" Heat surged to her face, and her heart pounded against her ribcage like a sledgehammer. If he was trying to embarrass her he had succeeded.

"Just trying to act like this is the happiest day of my life." His lips curved upward.

"Come on, you two, it's time to cut the cake," her mother said above the buzz of voices.

He released her and picked up the knife.

With her hand over his they sliced into the cake while everyone applauded.

He held out a sliver of cake and she leaned in cautiously. She didn't put it past him to shove it in her face.

She took a small bite while the photographer snapped some shots.

She picked up a piece of cake held it out for him to taste.

His fingers wrapped around her wrist and he popped the whole thing into his mouth. She tried to pull her hand away, but he tightened his grip.

His tongue darted out and licked the icing from her fingertips.

She snatched her hand away.

He grinned.

She knew then she was in over her head.

THE SUN DIPPED BELOW THE horizon, leaving behind obstinate streaks of violet and persimmon across the fading sky. Celeste gazed out past the frilly pink curtains of her old bedroom window in silent contemplation.

With the reception in full swing, she managed to slip away from the celebration to change clothes.

She turned away from the window and glanced around, her gaze settling on her graduation picture.

Her throat burned as the memories washed over her.

She'd had goals and dreams of getting away from home and traveling and being independent. Dreams that were no longer a possibility.

"All because of my bad judgment." Frustrated tears slid down her face.

She had traded one prison of overprotective parents for the cage of a loveless marriage. She was no closer to finding out her true identity or even if she were human at all.

"Celeste."

She tensed at the sound of Eric's voice. Keeping her back to him, she plucked a tissue from a side table and dabbed her eyes.

"It's time to go." From the matter-of-fact tone in his voice she knew that he would no longer tolerate being put off.

"Right now?" Her heart amped up and she turned around. Everything was moving way too fast.

"Yes." He frowned. "Surely you don't expect me to stay away from my business another day?"

"I don't expect anything from you." She just wanted to be left alone. She deserved the chance to mourn the life she'd lost.

"Good. Then let's go."

"I can't leave now." Her chest tightened. "There are things I have to settle."

"What things?" He crossed his arms over his chest.

"I have to let my landlord know I'm moving, and get my stuff out of my apartment." She swept her arms out to the side. "Not to mention, I haven't even packed my clothes."

Without a word he crossed the room in two strides. She stiffened.

He lifted her chin with his fingertips, forcing her to meet his icy gaze. She didn't look away. She refused to show any fear, not to him. She couldn't afford to.

"I'll take care of your landlord. I can call him and have your stuff placed in storage. Your mother told me she packed a bag for you. We can buy whatever you don't have when we get to Vermont."

She blinked and her shoulders dropped. She was out of time. She had no more excuses to stay.

"I believe everyone is waiting for us downstairs. They were grabbing bags of rice when I came up here." Contempt dripped from his voice despite his neutral expression. He'd made it quite evident that he didn't care very much for her family.

"Birdseed." She headed for the stairs.

"What?"

"They throw birdseed, not rice. Rice makes the birds explode." She took the steps slowly with him at her side.

He cut his eyes at her, giving her a strange look. Once again, he made her feel like an idiot. She tried to shrug it off. "At least that's what I've always been told."

"I don't think they explode. I think it's an urban legend. Anyway it doesn't matter. Birdseed is going to be harder to get out of my car than rice," he groused.

"Eric?" She stopped at the bottom of the stairs, her sweaty palms clasped together.

Just on the other side of that door was a whole other life that she was about to step into. A life she didn't want.

She still had unfinished business here. She still needed that book.

He stopped with his hand on the door knob and turned to look at her.

"Are we staying in Atlanta tonight?" It might mean another shot at retrieving that book. She needed to know now, more than ever, what she was.

She pushed the curtain aside and glanced at the frantic movement outside. Her family was busy lining up along the walkway clutching bags of birdseed.

"No, we're headed to the airport."

"Airport?" The curtain fell from her fingertips.

He grinned. "Looks like you'll be seeing Vermont sooner than you expected."

☾

TWO HOURS LATER, THEY PULLED onto the tarmac at DeKalb-Peachtree Airport a few yards away from a sleek-looking jet.

Men near the jet hurried toward them. One swung open her door while the other strode toward the trunk.

"Thank you," Celeste shouted over the roar of incoming planes. The second she stepped out the vehicle, the overwhelming scent of jet fuel hit her. Her stomach churned violently. She clamped her hand over her mouth and forced herself to take slow deep breaths.

She refused to throw up.

Not in front of an audience, and definitely not in front of Eric.

The men hefted the luggage out of the trunk and into the plane. When they disappeared a man dressed in a crisp pilot's uniform descended from the jet.

"Eric, I hear this is a special occasion." The dark-haired man held his hand out to Eric.

Eric shook the pilot's hand. "James, I'd like to introduce you to Celeste." He pressed his palm to the small of her back.

"Nice to meet you." She smiled as she shook James's hand.

"The pleasure is all mine, Mrs. Nordstrom." He nodded. "I'm James, Eric's . . . I mean, Mr. Nordstrom's private pilot. If you ever need to fly somewhere I'll be the one to get you there." His white teeth glinted against his black goatee.

"I don't think she needs to be going anywhere with you." Eric slapped him on the back. "We need to get to Vermont. I already missed my board meeting tonight. I can't afford to miss the one in the morning."

"Not a problem. I figure with the tail wind we've got tonight we'll make it there in record time." James gave her a wink. "You sure you don't want me to fly you two lovebirds somewhere else? Like the Bahamas or Tahiti? Vermont doesn't sound very romantic for a honeymoon."

Eric stepped in front of Celeste to block James's view. "Just fly us to Vermont. You think you can handle that?"

James craned his neck over Eric's shoulder to look at her. "I can, if that's where you really want to go."

"That's where I really want to go, James." Eric scowled at the pilot and turned. He placed his hand on her back and escorted her up the stairs into the plane. When they reached the top, Eric stopped.

"I'll be right back. I forgot my briefcase in the car." He hurried back down the stairs, leaving her alone.

She stepped inside the plane, eager to get away from the scents of the tarmac.

She stopped in her tracks, startled by how elegant it looked inside. There were captain's chairs with a table in between and a large sofa covered in cream colored leather. A few more large seats were located behind the couch. There was a bar area near the back close to the bathroom and two TVs, one mounted to the wall near the bar and another one between the chairs.

Sinking into one of the captain's chairs, she sighed, running her fingers across the soft leather of the armrests.

Her eyes drifted closed.

"We should be in Vermont in two hours. Once we take off, you can stretch out on the sofa if you want."

"I'll be fine here." She didn't bother opening her

eyes. They were much too heavy.

A few seconds later the sway of the plane taxiing down the runway rocked her to sleep.

☾

CELESTE YAWNED AND GLANCED AROUND. She was lying on the sofa instead of sitting in her seat.

She sat up as Eric walked out from the cockpit.

"Did you move me?" She looked up at him under her lashes.

He lifted his shoulders. "You looked like you could rest better on the sofa instead of the chair."

She twisted the wedding band on her finger and nodded, oddly touched by his concern.

"I was just about to wake you. We will be landing shortly." He sat, angling his chair toward her.

She ran her finger through her hair and snagged a tangle. She probably had a first-rate case of bed head. "Do I have time to go to the bathroom?"

"If you make it quick."

She grabbed her purse and made her way to the back of the plane to the bathroom and shut the door.

Studying her reflection in the mirror at the vanity, she cringed. Dark shadows hung under her eyes, and her hair was disheveled. Since discovering she was pregnant, she hadn't slept well. When she did manage to sleep, she had vivid dreams.

"I look nothing like the wife of someone as powerful as Eric Nordstrom."

Not that it mattered now. The deed was done and there was no going back.

CHAPTER FOURTEEN

A SHORT WHILE LATER, THE JET touched down at their destination. As she followed Eric off the plane, the nauseating smell of jet fuel and rubber assaulted her nose once again. Even though it was well after midnight, the airport was still humming with activity—planes landing and taking off, luggage being loaded and unloaded, and workers scurrying around the tarmac.

"Celeste, I'd like you to meet Solomon, my driver." Eric nodded toward the man who greeted them on the tarmac.

She tilted her head back, taking in the large man standing before her. He was tall and muscular, his skin the color of midnight and brown eyes that shone with kindness.

"Nice to meet you, Solomon." She held out her hand.

He took her hand in his and squeezed gently, as if he thought she'd break.

"It's a pleasure to meet you, Mrs. Nordstrom." He smiled.

"It's . . ." She pressed her lips together and cleared

her throat. "Thank you."

She'd almost corrected him, but she was no longer Celeste. She was Mrs. Nordstrom.

Solomon opened the limo door and she slid in, relieved to be away from the sounds and smells of the airport.

The inside of the limo was just as elegant as the jet, with a mini fridge, drop-down TV, and a bar.

Eric got in beside her and glanced at his Rolex.

"The people who work for you are very nice." Kindness was something she appreciated in a person and hard to come by

"They are nice because I pay them well." He snorted.

"You don't really believe that, do you?" A tired laugh trickled out of her.

He lifted his eyes from his cell phone and glared.

She was too tired to let it hurt her feelings. Despite his wealth and power and prestige, she couldn't help but pity him.

"I'm sorry," she said quietly.

"For what?"

"That you find it hard to trust people." She glanced at him.

"I have no idea what you're talking about." He folded his arms across his chest and stared straight ahead.

"Says someone who's been hurt before. Who hurt you? Was she someone special?" The words tumbled out before she knew it. She blamed it on a combination of exhaustion and hormones.

He let a smirk settle across his lips. "I assure you no woman broke my heart."

The only thing that would scar a man this badly

was either a woman or his parents. It was common knowledge at Cryptic that his parents had died a few years ago, and she couldn't help but wonder if their death had caused him to be so distant.

She tried biting her tongue, she really did, but somehow her tongue wiggled free. "Were you close to your parents?"

"We grew up very differently, you and I." The smirk melted off his face and in its place a serious demeanor.

"You grew up very privileged and my parents had to work for everything they had." She added.

He let out a hollow laugh and looked at her. "You are very close to your parents. I can see how much they love you."

"All parents love their children, Eric."

"Not all." A muscle jerked in his cheek.

"My mother was a good woman, kind and gentle, always trying to make peace between me and my father." His lips curled into a slight sneer. "For as long as I can remember, my father was constantly reminding me that I didn't measure up to his standards, his expectations, and his objectives."

"Did he actually say that to you?"

He shifted in his seat and turned his attention toward the window.

Her heart ached for him. How could a parent say such a thing?

Without thinking she reached for his hand. His head jerked up, suspicion shining in his blue eyes.

"Your father was wrong. You should have told him to suck it."

An uncomfortable silence settled in the car.

She shouldn't have said anything. And now she

couldn't take it back.

"I did tell him to suck it." He laughed. "Many times."

She pulled her hand away, wondering what effect his childhood would have on their child. Would he be an involved, loving father? Or would he see their son as someone who didn't quite measure up to society's standards?

She had nine months to figure it out.

"You are a very… unique woman, Celeste." He cocked his head as if he were trying to see inside her head.

Her heart jerked in her chest. His words hit a little too close to home. She looked him straight in the eyes.

"You have no idea."

☾

CELESTE WAS BEYOND EXHAUSTED. THE second the limo rolled up to Eric's house she wanted to cry with relief.

Solomon opened her car door, and she climbed out grateful that she was finally at her destination. Maybe now she could get some sleep.

"Welcome home." Solomon smiled as he opened her door. Once she was out he skirted the limo and opened the trunk to retrieve the luggage.

Her mouth dropped as she stared at the massive house before her.

She knew Eric was rich. She just hadn't prepared herself for how rich.

"Wow."

"I take it you like it." Eric stepped to her side.

She opened her mouth to respond, but a yawn

escaped.

"Come on, let's get you to bed. You'll have plenty of time to look around tomorrow." He took her elbow and led her inside.

If she hadn't been dead on her feet she would have made more of an effort not to lean against him as he helped her inside and up the massive staircase that lead up to the next level of the mansion.

After brushing her teeth and changing into pajamas her mother had packed, she crawled into the massive king-sized bed and pulled the thick comforter up to her chin.

She heard Eric moving around the bathroom, and for a fleeting moment she wondered if she should go sleep in another room.

She was too tired to care. She was asleep the second her head hit the pillow.

CHAPTER FIFTEEN

"UGH, WHY IS IT SO bright?" Celeste shielded her eyes with her hands against the sunlight streaming in from the window and sat up in bed. Blinking, she glanced at the bedside clock. It was already eleven a.m.

She never slept this late. For the first time in weeks she had managed to sleep through the night without any nightmares.

"Holy shit." She was in Eric's bed.

Her hands slid across the luxurious beige comforter and she looked around the room.

The walls were covered in a soft cream color damask wallpaper with art carefully placed throughout the room. There was a large stone fireplace along the wall with a large chair positioned in front. A very large crystal chandelier hung from the enormous ceiling in the middle of the room. The furniture was large and ornate and probably cost more than she made in a year. There was a small sitting area over by the curved bay window with two overstuffed chairs and an ottoman. Lush curtains framed each window and pooled on the hardwood floor.

It looked more like a five-star hotel than a bedroom.

As much as she wanted she couldn't stay in bed all day.

She shoved the comforter off and padded into the bathroom.

The bathroom was just as elegant as the bedroom. The shower was large enough for six people and encased in glass. The floors were expensive tile and chandeliers lit up the room.

Once showered and dressed, she headed down the sweeping staircase. Steadying herself with the handrail, she took her time, examining the portraits hung along the wall. The Nordstrom trademark ice-blue eyes and blond hair were evident in each picture. It looked like a Viking reunion.

She stepped into the marble floor of the foyer and looked up at the high coffered ceilings. She'd never felt more out of place in her life.

After a few false starts she finally found the kitchen and rubbed her hand across her queasy stomach. If she didn't eat soon her hunger was going to turn into severe morning sickness.

A plump older lady with short gray hair bustled about the stove and rattled pans.

She froze. She should have realized she wouldn't be alone in the mansion. With a house this big, Eric had to have staff.

She didn't want to bother the lady. If she could just point her in the direction of fixings for a sandwich she could fend for herself.

"Mrs. Nordstrom." A stainless steel bowl landed with a clank on the quartz countertop.

She started to turn to see who the lady spoke to, but caught herself. The woman was referring to her.

"Please, call me Celeste." She held out her hand across the island.

The older woman smiled and her face crinkled into kinds lines. She hurried around the island and pulled her into a tight hug.

Celeste stiffened, surprised by the warm greeting.

"I'm so pleased to meet you."The woman pulled away and gave Celeste a warm smile. "I'm Mrs. Gambil. I'm the housekeeper and cook for Mr. Eric."

"Nice to meet you Mrs. Gambil."

"Mrs. Celeste, I can't tell you how excited I was when I heard the good news. This house has been lonely without a lady. But not anymore. You're here now." Her gray eyes sparkled and her face shone with joy.

Celeste's gut twisted. She felt like a fraud.

"Oh, for a while I was worried that Eric would never settle down." Mrs. Gambil waved her hands in the air as she talked. "Especially after that mess with that Humphries woman. But I knew deep in my heart that he would find love."

Her smile wilted. Apparently, Eric hadn't told Mrs. Gambil the real reason behind the marriage.

"Look at me, gabbing away when you must be starving." Mrs. Gambil clapped her hands together.

"You read my mind, Mrs. Gambil."

"Sit while I prepare your lunch." She waved her to a barstool at the island.

"I don't want to bother you. I can fix myself

something to eat."

"Absolutely not." Mrs. Gambil lifted her chin and pressed her lips together. "Sit. I'm going to make you something to eat. I insist."

"Thank you. I really appreciate it." Celeste gave the woman a grateful smile and slid into the bar stool.

Less than five minutes passed before Mrs. Gambil was setting a plate filled with chicken salad, yogurt, fruit and homemade apple pie in front of her.

She bit into the chicken salad and sighed. "This is delicious."

"It's my mother's recipe. I figured since it's close to noon, you wouldn't mind a sandwich instead of eggs." Mrs. Gambil held up a measuring cup of sugar and poured it into a mixing bowl. "Mr. Nordstrom wanted you to know that he's going to be late getting in tonight. He said he had a lot of catching up to do at work."

"Did he say how late he would be?"

"No dear, but knowing him, it will be after midnight." The housekeeper clucked her tongue and shook her head. "Some nights he doesn't even come home."

Unease spread in her chest like melted peanut butter.

Maybe he didn't want to come home because he was still upset over their conversation about his father?

She wished she hadn't asked. But her curiosity seemed to override her common sense.

She needed to be careful and not get him upset. She had to get along with him for the time she was here. She had more than herself to consider.

She had her child to think about.

❧

AFTER LUNCH IT STARTED RAINING, so Celeste decided it was the perfect opportunity to explore the mansion.

She made a mental map of each room's location as she went, hoping to remember where everything was located.

The formal living room, kitchen, dining room, library, and game room were located on the main floor. The walkout basement housed an indoor pool and sauna along with an extensive gym.

The basement led outside to a beautiful garden of topiaries and flowers.

The second floor housed six bedrooms, each with its own private bath and large sitting area.

Since her bedroom was on the third floor, she decided to go back to the library to pick out a book to read.

She shoved open the large wooden doors and stepped into the library. The scent of old paper and leather books wrapped around her like a warm hug. The rain pelted against the windows, making it a perfect afternoon to curl up with a book and a cup of tea. Too bad it wasn't cold enough for a fire.

Ever since she could remember, she always sought books as an escape from everyday life. She read at an early age and loved going to the library on Saturday mornings. But she'd never seen a library as grand as this.

Floor-to-ceiling bookshelves lined the massive paneled walls. Sconces hung on either side of the large fireplace and a large portrait of a man, who she assumed was Eric's father, hung above it.

She pushed the rolling ladder aside to examine the titles. She caressed the spines, finding familiar titles as well as some she'd never heard of.

She could stay in here forever. Maybe she could seal herself in the library until she and Eric were divorced.

She walked past the ornate mahogany desk and several pieces of paper floated to the floor. She bent to pick them up.

Maureen called. Wants you to return her call when you get back in town.

Lisa called. She said she misses you and wants you to call her back ASAP.

Leslie called. She wants to know if you are still meeting her for dinner Friday night.

Her heart lurched and the room suddenly grew hot. She tried to look away but her gaze was stuck on the intimate words. She wanted to be anywhere but here. She didn't belong here.

She scooped up the messages and placed them on his desk.

Grabbing the first book she touched she wrenched it off the shelf and hurried out of the library.

She spent the rest of the day in her room, trying to get her mind off Eric and the messages.

By nightfall, Eric still wasn't home.

She ate dinner alone that night.

By bedtime, he still hadn't called, and she couldn't sleep.

She slipped on a robe she found in the closet and made her way down to the library and turned on his computer. She tried to ignore the paper messages sitting on the desk from all those women, but it was impossible.

She grabbed a book and plopped it on top of the paper, covering them up. She typed in Eric's name and hit enter. She'd heard the rumors at work about him but wanted to search out the truth for herself.

Within seconds newspaper articles about Eric and Elizabeth Humphries popped up. The article stated that Elizabeth claimed Eric had raped her.

"That's not Eric." She thought back to their night together in the pool house. He had clearly given her the choice. He hadn't forced her to do anything she didn't want to do.

She narrowed her gaze on a picture of Elizabeth Humphries. She was dressed in an expensive designer suit with her hair and makeup perfectly done. She didn't look like a woman in distress.

She scrolled down to the bottom of the article. It stated that the case was dismissed for lack of evidence. She sat back in her chair and studied his picture on the computer screen

No wonder he didn't trust anyone. No wonder he didn't trust her.

He thought she was just another woman after his money.

She had no choice but to prove him wrong.

CHAPTER SIXTEEN

NAUSEA SWEPT ACROSS CELESTE'S STOMACH and rode up into her throat. She bounded out of bed and rushed to the bathroom just in time.

When she managed to drag her head out of the toilet she leaned back against the wall and closed her eyes to try to quiet the pounding in her head and stomach.

"What I wouldn't give for a ginger ale." Just the thought of walking downstairs to the kitchen made her stomach churn. But she had no choice. She was alone and had to fend for herself.

She gathered her feet under her and stood. Her stomach lurched. She clenched her teeth, forcing herself not to throw up again.

She made her way toward the bedroom door and opened it.

She glanced down. Sitting on the floor was a silver tray with a small ice bucket holding a can of ginger ale. On a small plate sat two pieces of dry toast.

Tears welled up in her eyes. If she had the energy

she would have cried with relief.

She carried the tray over to the sitting area and placed it on the ottoman. She opened the ginger ale and took a sip. The crisp cold carbonated liquid slide down her throat and calmed her angry stomach. When the nausea turned the hunger to reach for the toast.

After keeping the toast and soda down, she took a shower and headed downstairs to the kitchen.

Mrs. Gambil glanced up from kneading dough on the counter. "Good morning, Mrs. Celeste. You look lovely today."

"Thank you." She glanced at her tan pants and light pink blouse. She didn't tell the woman it was one of few outfits she had.

"I want to thank you for the toast and ginger ale. It was exactly what I wanted." She would have to bring a ginger ale with her when she went to bed to have it when she woke up. She had heard morning sickness was bad, but she hadn't expected it to be this bad.

"Mr. Eric called last night and instructed me to leave it." She cut her eyes up at her as she worked.

"He did?" She blinked.

Mrs. Gambil nodded. "Yes, dear. He said the board meeting was running late so he would just stay in his apartment in the city."

"He has an apartment in the city?"

"Yes, I'm surprised he didn't mention it." Mrs. Gambil frowned and looked up at her.

She shrugged. "I'm sure he was planning on telling me." She doubted he would let it slip to his new wife that he had a sex nest hidden away in the city, even if theirs was a marriage of convenience.

"Mrs. Celeste, may I ask something?"

"Sure."

"Do your stomach troubles mean we can expect a little one?"

Heat spread from her neck into her cheeks.

"Yes." She lifted her chin, preparing for a lecture.

Mrs. Gambil squealed and hurried around the counter to pull her into another tight hug. "Well, bless my soul. Mr. Eric is starting a family. And I guess he wants a boy?"

Celeste relaxed at Mrs. Gambil's obvious excitement. The few times they had discussed the baby, Eric had referred to it as a boy. She nodded.

Mrs. Gambil chuckled and patted Celeste's cheek. "I knew it. Mr. Eric always gets what he wants, does he not?"

"Not always." She snorted.

She may have agreed to this marriage, but she had made demands of her own. And after the baby was born, she'd have her freedom again.

"Come, now. I've made you a heartier breakfast. You're much too thin. You must keep up your strength. You are eating for two now." Mrs. Gambil reached inside the stove and shoved a warm plate of pancakes and bacon across the kitchen island toward her.

Her mouth watered at the smell and she sat down to eat.

After another wonderful meal, she headed outside.

"It looks so beautiful. Like something out of a fairy tale." The dreary rain from yesterday had dissipated, replaced by brilliant sunshine and endless blue skies.

She loved being outside. It was her natural environment. Her mood lightened with each step.

Numerous topiaries adorned the garden, varying from winding spirals to perfectly formed circles. A few were even shaped like animals. Roses in every imaginable shade lined both sides of the flagstone path.

"It's almost too perfect to be real." She ran her finger across the velvet petals of a pink rose and smiled.

A sweet floral scent wafted up around her as she took her time admiring each color.

She walked all the way to the back of the garden and stopped. There was a large decorative white arch that led further into the woods. A slender dirt trail led from the garden into thick lush forest. She glanced down at her flats. If she continued she'd probably ruin her shoes.

Wasn't like she was going anywhere else. Shrugging her shoulders, she continued on. The canopy of trees protected the trail from yesterday's rain and kept it relatively dry.

Mushy green leaves and ferns sprawled across the forest floor, filling the air with an earthy smell. Light danced off the fern fronds as a chipmunk flicked its tail from around some scattered stones. The shrill of birds chirping and squirrels chatting mingled with the occasional drone of a nearby frog in a cacophony only nature could inspire.

She wasn't sure how long she walked, but the forest seemed to beckon her to come farther.

Blinding sunlight broke through the tree tops, streaming a beam of warmth on the ground. She stepped off the trail and into the center of the light.

She lifted her face letting the warmth soak into her body.

"Hello."

She screamed and stumbled backward.

A few feet away sat a little girl on the ground. The girl laughed, her curly brown hair bouncing with the movement. "I didn't mean to scare you."

"I didn't know anyone was in here." She rubbed a hand over her fast beating heart and shook her head. "Do you live nearby?"

The child nodded and giggled behind her hand.

"My name is Celeste." She dropped her hand and took a deep breath. "What's yours?"

"Anastasia." The little girl stood.

"That's a very pretty name." Maybe she should to add it to her list of baby names in case she had a girl.

"You should be thinking of boy names, not girl names. A boy is what you will have."

Her hand dropped to her stomach. A shiver ran down her back. "How did you know I was pregnant?" And how did she know what she was thinking?

"It has been foretold." The girl spoke in a sing song voice that had every muscle in Celeste's body tense.

"What has been foretold?" Fear tingled up her spine like tiny spiders.

"The prophecy. Your child bears the curse of death." Anastasia bent and picked up a colored rock.

She couldn't speak. Her insides quivered. Had she brought this on her child because of what she was?

Damn Eric Nordstrom. If he hadn't been there the night of the party she wouldn't have been distracted. She would have found that book. And she would know what she was. But no, he had to distract her with his looks and his sweet words.

She knew better. She was in this mess because of herself, not anyone else. As much as she wanted to blame Eric, the fault lay at her feet.

The girl dropped the rock and glanced up at her. "It is your destiny. Your parents tried to hide you. But the Queen knows where you are, Celeste."

"What Queen? What are you talking about?"

"The Queen wants what you have. She wants the blood of your child." An orange butterfly landed on the child's tiny finger and for a moment she seemed mesmerized.

"My child's blood?" The bone-chilling words congealed in her veins.

She took a step back.

Anastasia looked up, her chocolate-brown eyes rooting her to the spongy green ground.

She bent and picked up a wilted flower, her attention distracted.

She needed to leave this place, to escape. She tried to move, but couldn't. Terror froze every muscle in her body.

The child blew softly on the flower in her palm. The flower twitched and then began to spin. It rose into the air, hovered inches from her hand and changed colors until it transformed into a fresh daisy.

"How did you do that?" The words whooshed out of her lungs.

The little girl's smiled disappeared. She cocked

her head to the side. "You really don't know what you are, do you?"

"What am I?" She swallowed and braced herself for the answer. After seeing what the girl had just done, she wasn't sure she wanted to know.

Anastasia giggled behind her hand. "You are like me."

"No I'm not."

The girl's laughter faded. She put her hands at her sides, her palms facing the ground. The earth beneath the child began to tremble. Dirt flew around her feet like a small dust tornado. Slowly her feet lifted off the ground and she levitated in the air.

Celeste's knees buckled and she slid to the ground.

"Your enemies are coming for you. Run, Celeste." The little girl disappeared into thin air, leaving behind a thousand glittery white lights.

"I'm going crazy," she whispered. Maybe the stress of the last few days was making her hallucinate.

Maybe the hormones of the pregnancy were making her delusional.

A thousand thoughts raced through her mind.

She needed to get out of here. She scrambled to her feet and ran.

CHAPTER SEVENTEEN

LIMBS SNAGGED HER HAIR AND stickers clawed her skin, but Celeste didn't stop running.

Her lungs burned, begging her to stop, but the fear spurred her on.

Through the prison of green forest and foliage, a pinpoint of light shone ahead, teasing her with the promise of safety. She just needed to keep going.

Her heart hammered, threatening to break through her chest while her feet pounded against the mushy ground.

Heart racing, she broke through the tree line and into the garden. She glanced behind her and slammed into something hard. Arms encircled her and held her tight. She screamed and struggled to get away.

"Celeste, stop, it's me."

Her legs crumbled at the sound of Eric's voice. He caught her before she hit the ground.

"What's wrong?" He held her at arm's length and looked down into her face. Worry and concern flashed through his ice-blue eyes.

"There's someone . . ." She glanced back at the woods, expecting the creepy little girl to be standing at the edge, levitating in the air and laughing at her.

She saw no one.

"Was there someone in the woods?" Eric asked.

She nodded unable to speak. She dug her fingers into his muscled arm, refusing to let go.

There was no way she was letting him go in there and leave her alone. If what the girl said was true, if she really was like her, a freak, then she was screwed. That was something he didn't need to know.

He yelled and waved the gardener over who had been busy working in the flower beds along the house. Celeste forced herself to let go of her hold and step back as he questioned the man.

The gardener insisted he'd worked all morning in the front of the house and hadn't seen anyone. Eric nodded and quickly dismissed the man who hurried back to work.

"I'm sorry. I shouldn't have gone in there." She wiped away her tears and shook her head. Maybe she had imagined the whole thing.

"Don't apologize. You had every right to go into the woods. This land belongs to me and no one is allowed to be in there." Anger flashed in his blue eyes. "They didn't hurt you, did they?"

"No, just startled me, that's all."

"What did they look like?"

"I didn't get a good look." She was not going to tell him a seven year old girl had scared the hell out of her.

"I can't help if I don't know what happened." He

lowered his voice and stepped closer.

"I'm fine, really." She gave him a tight smile and forced herself to step away. "I guess I'm just a little on edge, with everything that's happened."

She needed to reassure herself as much as Eric that everything *was* fine. She didn't need to give him a reason to find her crazy and an unfit mother. He would have no reason to keep his end of the bargain if that happened.

"I didn't sleep much last night. I'm sure that has a lot to do with it."

"Why don't you go lie down? I'll have Mrs. Gambil bring you some tea to help you relax."

"Thank you. That would be nice."

Time alone to herself would give her the opportunity to think things through, to rationalize what had happened in the forest.

If she couldn't find some reasonable explanation for what she'd witnessed, then her problems were bigger than she realized.

☾

CELESTE OPENED HER EYES AND glanced at the bedside table. According to the time on the clock she'd taken a two hour nap. She'd managed to sleep two hours without dreaming. Maybe because she'd been so exhausted, she'd imagined the whole scene in the forest with Anastasia.

She pushed herself up, saw Eric in bed with her, and froze.

Eric leaned against the headboard, a book in his hand. He smiled and closed the book he'd been reading.

"Feel better?" He stroked her hair away from her

face.

His fingertips skimmed her cheek. Her heart thumped a little harder and a little faster. She had to remind herself to breathe.

"I do." She cleared her throat, feeling unnaturally warm. "You just got back?"

"The meeting ran long, because no one could agree on a damn thing. So I spent the night." He continued to stroke her hair while he spoke.

She shoved the comforter off her body and wished she had a cold glass of water to cool her down.

Maybe being pregnant caused hot flashes as well as delusions.

"Do you want to talk about what happened?" His intense blue gaze searched her face.

"I'm okay. I really don't want to talk about it." She turned away.

Silence settled between them.

He cleared his throat. "We'll be having dinner tonight with some business associates. It's formal attire." He stood.

"I don't have a cocktail dress." She jerked her head toward him. Just when she didn't think the day could get any worse, it had.

"I picked up something for you to wear tonight. In the morning, have Solomon drive you into the city to do some proper shopping."

Her stomach clenched. She didn't have any money with her and there was no way she could afford the designer clothes he'd expect her to wear.

"I can't."

"Do you already have something else planned?" He frowned.

"No. I don't have enough money to go shopping tomorrow. My last paycheck will be deposited next Friday. I'll go shopping then."

"I didn't expect you to pay." His eyes widened and a look of incredulity stretched across his face.

"But . . ."

"I left some credit cards on my desk." He lifted her chin with a finger to meet his gaze. . "Use those tomorrow."

"I'll pay you back." She hated being indebted to anyone. Especially to him.

"I don't want you to pay me back. You're my wife. I'm more than able to take care of my own wife." His deep voice sent shivers across her skin. The kind of shivers one gets when standing too close to a fire.

"Thank you."

He nodded and then tugged on her hand. "Come on. I want you to see your dress. I hope it fits. I had to guess at the size."

He led her into the large closet that looked more like a boutique with all its shelves and built in cabinets. He stopped in front of a white garment bag. He slowly unzipped it, revealing a black evening gown.

The dress was one-shoulder and had crystal accents at the gathered bust and a sexy slit up the thigh.

It was absolutely gorgeous. She could only imagine how much he'd spent on the designer gown.

"If you don't like it, you can take it back." He rubbed the back of his neck and looked at her under his lashes.

"No, don't take it back. It's beautiful." She let her

fingertips trail along the silky material.

"You like it?" He sounded relieved.

"Are you kidding? I love it." She flipped the tag over and smiled. "And the size is right too." She snorted and touched her belly. "At least for a few more weeks."

Her heart warmed at his thoughtfulness. She stretched up on her toes and pressed her lips to his cheek to thank him.

He turned his face and their lips touched. That familiar thrum rippled through her body, tickling every nerve.

He wrapped her in his arms and pulled her tight against his chest. She melted against him.

His tongue slipped between her parted lips, hot and insistent. She kissed him back and locked her fingers behind his neck, unable to pull away.

Her stomach warmed as he deepened the kiss. She moaned as his hands cupped her butt and pulled her closer.

The images of those scraps of paper in his office flittered through her mind, mocking her and reminding her how little she meant to him.

Panic rose in her throat. What the hell was she doing?

"Stop." She shoved him away. She had to. She was going to lose herself if she didn't start putting up a boundary around her heart.

His eyes widened in confusion as he stared at her. Something shifted in his expression, and then hardened like stone. "Be ready in an hour." He turned and walked out of the room, his words hanging in the air.

She stared at the empty doorway regretting that

she had pushed him away.

She shouldn't have let him kiss her like that.

She had other things to worry about right now. More important things.

She hurried into the bedroom and dug her cell phone out of her purse. She punched in her parents' number. It rang and rang and rang and before the answering machine picked up.

"Damn it." She hung up without leaving a message and dialed her mother's cell phone.

"Pick up the phone." It rang a few times before going to voice mail.

She tried her dad's cell phone and got the same result.

She eyed the clock on the nightstand. She didn't have much time to get ready.

She hurried into the bathroom and turned on the shower.

What did Anastasia mean when she had said her parents hid her?

Did they know what she was? Had they known this whole time?

She picked up her cell and called her parents' home phone and left a message. She needed to talk to them more than ever.

She needed answers and she wasn't going to stop until she got what she wanted.

CHAPTER EIGHTEEN

"I HAVE AN EIGHT O'CLOCK RESERVATION." Eric addressed the female hostess at the restaurant. He let his hand drift down to her lower back. Since they'd walked inside she already gotten several male glances. He wanted to make it clear who she belonged to.

The platinum blonde with the blood-red lipstick completely ignored Celeste and gave him a sultry smile. "It's good to have you with us again, Mr. Nordstrom. Your regular table is ready. If you will just follow me."

"Perfect." He dismissed the hostess's gaze and leaned down to his wife. She was busy admiring the contemporary décor of the restaurant. The dress he bought fit perfectly, showing off her slender figure and accentuating her beauty.

"Are you ready, sweetheart?" He smiled.

Her eyes widened slightly. She looked at the hostess and then back at him before she pasted on a sugary smile. "Sure, pumpkin."

The hostess eyes narrowed into slits for a moment before she remembered herself and recovered with a polite smile. Even if he wasn't married, he still wouldn't give her the time of day. She wasn't his type.

He followed behind Celeste as the hostess led them to their table. He wrapped his hands on her waist and whisper in her ear. "Pumpkin?"

Damn, she smelled good.

"I figured the 'sweetheart' thing was more for her benefit." She pointed to the hostess's back and shrugged. "Pumpkin was the first thing that came to my mind. It was that or Snicker Doodle."

"Snicker Doodle?" His eyebrows shot up.

She stopped so suddenly his crotch bumped into her tight little ass. His heart thudded hard in his chest.

"I can't help it." She continued walking. "When I get nervous all I can think about is eating."

All he could think about right now was eating too. Eating her.

They passed a couple seated at a table. The man did a double take as Celeste walked past and craned his neck to try to get a better look.

Anger flashed in his gut. He stepped in front of the man's line of vision, making sure they made eye contact and shot him a warning look. *Yeah, that's right, buddy. If you want to keep your eyes, keep them off my fucking wife.*

The wide-eyed man quickly looked down, his focus now on his house salad.

Eric shook his head, forcing his possessive lust back into its cage.

"There's no need to be worried." He leaned and whispered. "The board members you will be meeting tonight are quite pleasant."

"And the rest aren't?" She looked up at him.

"Depends on their mood." He learned a long time ago that people liked him when they wanted something.

"Don't worry." He rested his hand on the curve of her lower back and urged her forward. "You'll do fine."

She nodded and looked away. She seemed to relax when her gaze landed on Uncle Stephen sitting at their table.

"I was beginning to wonder if anyone was going to show up." Stephen smiled, stood, and placed a kiss on her cheek. "My dear, you look beautiful."

"Thank you. Eric picked out the dress." She blushed and brushed her hand across the silky material.

"He did?" Stephen's eyebrows shot up.

He shook his uncle's hand and ignored his uncle's gesture. "It's not even eight yet. You act like you've been waiting here for hours."

Stephen waved off his comment. "Being early is the reason I am as successful as I am today."

"I thought it was because you inherited Grandfather's money."

"Yes, but I've managed to hang onto it, haven't I?" Stephen shot him a look of irritation before turning his attention back to Celeste. "Tell me how you're feeling, Celeste?"

Eric pulled out her chair and she sat.

"Mornings tend not to agree with me, but other than that I'm fine." She smiled and placed her linen napkin on her lap.

"I read somewhere that the first trimester is the worst." Stephen nodded thoughtfully. "After that morning sickness should dissipate, and you will have a burst of energy and start nesting."

Eric chuckled. "Thank you, Dr. Spock. I hope you don't plan on delivering my son as well as giving out your sage advice."

"Of course not, but you should be looking for a doctor." He scowled and pointed a finger at him.

"It's already taken care of. Celeste has an appointment in a few days with Dr. Sevalus."

She jerked her head toward him. "In two days? When were you going to let me know?"

He shrugged and placed the napkin in his lap.

"What if I already had something planned?" She narrowed her eyes at him. Her full lips were pressed into an insistent line. He knew she was trying her best to conceal her irritation with him.

"*Do* you have something planned?" He eased back in the chair and studied her.

"Well, no. The point is it would have been nice to know ahead of time."

"I was going to talk to you about it tonight when we got home." He shifted in his chair to see her better. Even irritated, she was still beautiful.

"Ah. Here comes some of our dinner party now." Stephen nodded past them.

Eric turned in his seat.

Loren Jamison smiled as she approached, looking every bit like a silver-haired Jackie O in her tailored gray dress and pearls, while her husband, Conrad, dressed in a black suit, gave a nod.

"I thought we were going to be late. The traffic on the interstate is horrible, some sort of wreck." Loren fingered her string of pearls and shook her head.

The men exchanged handshakes.

"Glad you two could make it. You look lovely, Loren." Eric kissed her cheek.

She smiled up at him and patted his chest. "And you know just what to say to make an old lady's day."

Loren's gaze landed on Celeste and a look of surprise flashed across her face.

"I'm afraid we haven't met." Loren drew her sharp gaze from Celeste back to him.

"Celeste, let me introduce you to Conrad and Loren Jamison. Conrad is on the board of directors. They are both longtime friends of the family."

Celeste smiled and shook Loren's hand and then Conrad's. "It's a pleasure to meet you both."

"The pleasure is all ours." Loren smiled glanced at him. "Where have you been hiding this lovely young lady?"

"In my dungeon," he answered dryly.

"That explains it, then." Loren grinned and looked back at Celeste. "Tell me, dear, are you new to the area?"

"Actually . . ."

"Sorry we're late. Sloan almost had to go in to the hospital right as we were leaving." Andrea Leigh sauntered up to their table in a black-and-white sleeveless dress. Her dark blond hair was swept up off her shoulders into some kind of twist.

"But you're not on call tonight, son." Loren patted Sloan's cheek. He wondered if Sloan realized how lucky he was to have two wonderful parents like Loren and Conrad.

"I know. But the ER called me when they couldn't find Dr. Henry, who is on call. Ten minutes later they called back saying they'd located him." Sloan wiggled his eyebrows at his mother. "In the ladies' locker room with one of the ICU nurses."

"My word. I thought you doctors were too busy to even think about that kind of thing at work." Loren arched an eyebrow.

"We're men, Mother. We're never too busy to think about that kind of thing." Sloan smirked.

"I'm telling you right now, if I ever catch you doing that with one of those young nurses, it will definitely be the last time you do it. Ever. With anyone." Andrea Leigh gave Sloan a saccharine smile.

Everyone laughed.

Andrea Leigh's gaze zeroed in on Celeste. "Eric, aren't you going to introduce us to your date?"

"Celeste, this is Andrea Leigh Jones and her fiancé Sloan Jamison. Sloan is another board member."

Celeste stood and handshakes were exchanged. "Nice to meet you both."

"Nice to meet you as well." Andrea Leigh sat next to Celeste while Sloan beside his fiancé.

Eric fought a grin. He waited until everyone was seated before he spoke. "This is Celeste Nordstrom. My wife,"

CHAPTER NINETEEN

ANDREA LEIGH'S MOUTH DROPPED AND Sloan spit out the water he'd just sipped. Andrea Leigh handed her fiancé a napkin without taking her astonished gaze off Celeste.

Exactly the respond he'd expected.

"Wife?" Loren narrowed her eyes. "Is this a joke?"

"No. We were married a week ago." He motioned with his hands for everyone to sit, then took a drink of the scotch the waitress had just dropped off at their table. Thank god, Uncle Stephen always put his drink order in for him.

"This certainly is a shock." Conrad frowned, looking from Eric to Celeste. And then the frown grew into a smile. "What the hell am I saying? This is wonderful." Conrad stood, stepped around the table and planted a kiss on Celeste's cheek.

Loren elbowed her husband out of the way and pulled Celeste into a hug, her face lighting up with joy. "I can't tell you how happy I am for both of you."

Eric cut his eyes to Andrea Leigh. She'd never been a fan of anyone he dated. She always said the women were pretty on the outside but empty on the inside. He tensed, preparing to come to Celeste's defense.

Laughter bubbled out of Andrea Leigh and she wrapped Celeste into a warm embrace. "Congratulations, Celeste. I see that Eric finally chose someone with taste." She cut her eyes at him before looking back at Celeste. "Tell me, do I detect a Southern accent?"

"Yes. I'm from Georgia." Celeste smiled brightly.

"Well, honey, we're practically neighbors. I'm from South Carolina." Andrea Leigh drawled. She cut her eyes at him. "Glad to see you finally picked a woman of quality."

He grinned. He shouldn't have been surprised. Andrea Leigh always spoke her mind.

"I am hurt that you didn't invite us to the wedding, Eric." Andrea Leigh narrowed her eyes on Stephen. "Did you go to the wedding, Stephen?"

"Yes, it was a lovely affair." Stephen picked up his scotch, took a sip and averted his eyes.

"Why weren't we invited?" Andrea Leigh took her seat and crossed her arms.

"We didn't mean to leave anyone out. It certainly wasn't our intent." Eric looked across the table at everyone's expectant faces. "It was a quick and a very small ceremony." He paused and frowned, as he looked over Conrad's shoulder. Everyone followed his gaze to the leggy brunette in a bright pink dress strutting toward them.

Shit.

"I hope I'm not too late." Leslie strode up to the table, looked at him, and smiled.

"Leslie. You're right on time." His eye twitched.

He hoped to god that Leslie would mind her manners. He wasn't in the mood tonight for her bullshit.

"Perfect." Leslie shifted her gaze from him and raked Celeste with an icy glare. "You must be new. Otherwise you'd know you are sitting in my seat."

Celeste stiffened at the spiteful words but didn't move.

Anger surged in his gut. He slid his arm around Celeste's shoulders and pulled her close.

"This is where Eric asked me to sit. Until he tells me to move, I'm afraid you'll have to find another seat." Anger flashed through her emerald eyes despite the polite smile on her face.

Eric grinned.

Apparently Leslie had met her match.

Leslie's eyebrows shot up.

"Celeste is exactly where she should be." He kept his tone level. "Celeste, this is Leslie Andrews, another board member. You'll have to overlook her lack of manners. She didn't have the training you did."

The look of shock that crossed Leslie's face was priceless. He knew he'd hit her where it hurt. Her parents had sent her to the best girls' school in Switzerland.

"Nice to meet you, Leslie," Celeste said.

"Leslie, meet Celeste Nordstrom. My beautiful wife." He took Celeste's hand in his and placed a kiss on the back of her knuckles.

Celeste met his gaze and blushed.

"Your what?" Leslie squawked. Her eyes bulged and the color drained from her plastic face.

"Isn't it the most wonderful news in the world?

They are married." Andrea Leigh's tone was too excited. She was obviously reveling Leslie's discomfort. It was no secret that the two women hated each other. "Oh, and guess what? She's Southern. Just like me." Andrea Leigh picked up her wine glass and took a sip.

Leslie's gaze darted back to him. "Eric, darling, when did all of this happen?"

"A week ago." He picked up his scotch and swirled the straw colored liquid. There was going to be hell to pay if the board caught wind of the true reason behind the marriage. And Leslie was vindictive enough and had a big enough mouth to make that happen.

"Yes, well, congratulations of course." Leslie's thin lips pressed into a semblance of a smile. "I'm just surprised, that's all. I mean, after all, you did say you were never going to get married."

"I guess when fate intervenes, you can't fight it." He looked into Celeste's green eyes and he couldn't help but wonder what it was about her that had him captivated.

Keeping his distance from her for a year was going to be walking straight into hell. He just hoped he had the fortitude for it.

"I WORKED AT CRYPTIC. THAT'S HOW I met Eric." Celeste smiled politely as Leslie barraged her with yet another question.

She clutched the water glass and took a sip, trying her best to tap down her irritation. She usually didn't let people get to her, but Leslie was an exception.

She bet that this was the same Leslie whose name she'd seen on those scraps of paper. One of Eric's girlfriends.

Her stomach tightened and suddenly she wanted to be anywhere but at that table. She didn't fit in here. She wasn't one of these people.

"Why the hurry? Why the need to get married so fast? I wonder if there is more to the story than you are telling, Celeste." Every time Leslie gave her a smug smile, she wanted to rip the woman's gorgeous black hair out by the roots.

Or maybe even scalp her. Yeah, scalping would be better.

"I knew I had to return to Vermont. And I didn't want to wait." Eric answered without hesitation.

"You couldn't wait at least . . ." Leslie batted her eyes at Eric but he quickly interrupted her.

"Enough." Eric glared at Leslie. "This is a business dinner, not an inquisition."

Celeste fought the overwhelming urge to kiss him.

The men and Leslie settled in to talk business which gave her the opportunity to visit with Andrea Leigh and Loren.

"Andrea Leigh, do you work?" She took a small bite of her filet and focused her attention on the pretty blonde.

"I used to when I lived in Charleston. I was a drug rep. That's how I met Sloan. I wasn't even looking for love." She beamed.

"That's usually the way it happens." She smiled despite the twinge of envy that tugged at her heart. She could tell from how they looked at each other that they were crazy in love.

"Exactly. I mean, look at you and Eric. You guys were probably not even looking for love, and the next thing you know, you're married."

She forced herself to smile. She was a liar and an imposter. Their marriage was a business deal, nothing more.

Since that one night together, Eric hadn't shown any interest in her other than one kiss. She was beginning to think he'd found another woman to fill his bed at night. That was a possibility. It wasn't like he was spending nights at home.

"If you're not doing anything tomorrow, I'd love for you to come over for tea." Andrea Leigh's eyes lit up.

"Tomorrow? Sorry, I had a day of shopping planned."

"Now you're speaking my language." Andrea Leigh's eyes sparkled.

"Would you like to go?" Celeste asked.

"I would love to."

"That would be great. I'm not familiar with any of the local stores and I'm not sure what I might need here." A weight lifted off her shoulders.

"Shopping is my second language. I'd love to help you pick out some things. How about I pick you up at nine? That way we can shop and then have lunch out." Andrea Leigh took another sip of her wine.

"Thank you. I would like that." Celeste smiled. She'd made her first friend since moving to Vermont.

For the first time since she'd arrived, she began to feel like she wasn't completely alone.

CHAPTER TWENTY

"THANK YOU FOR THE LATER appointment." Celeste smiled at the receptionist and stuck the appointment card in her purse. Eric had made her first appointment with the doctor early in the morning. With her morning sickness she'd made sure to schedule her next appointment for noon.

She hooked her purse on her arm and headed for the elevator.

Her first prenatal appointment with Dr. Sevalus had gone well. He was a soft-spoken older gentleman with gentle eyes who patiently answered all her questions. More importantly, he didn't ask why her husband hadn't come with her.

Not that she'd expected Eric to come. But it was embarrassing to sit in the waiting room with all the other pregnant women who had their doting husbands with them while she sat alone with only a magazine to keep her company.

Being alone was a feeling she was getting used to.

She'd barely seen Eric since they'd gotten married. He went to work before she even got up, and arrived home late at night when she was already in bed. The only way she knew if he'd even come home was through talking to Mrs. Gambil over breakfast.

"Mrs. Celeste." Solomon gave her a kind smile and opened the door to the limo. She slid in and leaned back against the leather seat.

Her stomach turned and a fresh wave of nausea washed over her. She sucked in slow breaths to calm her stomach while Solomon drove onto the street.

She'd already been sick before they left the house, and she wasn't prepared for another round on the ride back.

She pressed her hand against her stomach in a futile attempt to get her body under control.

It wasn't working.

She groaned and slapped her hand across her mouth, meeting Solomon's concerned gaze in the rearview mirror. He nodded and pulled into a gas station.

She opened her door and sprinted to the bathroom, praying she'd make it in time.

When she walked back to the car she gave him a grateful smile. "Thank you, Solomon."

"I thought you might need this." He handed her a brown paper bag.

"What is it?" She opened the bag and looked inside. A can of a ginger ale and box of vanilla wafers.

"How did you know that was what I needed?" She slid into the car and sank into the leather.

"It's what my mother gave me when my stomach didn't feel good." He shrugged and shut the door behind her, then climbed into the driver's seat. "Figured it might help."

"God bless you, Solomon." She popped the top of the soda and took a sip. The sweet bubbles calmed her offended stomach.

"He already has blessed me, Mrs. Celeste, when he sent me to watch over you."

She froze.

The image of Anastasia flashed through her head.

He started the engine and pulled onto the street.

"Solomon, may I ask you something?" She watched him in the rearview mirror.

"You can ask me anything."

"Have you ever seen anything you couldn't explain?" she asked.

"That's a strange question." He glanced at her in the mirror and then looked back at the road.

How much should she say? How much could she say? After all, he did work for Eric, so his loyalty lay with him, not her.

She met his gaze again and decided to press on. "I suppose you don't know anything about a queen, do you?"

His eyes widened slightly. If she hadn't been staring at him in the mirror, she would have missed it.

"Solomon?"

"Which country are you referring to—England, Monaco?"

Her heart fell. Once again she was making something out of nothing.

She laid her head back against the seat and glanced out the window.

"Never mind. It's not important."

☾

THE MORNING SICKNESS GREW WORSE over the next few weeks that Celeste thought she'd die. Sometimes she would be so sick that she didn't have the strength to get out of bed.

Fatigued and miserable, didn't leave home much. With Eric always at work, she entertained herself by reading, exploring the gardens, or helping Mrs. Gambil in the kitchen when had the energy. She was homesick and desperately missed her parents.

But she knew this was her home now, even though it didn't feel like it. She had to make the best of the situation until the baby arrived.

Though there was a lot to keep her occupied, there was one place she avoided: the woods. The eerie encounter with Anastasia was never far from her mind, especially at night.

Some days she sat near the window of her bedroom and gazed down at the narrow dirt path that led back into the woods and wondered...had she imagined the whole thing?

Some nights she felt drawn to the path, as if she were experiencing a magnetic pull to find the truth. But fear for her baby kept her from acting on those feelings. Fear—and the nightmares that continued to plague her at night.

She continued to have nightmares, nightmares about animals with sharp teeth ripping into her skin while her baby cried in the dark. At night she prayed for the dreams to stop.

But unlike before, this time her prayers went unanswered.

"COOKIES." CELESTE COULDN'T MOVE FAST enough down the stairs as she followed the aroma of freshly baked cookies to the kitchen. Since she'd entered her second trimester, her morning sickness had vanished and her appetite had increased, much to the relief of her doctor.

Dr. Sevalus had voiced his concern about her not gaining enough weight. He'd even threatened to put her in the hospital if she didn't start eating more.

Something she was about to rectify right now. Plopping down on a barstool at the kitchen counter, she grabbed a warm oatmeal cookie.

She took a bite and moaned as the sugary confection melted on her tongue.

"Does this mean the morning sickness has passed?" Eric came up behind her and grabbed a cookie off the platter. She frowned and fought the urge to pull the plate closer.

"I've not had any nausea for about a week now." A real husband would have known that. She pointed the half eaten cookie at him. "I thought you would be at work by now. Is something wrong?"

"I don't have anything scheduled until this afternoon." He popped the rest of the cookie in his mouth.

"Are you feeling okay?" She leaned over and pressed her hand across his forehead.

"I'm fine." He ducked away from her hand and his gaze flicker toward the ceiling. "You act like work is all I do."

"Work is all you do. I'm not even sure you sleep."

She hooked her arm around the platter and pulled it out of his reach. She picked up another cookie and paused, the cookie halfway to her mouth. "For all I know, you could be a vampire who pretends to be at work but is actually stalking helpless victims in dark alleys."

He chuckled and shook his head. "You clearly watch too many vampire movies."

"I don't watch vampire movies. I read vampire books. Books are always better than the movies." She bit into the cookie and closed her eyes in appreciation. "I love Mrs. Gambil."

He pulled the platter away.

"Hey! I need those." She made a grab for the plate but he held it out of her reach.

"What you need is to eat something healthy, like a real breakfast with eggs, toast, and fruit." He frowned and glanced around. "Where is Mrs. Gambil, anyway?"

"She left to go to the grocery store. And what I need is an oatmeal cookie." She snatched another cookie off the platter and took a bite before he could stop her.

His gaze dropped to her mouth, his eyes darkened. He placed the platter on the counter and stepped closer. "Oh I think I know what you need." He ran his thumb across her bottom lip.

Her breath caught in her throat and her heart raced.

He moved his hand away but continued to gaze intently at her. Warmth spread throughout her body. He was going to kiss her. And she wasn't going to stop him.

"I want to have a cocktail party Friday night. It's

time to make our announcement about our child."

Her shoulders slumped with disappointment. "A cocktail party?" She cringed, thinking of all the work that would be necessary to insure a successful event.

"I know that Andrea Leigh has been trying to get you to go out and have martinis. Now she will know the reason you keep refusing."

"How did you know about that?" She hadn't said anything to him about Andrea Leigh's weekly invitation.

"She made Sloan ask me if you were mad at her." He cringed.

"The first friend I make and she thinks I'm mad at her. I need to call her." Unease welled in her chest. She hopped off the barstool and looked around, trying to remember the last place she'd put her cell phone.

"Hold on." He wrapped his arm around her waist. "Just tell her at the party. Besides, I am sure Andrea Leigh will insist on taking you shopping for baby stuff."

"But I don't want to wait."

"Here." He grinned and held out two cookies to distract her. She happily accepted.

"I want to talk to you about something," Eric said.

"What?" She finished off the first cookie and started on the next.

"We need to have one of the rooms upstairs decorated for a nursery. There are plenty of rooms on the second floor to choose from."

"The second floor?" The second floor was too far away from their bedroom. What if her baby needed her? What if something happened? What if the dreams came true?

"What's wrong with the second floor?"

"I don't like the idea of the baby being on a different floor from our bedroom. I mean, he'll be little, and what if he needs me in the middle of the night?" She wasn't going to give in. Not this time.

Panic rose in her as the nightmares flooded back—followed by Anastasia's warning.

"There is a small sitting room on our floor that's not used. Would you rather use that for the nursery?"

"Can I?" She grabbed his arm.

His lips tilted upward. "If it makes you happy, yes."

"Thank you." She threw her arms around him and buried her face in his chest.

He stiffened in her arms.

She took a step back, embarrassed that she'd leaned into him, but his arm slid up her back, holding her against his body.

His hand cupped her cheek and he stared down into her eyes.

"It's not wrong, Celeste." His fingers brushed against her cheek.

"What's not?" Her breathing changed and grew labored. She also knew she should stop him, knew this would complicate things, knew the danger of getting this close.

"It's not wrong to want to be touched. We are married, you know."

"Hmmm." Her eyelids slid closed and she leaned into him. She couldn't help it.

His lips covered hers in a possessive kiss. A flood

of emotions rushed out, just as intense as their first night together.

He nipped at her bottom lip and she let resolve go and kissed him back.

He kissed his way to her neck, his mouth hot and insistent. His lips heated her flesh, causing tiny pinpricks of pleasure to skit across her skin.

His hand trailed up her thigh and her breathing increased.

His cell phone chirped to life. "Damn it." He pulled away and dug the phone out of his pocket. "Hello?"

She wrapped her arms around herself and walked to the window, trying to slow her breathing.

She had enough problems without adding to them by getting her heart involved with Eric.

She needed to figure out what her dreams meant and what she was exactly. But she needed that book in Stephen Nordstrom's library. They were in Vermont, and that book was in Atlanta.

James.

A small smile curled her lips. She'd forgotten about Eric's pilot.

On a private jet, she could go to Atlanta and be back home before dinner. Eric would probably find out about the trip, but she would tell him she'd needed to get some of her things before she had the baby. Surely he couldn't get mad at her for that.

She turned and looked over at him. He was staring intently at her. His gaze never left her as he continued his conversation on the phone.

She looked away, afraid he might see the secret in her eyes.

"I'm sorry. I have to get back to the office." He walked slowly over to her.

"Is everything okay?" She pressed her hand to her stomach.

"There's an issue with a contract." He kissed her cheek and stepped back. "Oh, I expect that Leslie will offer to decorate the nursery when she hears the news. She has a degree in interior design. Some of the board members have had her remodel some of their vacation homes." He walked to the door and spoke over his shoulder. "If you don't want her involved, just ask Andrea Leigh to recommend someone. She's always having her house redone."

Her heart frosted over. Leslie was obviously interested in Eric. It didn't matter whether he returned her advances or not. Woman like Leslie didn't quit until they got what they wanted.

Leslie might get Eric eventually, but there was no way in hell that woman would ever get near her son.

CHAPTER TWENTY-ONE

"I'M NOT READY TO DO this." Celeste wiped her clammy hands on her thighs and took a deep breath.

In a few short minutes, the party would be starting, and everyone would be there, judging her as Mrs. Eric Nordstrom.

She glanced down at her silver halter dress and pressed her hand down the front of the empire waist that concealed her rounding belly. Her hand went to her bare neck. She'd pulled her hair up in a French twist and left just a few tendrils on either side of her face.

She'd never thought she'd miss her small boobs. She cupped her full breasts and looked down. They were sore and they were getting in her way and she couldn't' wait until she went back to her normal size.

She glanced at the clock and her heart sank.

She needed to head downstairs to check on the caterers and make sure everything was in place. She didn't need her first party to be a disaster.

Coming down the stairs, she was hit with the

delicious aroma of food. She couldn't believe how pregnancy heightened her sense of smell. She could be upstairs in the bedroom and still smell Mrs. Gambil baking fresh bread downstairs in the kitchen.

She stepped into the lavish dining room. Her mouth watered at the table laden with elegant appetizers and delicious desserts.

On the other side of the dining room, a full bar was set up along a wall with expensive bottles of wine. Wait staff dressed in black-and-white uniforms bustled around, stacking plates, polishing glasses, and lining up champagne bottles.

"You look lovely, Mrs. Celeste." Mrs. Gambil came out of the kitchen carrying a fresh arrangement of roses and hydrangeas and placed it on the table. "What do you think of these flowers, Mrs. Celeste? Are they what you wanted?"

"They're perfect. Everything looks wonderful. Thank you for your help." She had told Mrs. Gambil she didn't have to work the party, but she'd insisted on being here because she didn't like anyone else meddling in her kitchen.

"You're very welcome, dear." Mrs. Gambil's face brightened at the compliment.

A loud crash came from the vicinity of the kitchen. "I better go see what that was." Mrs. Gambil scrambled away with a worried scowl on her face.

"That was very kind of you." Eric spoke behind her.

Her heart skipped a beat and she turned.

He stood in the doorway dressed in a black tux, his blond hair gelled back. He looked like he'd stepped out of a magazine.

His blue eyes appeared darker, more intense. Even his lips seemed sexier, like he had a thousand dirty thoughts and he planned on using every one of them on her. His ice-blue gaze roamed her across her body taking in her appearance.

He met her gaze and grinned.

She cleared her dry throat. "I couldn't have done this without Mrs. Gambil's help." She glanced down and pretended to straighten the already perfect floral arrangement on the table.

"You're too modest. You have been on the phone all week with the caterers and decorators, checking on every detail."

She blushed. The majority of those calls had not been to the caterers. They had been calls home.

She had almost given up trying to reach her parents when her mother had finally answered. The moment she'd asked if she knew who the Queen was, her mother said she was late for an appointment and hung up. After that, Celeste called back every day but only got the answering machine.

"I hope everything goes well. I've never hosted a party like this before." She turned, only to find him right behind her. She was trapped between him and the table.

His arms wrapped around her back then slid his hand down her hip and he nudged her closer.

Her heart raced.

"You look stunning. I can already see I'll be busy keeping the men away from you tonight." His voice, low and sensual, rippled through her veins like a cool breeze across water.

"Men don't look at pregnant women." Her voice

cracked. "And they certainly don't look at me."

Desire flashed in his eyes and he cupped her cheek, leaning in so close, she could feel the heat from his body.

Her heart sped up at his touch and she held her breath, waiting for the touch of his lips across hers.

The doorbell rang.

"Damn," he mumbled and dropped his hands.

She stepped around him and inhaled deep to gather her composure. Now was not the time to get flustered. She had a party to host.

He captured her hand and brought her fingers up to his lips. A slight smile played at the corners of his lips.

"We're going to finish this, Celeste. That I promise."

☾

"THE LAST TIME I HAD this many people here, it was my parents hosting the party." Eric had leaned down to whisper into Celeste's ear. Her sweet scent made him want to kiss her neck and work his way down her body.

She looked up at him, her green eyes sparkling. "How am I doing?"

"Wonderful." Her smile hit him like a bat in the gut. It felt right to have her at his side and in his home.

She turned back to speak to the wife of one of his board members. Watching her, he marveled at how she effortlessly charmed them all with her genuine smiles and polite conversation.

Needing to touch her, he rested his palm on the small of her back.

She glanced up and met his gaze. With those emerald eyes on his, something stirred in his chest, an emotion he couldn't put a name to.

"Are you all right?" Celeste leaned in and whispered.

"I'm fine. Why do you ask?" He smiled and looked away, hoping she hadn't noticed that he'd been staring at her like an idiot.

Thankfully he was saved when the door opened. He turned his attention to Andrea Leigh and Sloan as they entered.

"Andrea Leigh, you look beautiful." Celeste hugged her new friend while Eric shook Sloan's hand.

"Sloan loves red, so I wore it for him." Andrea Leigh propped her hands on her hips and posed, showing off her short red dress.

"I believe the night I met Celeste, she was wearing red. Red's a good color." He pulled Celeste into his chest.

"Well, well, well. Isn't this a cozy domestic scene?" Leslie elbowed her way in between Sloan and Andrea Leigh.

"Hello, Leslie." He mumbled and shot the woman a warning look.

"What were you saying about red, darling?" Leslie tossed her dark hair back across her shoulders and leaned toward him.

"Eric was saying when he fell in love with Celeste, she was wearing red." Andrea Leigh said. Not exactly his words, but he didn't bother correcting her.

"What a shame she's wearing that dull gray tonight," Leslie purred, fluttering her eyelashes at him.

"It's silver and it's what's in style." Andrea Leigh glared. "If you would bother to keep up with fashion, then you would know that. And you wouldn't have worn that hideous pink prom gown to dinner the other night."

Celeste snorted and tried to cover with a cough.

Leslie narrowed her eyes.

"Come on, Sloan, let's grab a drink." Andrea Leigh kissed Celeste's cheek and then headed for the bar.

More guests entered, forcing Leslie to move away and mingle with the rest of the guests.

Alone with his wife, he relaxed and greeted the next guest.

"NOT BAD FOR A COUNTRY girl from Georgia." Celeste indulged in a satisfied smile. Everyone was eating, laughing, and having a good time. She had to admit that she was enjoying herself.

Her first party had gone off without a hitch.

"You did a fabulous job." Eric wrapped his arm around her waist. He'd not taken his hands off her the entire evening. For a moment they almost seemed like a real couple.

She looked up at him and smiled.

"It's time," he said.

"Time for what?"

"For our announcement." He grinned, grabbed her hand and escorted her to the middle of the room.

"Can I have everyone's attention for a moment?"

His deep voice carried across the crowd.

Her stomach clenched as the room quieted and the wait staff stilled their movements.

"I have an announcement." Eric looked out into the crowd.

They were all looking at her. She could feel the heat rising in her cheeks. She tightened her grip on Eric's hand.

"As you all know, this is the first party hosted by my beautiful wife. She's done a wonderful job, don't you think?" He looked down at her and smiled. It was the kind of smile that made her stomach melt.

Applause broke out in the room before he motioned for everyone's attention again.

"Tonight is special for another reason, the real reason we brought you all here." He gave her hand a reassuring squeeze.

"We are excited to announce that Celeste is pregnant with our first child."

Cheers, claps, and whistles erupted around the room. He tugged her tighter against him as he picked up her hand and kissed the back of her fingers.

She smiled as everyone pressed toward them, offering congratulations, hugs and handshakes. Champagne bottles popped and crystal glasses clinked while the atmosphere grew festive.

Her heart swelled with joy. Everyone seemed genuinely happy for them. Not once did she see a judgmental gaze pass over her. She straightened her shoulders, feeling a weight liftoff her shoulders. She'd been worried for nothing.

"Oh, I'm so happy for you guys." Andrea Leigh squealed and hugged her tight. "This is going to betoo much fun. We must go clothes shopping since you'll be having," she stopped and her gaze flickered from her to Eric. "Wait, do you know what you'll be having?"

"No. I want it to be a surprise." She'd told the doctor she didn't want to know the sex of the baby, and he complied.

"Well, we'll just have to buy stuff for both a girl and a boy." Andrea Leigh's eyes twinkled.

"Why don't you recommend a decorator first?" Eric chuckled.

"I know just the person. How about I come over tomorrow morning and we'll start working on ideas?" Andrea Leigh clapped her hands together.

"I would love that. I feel like there is still too much to do."

"Well, well, well." Leslie pushed past Andrea Leigh and stopped in front of her and Eric. She stood there with her lips curled in a smirk and her eyes narrowed in an accusatory stare.

Celeste swallowed. She realized from the look in Leslie's eyes that she was about to make a scene.

She felt the blood drain from her face and for a second she thought she might faint.

In that moment she knew she had two choices. She could make her escape before Leslie embarrassed her, or she could stand her ground. If she didn't stand her ground now, then Leslie would continue to torment her for the rest of her marriage to Eric.

She knew what she had to do.

CHAPTER TWENTY-TWO

"NOW EVERYTHING IS MAKING PERFECT sense. How far along are you?" Leslie's tone was laced with bitterness.

"Leslie, that's none of your business," Andrea Leigh hissed.

"I'm not talking to you. I was talking to the other Southern belle." Leslie kept her serpent-like gaze leveled at Celeste.

A hush fell over the room and everyone stared.

All those horrible high school moments came flooding back. Being chosen last in gym class. Being bullied by the popular girls. Being teased by the pretty girls.

She opened her mouth, but Eric stepped in.

"You're drunk and being disrespectful to me and my wife. You need to leave." His tone held a lethal edge, sharp enough to slice a hair in half.

"Wife?" Leslie laughed. "Now I know why you married her so quickly. You know, Eric, women get knocked up all the time. That's no reason to go and marry a no-body from Podunk, Georgia. How do you even know it's yours?"

Celeste's lungs constricted and she couldn't breathe. Didn't want to breathe.

Tears bit the back of her eyes, clawing to be freed. She blinked and held them in. She refused to drop her head in shame.

She steeled her spine and waited for others to join in.

RAGE SLICED THROUGH EVERY CELL of Eric's body in a deadly torrent. "I will not tolerate a vicious drunk slandering my wife." He grabbed Leslie by the arm and walked her to the front door.

Leslie's eyes bulged in disbelief and her hand clutched her throat in shock.

He didn't care. He was tired of her bullshit. He was putting a stop to it once and for all.

He lowered his voice.

"Not that it's any of your business, but I know it's my child because she was a virgin when we slept together. No man had touched her before me, and no one will ever touch her but me."

He opened the front door and motioned for Solomon. "Please drive Ms. Andrews home. Have one of the wait staff follow you with her car. I don't want to give her any reason to return to my home."

"Understood." Solomon nodded and escorted a sputtering Leslie into the back of a limo.

He slammed the door. He turned and glared at his guests, daring anyone else to say a

word. If they did, he'd rip their fucking tongues out.

The music started up and people went back to

their drinks and conversations, ignoring the obvious scene that had just taken place.

He searched the room for Celeste, but he didn't see her.

He'd seen her expression, the pain as evident as if someone had slapped her.

Damn Leslie. He wanted to strangle that bitch.

First thing in the morning he was going to call a board meeting and do whatever it took to get her ass voted out.

☾

CELESTE HURRIED INTO THE KITCHEN and dabbed at the tears with a napkin. She picked up a silver tray and glanced at her reflection. She sucked in some deep breaths and tried to dry her eyes and fix her makeup.

"Don't let that nasty bitch make you cry. It's what she wants." Andrea Leigh took her by the arm and forced her to look up. "Leslie has been after Eric for a while, and she's pissed because you have him now."

"Did they date?" She swallowed back the lump that had formed in the back of her throat and set the tray down.

"I wouldn't use the word 'date.' I would say that Eric banged her one night while they were in Canada."

Her heart sank to her toes. Just when she didn't think she could feel any worse, she did.

A one-night stand. Just like she was. Only he'd gotten her pregnant.

"Sloan was there with Eric on business. Leslie showed up at the restaurant they were at and started coming on to him. He kept telling her he wasn't interested."

"The next morning, Eric told Sloan that he must have drunk way too much because he woke up with Leslie in his bed. Eric swore he didn't remember a thing."

"Leslie must have been mad that he didn't remember." Celeste looked away, afraid that Andrea Leigh would see the truth in her eyes.

At least Eric never denied the fact that they'd slept together. But then again, he'd only had that one drink, he wasn't exactly shit-faced.

"Leslie manipulated Eric into feeling guilty about not remembering they'd had sex. She used that to her advantage."

"What do you mean?" She leaned forward, intent on hearing every word.

"Leslie would come crying to Eric every time she needed something—money for her mortgage or car payment. And he'd give it to her." Andrea Leigh's mouth stretched into a sneer.

"But she's on the board at Cryptic. Doesn't she make a lot of money?" That didn't make sense.

Andrea Leigh snorted. "Rumor has it, she's blown through her inheritance money and is so far in debt that her paycheck just keeps the bank from foreclosing on her condo. Even Eric has told her she needs to manage her money better, but she continues to live beyond her means."

"You're kidding."

"No, I'm not. You have no idea how miserable she has made his life. She even started telling people that she and Eric were about to become engaged."

"She was using him for his money." She was willing to bet this wasn't the first time people had tried to use him for their own advantage.

No wonder Leslie hated her. And no wonder Eric kept people at a distance.

"But when he came back with you, that shattered any control she had over him. Since he's been married he hasn't given her one red cent. I know this because Sloan told me. Eric tells him everything." Andrea Leigh squeezed her hand. "You saved him, in more ways than you will ever know."

"I doubt that," Celeste murmured and looked away.

"There you are." Sloan walked up and rested his hand on Andrea Leigh's shoulder. "Celeste, can I borrow Andrea Leigh for a minute? I've got some friends I want to introduce her to."

"Of course." As the couple walked away, her heart squeezed with the tiniest bit of jealously. She longed for a relationship built on love and trust instead of the mountain of lies hers was anchored to.

"I'm sorry about Leslie." Eric's low voice came from behind her.

She nodded but couldn't look at him. Leslie's words still echoed in her head. What Leslie had said was true.

"Are you okay?" He stepped in front of her and took her hand in his.

"I'm fine." She gave him a sliver of a smile. "You didn't let her drive home, did you?"

"After how she acted, you are still gracious enough to think of her safety?" His brow furrowed and he shook his head.

"No, not really." She shrugged. "I just didn't want her to wreck and then sue you. Blaming someone else for her actions seems to be working out well for her."

A ghost of a smile hung at the corners of his lips. "Actually, Solomon drove her home."

"Ah."

He gently cupped her face. "I apologize for the awful things she said."

"Why are you apologizing? You didn't say them."

"I've never seen her act that way before. What she said is inexcusable. I'm going to have her voted off the board."

If Leslie were off the board, then Celeste would have no reason to ever be around her again. Yet thoughts of Andrea Leigh's revelations about Leslie's financial situation tumbled through her head, despite her attempts to ignore them.

"That's not necessary." She hated the idea of making anyone—even Leslie—destitute.

"After what she said? I think it is." He lowered his voice and the corners of his eyes.

"Think about it. She would cause more trouble if you tried to get her thrown off the board. Besides, from what Andrea Leigh was telling me, she doesn't really have any other income."

She hated the fact that deep down inside she knew she could be Leslie. She could be desperate and destitute. Putting herself in others' shoes was the thing that kept her from striking back at others, no matter how much they'd hurt her.

"Hello, gorgeous."

She froze. For a second she wondered if she'd imagined that familiar deep voice. One she'd known since childhood.

"Donovan?" She turned around. Her favorite cousin was dressed in a tux and looking like a million dollars, as always.

Donovan smiled, swept her up in a hug and lifted her off her feet. "How's my girl?"

Laughing, she hugged him back. He finally set her back on the ground.

"What are you doing here?" She smiled up at his blue eyes that crinkled at the corners when he laughed.

His dark brown hair was a little on the long side, but he still looked good in his tux. In fact, he had never looked better. He was the one person who always seemed to show up just when she needed a friend. As always, he had perfect timing.

"Are you surprised to see me?" Donovan grinned, his blue eyes sparkling with unspoken mischief.

"Of course." Laugher and joy bubbled out. He was exactly what she needed.

"Good." Donovan raked his gaze over Eric, and the amusement left his eyes. "It seems I've stayed away too long this time. Apparently there have been some changes to our *family*."

"Eric, this is my cousin, Donovan Finley." She touched Eric's arm and smiled.

"Eric Nordstrom, Celeste's husband." The men exchanged a handshake.

"I get no invite to the wedding and I have to find out from Aunt Agatha that my girl is married." Donovan crossed his arms over his chest. From the tone of his voice, she knew he was hurt.

"It all happened quickly. I assumed someone had called you." She cleared her throat.

"You know I'd have been there if I had known. Apparently they were afraid that I might make some trouble." He cut his eyes at Eric. For that brief second, she saw a hardness flicker through his gaze before he brought it back to rest on her.

"How did you know where we live?"

"I have my ways, dearest." Donovan took her hand and pressed a gallant kiss to her knuckles. "Now if you don't mind, I think I'll go grab a drink." He hesitated and arched an eyebrow at Eric. "It's not a cash bar, is it?"

"Absolutely not." A muscle twitched in Eric's cheek.

"Good." Donovan smiled, slapped Eric on the back, and sauntered away.

"*He's* your cousin?"

"Yes. We practically grew up together." She shrugged. "He usually got shipped to our house for the summer because of the trouble he got into."

"Sounds like someone I need to keep my eye on," he mumbled.

She followed Eric's narrowed stare to the bar, where Donovan sat charming a group of ladies.

"Women do seem to fall at his feet." She snorted.

"I hope you're not one of them." Eric's serious tone had her jerking her head toward him.

"You did not actually say that." Her eyes widened. "He's my cousin, Eric. Just because I grew up in the South doesn't mean I lived in Deliverance."

He blinked and then barked out a laugh.

"You're such a jerk sometimes." She gritted her teeth and took a step, her good mood lost.

He grabbed her arm, halting her escape.

"You're right. I shouldn't have said that. I'm

sorry." His serious gaze matched her own. He shifted his weight. "It's hard for me to watch men stare at you."

Her mouth dropped open. "You are delusional if you think men are looking at me. Look how big I'm getting."

He trailed the back of his finger gently down her cheek. Her heart amped up.

"You have no idea how breathtaking you are, do you?" His gaze darkened.

"Eric, I'm getting fat." She let out a shaky laugh.

"You are carrying my child. Our child. And getting more beautiful by the day."

She swallowed, not sure what to say. It was the most open he'd ever been with her.

In that moment, she saw Eric for who he really was, a man who'd never really had the chance at being loved for himself and not his wealth.

She wasn't sure if he'd ever let someone get close enough to love him.

In that moment, she considered giving their marriage a real try.

CHAPTER TWENTY-THREE

"IT CAN'T BE MORNING. I just went to sleep." An insistent stream of sunlight pounded against Celeste's closed eyelids. The party had lasted into the wee hours, and she hadn't gotten to bed until around four a.m.

She tried to ignore the blinding light, squeezing her eyes tighter and burrowing into her pillow. The top of her head bumped something soft.

She stuck her arm out from under the warmth of the covers. Her fingertips brushed something furry.

She snatched her hand back and bolted upright.

A sleek black cat with blue eyes perched on her pillow and stared back at her.

"Where did you come from?" She ran her fingers through the soft fur, letting the cat's purrs resonate through her.

Eric hadn't mentioned he had a cat. She would have pegged him as a dog person.

She eased out of bed and slipped on her robe.

"Come on, little guy. Let's see what there is to eat downstairs."

She walked into the kitchen with the cat trotting

close behind.

Mrs. Gambil was bent over the counter writing out a list. She straightened when Celeste entered the kitchen. "Good morning, Mrs. Celeste. I expected you would be sleeping in today."

"I planned on it, but my company wouldn't let me." She lifted the top off the cake plate grabbed a warm muffin. "I woke up and found him curled up on my pillow. I didn't know we had a cat." The cat weaved between her legs, purring while she munched on the strawberry pastry.

"We don't have a cat." Mrs. Gambil bent and rubbed the cat between its ears. "Sometimes we get a stray out in the gardens, looking for birds, but we've never had one get in the house before. I'll ask around when I go to the farmers market today to see if someone lost their pet. Is there anything in particular you'd like for me to make for dinner this week, dear?"

"Everything you make is delicious, Mrs. Gambil." She cocked her head. "But if you could make some more of your homemade cookies, I would appreciate it."

"Of course, dear. I've got a ton of recipes. I'll surprise you."

After breakfast and getting dressed, Celeste spent the morning on the Internet, poring over pictures of nurseries. She narrowed down her wish list and printed off her ideas, to be ready to discuss them with Andrea Leigh.

She glanced at the grandfather clock. She still had some time before Andrea Leigh arrived. She picked up the phone and dialed her parents' number. She tapped her fingers on the massive desk as it went straight to voicemail.

If her parents wouldn't answer her calls, then she would email them. She would get James to fly her to Atlanta later this week to look for that stupid book and check on her parents.

She moved the mouse and opened her email. There was one new message with nothing in the subject line and an unfamiliar address.

She bit her lip. If she opened it and it turned out to be a virus that infected Eric's computer, she could only imagine what he would say.

It wasn't like he didn't have the money to buy another computer. Plus, she bet he backed everything up since he was such a control freak.

She pointed and clicked before she could change her mind.

You cannot hide, Celeste. I'm coming for you!

Wet chills marched up her spine and seeped into her veins. The ominous message resonated deep in her heart.

Anastasia. The woods. The monsters. The images pounded through her head at breakneck speed.

A sharp tap at the window made her jump in her chair. She pressed her hand to her chest, her heart beating against her palm, and stared at the window, expecting to see eyes staring at her.

She saw nothing.

Something was off. Something was wrong.

Her skin prickled with unease, with fear, with terror.

Frantically her gaze darted about the room looking for the unseen danger.

Tap, tap tap.

Like fingers strumming against the glass.

She shoved away from the desk and bolted downstairs to the kitchen.

It was empty.

She'd forgotten that Mrs. Gambil had gone shopping.

She was alone.

Her heart beat against her ribs, and stole the air from her tight lungs.

As panic closed in on her, she scanned the room with jerky movements, afraid that any moment something would jump out and grab her.

She was trapped in her own home.

She couldn't stay here.

She flung open the door and bolted out into the garden.

The shrill of breaking glass echoed behind her and she screamed.

Every cell in her body was on fire with fear.

She raced through the garden on trembling legs. She needed to hide. She needed to be invisible.

When she reached the woods, she jumped over a fallen tree and ran deeper into the underbrush, hoping to camouflage herself among the thick green foliage.

Deeply ensconced in the woods, she leaned against a tree and sucked in quick breaths.

"Meow." The black cat wove itself between her legs.

She yelped.

"You scared the crap out of me." She slapped her hand across her mouth. Her eyes darted around the area searching for anything moving.

An eerie hush swept across the forest.

Everything went silent. Eerie silence. No chirping crickets. No singing birds. No rustling leaves.

The only sound was her harsh breathing.

Her gaze landed on a bright yellow daisy on the forest floor. The same daisy the mysterious little girl had brought back to life.

She pressed her body against the rough trunk of the tree and wished she could sink inside the protective bark. She felt exposed, naked, and vulnerable.

A loathsome laugh cut through the trees, shredding the silence like razor blades.

Terror buckled her legs and she slid to the ground. Moisture from the moss seeped into her pants and soaked her skin, racking her body with shivers.

She frantically looked around for something, anything, to use as a weapon. She spotted a heavy stick and grabbed it. Forcing her legs under her, she stood and tightened her fingers around the weapon.

Despite the heavy green foliage, the woods didn't seem like a good place to hide.

"Where do you think you are going, Celeste?" The male voice, low and gravelly, made the tiny hairs on her neck stand up.

Horror bleed into the very marrow of her bones. Nightmares of having her skin ripped from her body flashed through her mind.

A hot putrid odor stung her eyes and reached into the back of her throat, making her stomach churn. Out of nowhere, a pair of eyes the color of gunmetal and rimmed in yellow appeared and hung in midair only a few feet in front of her.

What the hell was going on?

"Come to me, Celeste."

"No." Her voice cracked.

"Come to me!" it screeched.

She clasped her hands over her ears. The noise was so painful she expected to feel blood dripping from her ears.

The horrendous noise stopped, drowning everything once again in a vacuum of silence.

She slowly dropped her hands, unsure what was coming next.

Her heart climbed into her throat.

The eyes were still there, hanging in midair and glaring at her. Something began to happen. The evil yellow eyes blinked and began to transform.

A face began to appear, then a torso. Out of the torso, legs grew, then arms, until a man stood in front of her.

He was tall with dark features, a black beard, and hair to match. But it was his eyes that terrified her the most. They were different now, blacked out, rimmed in yellow and overflowing with rage.

"This is not real, this is not happening." She blinked furiously and shook her head. She pinched herself, but the pain didn't wake her from the nightmare she'd found herself in.

"Oh, but it is real. This is more real than that pitiful charade of a life you've lived. Your life has been nothing but a lie, a desperate attempt to hide you. But I found you."

Panic squeezed the air out of her lungs.

She could stay here and die, or she could run and have a slim chance to live. Her body decided for her. She ran.

The man slammed into her hard. She landed

on the ground with a thud, knocking the breath out of her lungs. He straddled her and snarled, his rancid breath hitting her cheek. Those same teeth, sharp and shark-like, were anything but human.

She screamed and hit him across his face. The tiny stones on her wedding band ripped into his cheek. The gash on his face oozed black and reeked of decaying flesh.

"What are you?"

"I am Wrath."

In that instant, vivid flashes of every unspeakable thing he was going to do to her spilled out from his soulless eyes.

Panicked, she struggled under his massive weight.

He grabbed her arms and pulled them above her head. He secured her wrists in one hand while his free hand grabbed her breast and twisted her nipple.

Another scream tore from her throat as his talon-like fingers clawed into her breast. He inhaled deeply. His eyes rolled back in his head, and his lips curled up into a sadistic grin.

"I'm going to enjoy making you scream."

From out of nowhere, the black cat hissed and launched itself at the man. It buried its claws into the creature's cheeks. The evil man screamed while black blood streamed down his face in rivulets. He let go of her and cradled his face in his hands.

She saw her chance.

She scrambled to her feet and ran. She stumbled on the uneven, spongy ground with every frantic step. She forced herself not to look back, too afraid that he would be right over her shoulder, ready to capture her.

She didn't stop running after she broke out of the woods. She didn't slow down until she was inside her house with the door locked.

Shaking uncontrollably she hurried from room to room, checking every door and window downstairs.

She collapsed on the sofa and curled up in a fetal position and cradled her stomach with her hands.

What the hell was going on? Nothing made sense anymore.

The doorbell reverberated throughout the house.

She jumped.

Easing to the door, she peeked through the glass and wrought-iron doors. Relief slid through her when she saw Andrea Leigh's smiling face.

She opened the door.

"Hi honey. I hope you picked out some ideas for the nursery." Andrea Leigh walked inside. Her smile dropped. "Hey, are you okay?"

"Help me," she whispered. The room swayed, and then everything went dark.

CHAPTER TWENTY-FOUR

"CELESTE, CAN YOU HEAR ME?"

She blinked against the blinding light beaming into her closed eyes. When she opened her eyes, she spotted Dr. Sevalus standing over her with a penlight pointed in her face.

She squinted and looked around. They were not alone. Eric, Andrea Leigh, and Mrs. Gambil gathered around the bed, all wearing serious expressions.

"Drink this." Dr. Sevalus handed her a glass of water. Eric's arm slid down her back and helped her sit up.

She took a sip and winced as the cool water slid down her raw throat.

"How are you feeling?" Dr. Sevalus pressed a cold stethoscope to her chest.

"Okay."

Eric eased onto the bed beside her, while Dr. Sevalus pressed the stethoscope to her chest and then to her belly.

"Do you remember anything?" Dr. Sevalus pressed two fingers against the pulse in her wrist and studied his watch.

Andrea Leigh stood at the foot of the bed. Her mascara had bled onto her cheeks from crying. Mrs. Gambil wrung a tissue in her hands, and her face was twisted in concern.

She had been attacked in the woods by something evil that had appeared out of thin air. There was no way in hell she was going to say *that* out loud.

She slowly shook her head.

"Are you done?" Eric glared at the older man.

"Yes. But I would like to do some bloodwork, run some tests." Dr. Sevalus put his stethoscope in a bag.

"Andrea Leigh, tell us again what happened." Eric looked toward the foot of the bed.

"She answered the door looking white as a sheet. She said, 'Help me,' and then she just fainted. That's when I saw the marks on her arms." Andrea Leigh's voice cracked and she looked away.

What marks?

She handed the glass back to Dr. Sevalus. She glanced down at her arms. Bruises, in the shape of fingers, wrapped around both wrists from where she had been pinned down.

"Everyone out," Eric bellowed. "Now."

The room emptied, leaving her alone with Eric.

He took her face between his hands, his eyes serious and his face lined with worry.

Dread settled in the pit of her stomach.

"It's the baby. Something's wrong with the baby, isn't it?" Purple spots swam before her eyes and she tried to get her breathing under control. She cradled her stomach with her hands.

"The baby is fine. Dr. Sevalus said so."

A relieved breath slid through her lips. She slumped against the pillows behind her. "Then why do you look worried?"

"When I saw those marks on you, I didn't know what to think. How did you get them?" He lifted her wrist and rubbed his thumb softly across the bruises.

Her heart ached. She wanted to tell him. But would he believe her? Or would he have her committed and get full custody of their child?

She couldn't take that chance.

"I don't remember."

"I can't help if I don't know who hurt you." His gaze bore into hers. Her heart caught within her chest. She wanted to trust him, more than anything, but—

"You can't protect her, Nordstrom. You have no idea what you are dealing with." Donovan stepped into the doorway, arms crossed over his chest.

"How the hell did you get in my house?"

Donovan ignored him and gave her a warm smile. "I've called Aunt Sarah and Uncle Ben. They're on their way here. I sent Mrs. Gambil and Andrea Leigh home, along with the doctor. This doesn't concern them. This is family business."

"Then why are *you* here?" Eric growled.

"Like it or not, I'm family." Donovan sneered.

"You're not my family." Eric took a threatening step toward Donovan.

"Stop it, both of you." She pressed her hand to her head. She didn't have the patience for them right now. "Donovan, what are you doing here? I thought you went home after the cocktail party last night."

"I had a… date." He smirked.

"I don't understand. Why did you call my parents to come?"

"Because they can give you the answers you've been searching for." His smile faded. "They are going to tell you everything."

☾

"MOM, DAD." CELESTE'S EYES STUNG with tears as her mom and dad walked through her front door. They took her in their arms, and she burst into tears. She was hormonal, exhausted, and terrified, and she couldn't hold it in any longer.

"I want to know what's going on." She pulled out of their embrace and wiped at her tears.

"Why don't we sit down first?" Her mother's forced smile and pain-filled eyes had Celeste's stomach twisting into a thousand knots.

Eric led everyone into the library. The tension in the room was palpable, like humidity on a hot Southern day.

"Donovan has indicated that you two know what's going on with Celeste." Eric narrowed his gaze at them.

"Maybe. But we need to ask Celeste some questions first." Her mother sat next to her on the leather sofa. "Donovan said something happened in the woods. Honey, we need to know exactly what you saw."

"You won't believe me." She chuckled. "I don't even believe what I saw."

"Is that why you didn't tell Eric? Because you

were afraid he wouldn't believe you?" Her mother gave her an encouraging smile.

She glanced at Eric and nodded.

"You know you can tell us anything, right?" Her mother gave her hand a reassuring squeeze.

She looked at her mother and frowned. Could she tell them anything? Could she tell anyone?

"Is this the first time something has frightened you?" her mother asked.

She shook her head.

"About a month ago she came running out of woods, obviously upset. She said she had seen someone then, but didn't elaborate. She wasn't hurt, so I didn't press her for answers." Eric sat in the chair across from her and rested his elbows on his knees.

"What did you see?" her mother asked.

She closed her eyes, took a deep breath, and told them about the little girl in the woods. Once she started talking, she couldn't stop. She even told them how Anastasia had levitated in midair and breathed life into the dead flower.

"What exactly did Anastasia say?" Her father tapped his lip with his finger and gave her his full attention.

"She said you both hid the truth from me." She searched her father's eyes, waiting for him to deny it.

"But the girl did not harm you, right?" Her father's brows furrowed.

"No." She shook her head. "But it scared the hell out of me, seeing her do something so … so …"

"Magical?" her father asked.

" Powerful?" Donovan chimed in.

"No! Something so unnatural, evil." She shivered with the memory of the girl's words.

Donovan and her father exchanged a look.

"Wait a minute. Why aren't you all giving me a logical explanation for what I saw?" She looked from her mother to her father.

"What kind of explanation?" Her mother gave her an innocent look.

"Like maybe I was hallucinating, or maybe I fell asleep and it was all a dream, or maybe I'm just crazy."

"Oh, honey, you're not crazy." Her mother laughed.

"Of course not." Her father smiled.

She looked to Eric for his reaction.

He said nothing, his face stoic.

"Celeste, tell us what happened today," her father urged.

She took a deep breath. "I guess it started with that email I got."

"Show me." Donovan walked over to the computer and sat. Celeste leaned over him and pulled up her email and clicked on the message. Everyone crowded around the desk.

She expected the cryptic message to be gone, to be erased. But it wasn't. It was still there, taunting her.

The words seemed to leap out at her from the screen. She took a step back and bumped into Eric.

"Sorry," Celeste muttered, stepping away. He wrapped his arms around her waist and held her close. Just for a second, she closed her eyes and soaked up his strength.

"Then what happened?" Her father narrowed his

eyes at Eric's possessive hands across her stomach.

She blushed and cleared her throat. "It scared me. It felt like someone was in the house with me, watching me. I had to get out, so I ran. As I was running, I heard breaking glass coming from the house."

"That explains the broken window in the master bedroom." Donovan rubbed his jaw. "You were right to run. Whoever sent you the email was trying to get into the house."

The energy seemed to seep out of her body, and she felt legs give out. Eric held her tighter.

"It's okay. While you were sleeping, I had the glass replaced and rewired for the security system," Eric whispered against her ear.

"And then what happened?" Donovan spoke up.

"Before I realized where I was going, I was in the woods again." Celeste hesitated, unsure of how to proceed.

"And what next? Don't leave anything out," her father encouraged her.

"When I stopped running, I realized I stood in the exact same place where I'd met the girl. But this time it was different."

"How?"

"It was silent. There were no sounds. You couldn't even hear the leaves rustling. It was like everything had stopped. Like sound and time had stopped."

"That's when I saw it. Well, I just saw its eyes." Celeste pressed harder against Eric. He tightened his embrace.

"Because the rest was hidden?" Donovan looked up at her.

"No." She was too embarrassed to continue.

Even if her family had believed the first part of the story, this would definitely be too much for them.

She eased out of Eric's arms and faced everyone. "The eyes were all I saw because that's all that was there." She waited for their skeptical remarks, but no one said anything.

"It got angry. Then it transformed into a human form." She cringed, remembering the malice in those eyes.

"Morphed from what?" Donovan gave her a quizzical look.

"It morphed out of thin air." She squeezed her eyes shut, embarrassed at the words coming out of her own mouth. "I know this sounds crazy, but I know what I saw."

"It must have hidden its body in the under-realm." Donovan's voice was calm and thoughtful.

She cracked an eye open. "Under-realm?"

"The dimension where evil resides." Donovan shrugged.

"You mean like hell?"

Donovan shook his head. "Not exactly. Once you are in hell, you can't escape, whereas the under-realm is a portal that allows evil to come and go. What you saw was a demon."

"Celeste, you said it got angry. Why?" Eric asked.

"It told me to go to him. I didn't. It got angry. That's when it changed."

"What did it look like, honey?" Her mother tilted her head expectantly.

"Well, it changed into a man, but I don't think it was human. It was something else, something evil. When it held me down, I could see its thoughts in its black eyes."

"It touched you?" Eric reached out and turned her wrists over. "Is that how you got these bruises?"

"Yes."

Rage flashed in Eric's eyes.

"How did you get away?" Her father's voice brought her back to the present.

She inhaled and pulled her hands from his grip. "Oh, my god. I forgot. The cat."

"What cat?" He gave her a blank look.

"When I woke up this morning, there was a black cat sleeping on my pillow. It followed me into the woods and attacked the man, or whatever it was, to let me get away. Poor little thing. There's no way it could have survived." The cat had saved her life, and she hadn't even given it a second thought.

"Cat, indeed." Her father snorted.

"Don't worry Celeste. I bet that brave cat is fine." Donovan smirked.

Her parents exchanged a glance.

"Did anything else happen?" Eric asked.

She shook her head. "No. I ran as fast as I could back to the house." She looked around the room at everyone and pressed her palm to her stomach. "It knows where I live. I led it straight to the house."

Donovan gave her a sympathetic smile. "I'm afraid it's always known where you lived. It was just biding its time."

CHAPTER TWENTY-FIVE

ERIC STARED OUT HIS LARGE library window into the sprawling night. He'd always found solace in the night sky. He hoped he might find some peace in the sparkling skies tonight.

Everyone else had gone to bed, and he was left alone in the library to absorb the strange explanation of what had happened to his wife.

He'd seen the look of fear in Celeste's eyes when she'd recounted her experience in the woods. Her story might be fantastical but the purple bruising on her delicate wrists was not imagined.

Someone had definitely hurt her.

It was her explanation of who had hurt her he didn't believe.

A quick knock on the door had him turning away from the window. "Come in."

The door opened and Ben walked through. Eric braced himself for what her father was about to say.

"Do you have a second to talk?" Ben asked quietly.

"Sure." He walked over to the couch and sat. "Have a seat."

Ben sat in the wingback chair across from him and placed a book in his lap. "I know what Celeste said is difficult to believe."

"You mean impossible. I need solid answers not hallucinations."

Ben's gaze hardened. "Like I said, I know it's impossible. I also know there are some questions she has about why this is happening at all."

"Why don't you tell me what you know? And please don't tell me that insanity runs in your family." He forked his fingers through his hair and studied the floor.

Ben jumped up. "Look, Viking. If you ever say anything like that again, I will personally peel the flesh from your bones."

Nice visual.

"You didn't let me finish. I was going to tell you I don't think Celeste is crazy."

"But you don't believe she actually saw what she described." Ben narrowed his eyes and eased back down to his seat.

Eric sighed. "I think she is confused. I think she saw someone. And that someone hurt her. But I don't think it transformed like she said." He shook his head. "Maybe the perpetrator wore some kind of mask. I think she was traumatized, and her brain is trying to protect itself."

He expected Ben to shout and yell and possibly try to punch him. What he didn't expect was for Ben Hart to smile.

"Boy, I tell you what. You've got a lot of learning to do." Ben laughed. "That's why I brought this." Ben handed him the book.

"What's that?" He ran his hand across the antique

leather-bound book with a Celtic cross stamped across the front.

"I think it will help explain what's going on." Ben stood and headed for the door. "It's been a long day. I'm going to bed."

"Wait." He held up the book. "Where did you get this?"

Ben turned and shrugged. "I stole it out of your Uncle's Stephen's library."

☾

"SORRY, I DIDN'T KNOW YOU were in here." Celeste stopped short when she saw Eric sitting at his desk in the library. She turned to leave, not wanting to discuss last night's conversation.

"Wait." Eric stood. "I want to talk to you."

She laced her cold fingers together and turned. She hadn't slept at all last night, worrying what he might do after hearing about her experience in the woods. Would he think she was crazy? Take the baby and prevent her from even seeing it?

Maybe she *was* crazy.

With heavy footsteps she walked over to the sofa and sat. He sat beside her.

"Why didn't you tell me what happened in the woods with the girl?"

"I didn't get hurt the first time, so there was no point in telling you. Plus, you'd think I was crazy."

"But yesterday you did get hurt. As your husband, I have the right to know who is threatening my wife."

She opened her mouth to tell him they were only husband and wife on paper. He was only bound to her because of their baby. She was just an obligation, nothing more.

"You said you saw what he was going to do to you."

"Yes." She swallowed back her terror of what she'd seen in those evil eyes. It had been like watching a movie.

"Was he going to rape you?" Eric's strained voice compelled her to meet his gaze.

"To start with." She swallowed.

"Was he going to kill you?" He reached for her hand.

"He would have done that, too." She blinked back the hard sting of tears.

"What else?" His voice was hard and demanding.

She didn't want to say it out loud. For some reason, she knew if she said it out loud it would make it all too real.

"What else, sweetheart?" He cupped her cheek and gently forced her to look at him.

"He was going to cut my baby out while I watched."

"Fuck." He groaned low and deep, like an enraged animal. The anger in his eyes frightened her.

He grabbed her by the waist and lifted her into his lap. He didn't say a word but held her against his chest.

His gentleness undid her. The dam shattered, and she let go of the tears, sobbing into his strong chest.

After a while, she lifted her head and swiped at the tears with her fingertips. "I've messed up your shirt.

"I don't care about the damn shirt." He raised her hands to his lips and pressed his lips to each wet fingertip, kissing away her tears.

Heat pulsed through her stomach. His warm breath ticked her cheek and sent shivers across her skin.

With a feather light touch, he stroked the nape of her neck and gently touched his lips to hers.

She wanted more.

She wrapped her arms around his neck and pulled him closer. She wanted nothing between them. Not air. Not clothing. Not space.

He deepened the kiss, his tongue sliding against hers in a wicked promise. She moaned at his spicy taste and clutched at his shoulders. In that moment, they were free from expectations, and driven by want and desire.

"I need you." He groaned and lifted her in his lap. His warm fingers slipped under her shirt and trailed up her naked back, leaving her skin pebbling in his wake. She arched into him, needing to be closer.

His hands slid around to the front to her stomach.

She stiffened and placed her hand over her protruding belly.

Embarrassed, she scrambled off his lap.

"What's wrong?" He stood, his pupils dilated, his chest heaving.

How could he be attracted to her in her condition? He dated supermodels. Not pregnant country girls.

"Here you are." Donovan's voice made her jump. "I've been looking everywhere for you, Celeste." Donovan cut his eyes at Eric. "Hope I wasn't interrupting anything."

"Of course not." The heat crept up in her face and she cupped the back of her neck and looked away.

"Great. I'll go get your parents." Donovan reached for the doorknob and looked over his shoulder at her. "I hope you're ready for the truth, Celeste. After today, there's no going back."

☾

TENSION WEIGHED DOWN THE ROOM like an elephant on a tightrope.

Her parents sat on the couch, while Donovan lounged in a wingback chair. She and Eric sat together on the love seat.

"So, who is going to tell me what's going on?" Her gaze flitted between her parents.

"What we are about to tell you is going to make you question everything you ever knew. I need you to listen with an open mind." The urgent tone in her father's voice had her sitting up straight.

"Okay." She had a bad feeling, like getting a two a.m. phone call. Two a.m. phone calls were never good.

Her father cut his eyes to Eric. "We are asking you to listen with an open mind as well."

"I can do that." Eric rested one arm on the back of the sofa and nodded.

"We've always taught you about your heritage. But being Irish is only part of who you are. We have royalty in our blood that spans back thousands of years."

"Like kings?" She'd never heard about this.

"And queens," Donovan murmured.

"Yes. But not like you might expect." Her father

shifted in his seat. "Our blood runs a bit richer than an ordinary king's or queen's."

"What do you mean?"

Her father leaned forward. "We have Fae blood."

"What?" She stared at her father. Oh, god. Crazy did run in the family.

"Fae? As in fairy? Are you really saying you have fairy blood?" Eric rubbed his temple.

"That's exactly what I'm saying." Her father glared. He turned his attention back to her and his expression softened. "I told you there would be things we were going to tell you that were hard to believe, sweetheart."

"Yeah, and I thought that meant something along the line of 'Honey, we need to tell you that you are adopted,' or 'Me and your mom used to be carnies.'"

"Carnies?" Donovan smirked. "Circus people?"

Celeste cut her eyes at him and then looked back at her father. "Do I have Fae blood?"

"Yes," her father answered.

"Do you and Mom?"

"Of course. As does Donovan." Her father looked over at Donovan.

"But fairies are just a myth, a legend. Fairies are not real." She shook her head.

"Fairies originated from fallen angels. Fallen angels were cast out of heaven during the Great War. Once they fell to earth, they fell in love with humans and begin to intermarry. The children who were born out of those unions were fairies."

This was crazy. What her father was telling her was abso-freaking-lutely crazy.

Why was there some little part in her that wanted

to believe him? Why was there some smidge of her heart that sighed with the knowledge that now she knew why she was never accepted? All her life she'd known that she was different and that she never really fit in.

"Go on." She swallowed the lump in her throat.

"Fairies lived among humans for hundreds of years. Their true identity was hidden until something happened that changed everything." Her father sat back and continued. "Like all nations, the fairies had a ruler, a queen who lived in Ireland. The Queen had a sister named Isa whom she dearly loved."

"Isa was beautiful, and any man who looked upon her fell in love. It started causing trouble among the villagers."

"The wives accused Isa of being a witch. Afraid for her sister's safety and worried about the risk of exposure for the other fairies, the Queen commanded her sister to only come out at night. Isa obeyed and only ventured out under the moonlight to swim in the ocean."

"One night a Viking named Naddoddr anchored just off the coast of Ireland, not far from where Isa was singing and swimming. When Naddoddr saw Isa, he instantly had to have her. That night he took her and sailed back to his Norse homeland with Isa."

"He was enchanted and fell in love with her. But he never touched her. He wanted her to love him as much as he loved her. He did everything in his power to make her love him back. He brought her jewels, gold, spices from exotic lands, yet she resisted him."

"One night there was a raid on the neighboring village. Naddoddr went out to fight along with his men. The battle lasted all day and night. When he didn't return the next day, Isa became frightened. It was then that she realized she had fallen in love with the Viking."

"Finally, as dawn broke, Naddoddr walked back into the village. He collapsed at his front door with a mortal wound to his chest. Isa rushed to his side and began to weep. She was a very powerful fairy and had the ability to heal others. As her tears fell on his wound, he began to heal and she saved him."

"Naddoddr and Isa went on to live a happy life with a home filled with children and love. It was through their children that the Fae blood continued in the Norse land."

She cut her eyes at Eric. His ancestors were from Sweden.

"Then everything turned out all right." She crossed her legs.

"Not exactly. You see, there are always consequences to our actions." Her mother gave her a sad smile.

Her stomach twisted. Her father had said those very words to Eric.

"When Isa was kidnapped, the Queen tried to send her army of fairies to stop the Viking ship, but they were too late. The Queen was infuriated. Stricken with grief, the Queen wanted Naddoddr to feel the anguish of losing someone he loved."

"In her anger, the Queen went to the King of the Pixies and asked for his help."

"Pixies?" Celeste blinked. "There are pixies too?"

"Yes. Don't underestimate pixies, Celeste. They

are just as powerful as a fairy and more devious," her father said.

"What did the king do?"

"The king agreed to help, on the condition that the Queen of the Fairies would owe him a debt. An agreement was made. The Pixie king placed a curse on the Viking that any child born through him would die."

"A curse? Pixies can do that? I thought they had pointy hats and were always smiling."

"You're thinking of gnomes, dear." Her mother patted her hand.

"Pixies are very skilled at black magic," her father said.

"That means pixies are evil?"

"Hey! That's racial profiling." Donovan jumped to his feet. "Not all of us are evil."

"You're a pixie? I thought you were a fairy." Celeste gaped.

"So did I." Eric snorted.

Donovan shot Eric a glare and then turned to address her. "You asked whether I had fairy blood in me. The answer is yes. There are different types of fairies. Pixies are a variation of fairies."

"This is very confusing." She frowned and rubbed her temple.

"What happened to Isa and Naddoddr?" Eric asked.

"Ah. You see there's a twist. Isa and Naddoddr fell in love, inactivating the curse."

"So everything turned out well." She looked from her father to her mother. Something in their eyes told her she was wrong.

"Celeste, the curse was inactivated until a child

from the linage of Naddoddr and Isa is born. For thousands of years this hasn't happened. Until now."

"What do you mean?" A chill swept up Celeste's spine.

"Naddoddr and Isa had two children, a son named Seger and a daughter named Agatha. When they were old enough, Seger married and stayed in Sweden while Agatha married an Irishman and moved to Ireland. Each sibling fell in love, therefore inactivating the curse."

"Isn't Aunt Agatha named after an ancestor?" Unease snaked up her spine.

"Yes." The muscles worked in her mother's throat as she struggled to speak, sadness and despair etched in her frown.

"I'm guessing Eric has an ancestor named Seger."

Her mother nodded and then glanced away, but not before Celeste caught the tears swelling in her eyes.

"You are both from the linage of Naddoddr and Isa. For the first time in one thousand years, a child will be born from that lineage."

"You can't possibly expect me to believe this." Eric stood. "It's a nice story, but I'm afraid that's all it is. Just a story."

"I told you he wouldn't believe it." Donovan's face tightened in rage.

"When we found out about the pregnancy, we traced your heritage, Eric. It's true." There was a sadness in her father's eyes as he stared at Eric.

"Wait. Wouldn't that make Eric and me related?" She placed her hand on her stomach and quickly sent up a prayer that her child wouldn't have duck feet.

Her mother shook her head. "It's been hundreds and hundreds of years. You may be twenty-third cousins twice removed."

"I agreed to hear what everyone had to say, and I've done that. But what you are telling me is ridiculous." Eric walked over to his desk and sat. He pulled out a large book from one of the drawers. He narrowed his gaze on her father. "I would give this back to you, but I'm afraid you're not the rightful owner."

She craned her neck to get a better view of the book but her father stepped in front of her.

"Did you read it?" Her father cocked his head.

"I did. And it is nothing more than a fairy tale." Eric pushed the book to the edge of the desk.

"I told you I was the better match for Celeste, but you wouldn't listen." Donovan's menacing tone echoed in the library. "She should have married me."

"What are you talking about, Donovan? We're cousins." She cringed. Now everyone was losing their mind.

"Apparently we are too." Eric deadpanned.

"I'm not your cousin," Donovan thundered.

"Of course you're my cousin." Celeste smiled and looked to her father.

Her father shook his head. "Remember the debt the Queen had to pay the King of the Pixies? Well, he's it." Her father shoved a thumb at Donovan. "Every generation has to agree to take in a pixie that has caused the most trouble, the one who might risk exposing the pixies to the world. And well, here he is, Mr. Troublemaker himself."

"Donovan is not my cousin?" She frowned.

"No, honey. We told you that so you wouldn't be interested in Donovan."

She rubbed her temple again fighting away the growing headache. This was all getting too weird.

"How is the little girl connected to the man who attacked me?"

"You said she had a flower in her hand." Her mother leaned in.

"Yes."

"Do you remember what kind it was?"

"I think it was a daisy."

Her mother's expression relaxed. "She wasn't there to harm you, just warn you. Flowers have different meanings to fairies. Daisies mean compassionate and empathy. She meant you no harm, Celeste. Did she say anything else?"

"No." Celeste looked out the window. "Oh, wait. She said that I was going to have a boy."

"Oh, Celeste, I haven't even asked anything about the baby." Her mother's bottom lip quivered and she had that "I'm the worst mother in the world" look on her face.

"It's okay. The morning sickness is over and I'm feeling better now."

"Do you have a good doctor? Does he know what he's doing?" her father added.

"Yes, Daddy. He's very good. I like him a lot. I have another sonogram tomorrow. You both are welcome to come with me if you want."

"Well, we don't want to intrude. I mean, I'm sure Eric wants to be there." Her mother looked at Eric.

Everyone turned to Eric. He averted his eyes and didn't say a word.

"You've been going to the doctor alone?" Her

father's voice echoed in the room.

"Eric is very busy with work. He can't take time off to go to every doctor appointment I have." She lied.

"How many appointments has he gone to?" Her father narrowed his eyes.

She looked away.

"You know, I'm beginning to think that we made a mistake agreeing to this marriage." Her father glared at Eric.

Eric narrowed his eyes yet said nothing. From his silence, he appeared to share her father's opinion.

Her mother went to her and rested her hands on shoulders.

"I'm the one who agreed to this marriage. What's done is done." Her insides ached with anger and frustration. She brushed off her mother's hands and hurried out into the hallway.

The voices of Eric and her father arguing followed her down the hall.

She ran outside. She couldn't go back inside to face her parents' looks of pity.

She needed to be alone and to calm down before she did or said something she'd regret.

She headed for the garage.

CHAPTER TWENTY-SIX

CELESTE RAN INTO THE GARAGE. Solomon straightened from polishing the Mercedes.

"Well, hello, Mrs. Celeste. I didn't expect you." He smiled and folded the polishing cloth into a neat square. "Do you need me to drive you somewhere?"

"No thank you, Solomon. I was just walking around and realized I'd never been inside the garage." She walked between a black Mercedes and silver Porsche. "I didn't know Eric had so many cars."

"Mr. Nordstrom loves his cars, that's for sure." Solomon chuckled. "You haven't seen your car yet, have you?"

"My car?"

"Yes. Mr. Nordstrom had it ordered for you. You were supposed to see it, but you had such bad morning sickness, and he said that you wouldn't feel like driving."

Eric had bought her a car? Just for her?

Solomon walked over to a cabinet and pulled off

a set of keys. He dangled them in front of her.

She snatched them up and grinned. "Which one?"

Solomon walked down the line up of cars and stopped at the last car.

Holy crap.

A dark gray Infiniti.

"Go ahead, get in." Solomon gave her a cat-who-ate-the-canary grin.

She slid in behind the wheel. Her body melted against the expensive leather seats.

Solomon pointed to the dash. "Now, this is your navigation system and here is your satellite radio. It has Bluetooth for your cell phone and there is a screen in the back of each headrest for movies—you know, for when the baby gets older and you and Mr. Eric take family vacations."

Her chest tightened. There would be no family vacations.

"You go have fun, Mrs. Nordstrom." Solomon hit a button and opened the garage door.

She powered down the windows, turned up the radio, and pulled out of the garage.

She remembered in college riding around the campus with Donovan, laughing and singing along with the radio. Back then, her dreams had seemed very attainable.

All she'd ever wanted was a place of her own, a job she loved, and a man who loved her above all else.

Now she was living in a house that didn't belong to her, had no income of her own, and was married to a stranger who didn't believe in love.

She was as far from her dreams as possible.

She drove in the opposite direction from town, taking her time and noticing the rolling hills, ambling cows, and sweet farmhouses in the countryside. The sky was a brilliant blue, the kind of blue that promised a new day and good things in the air. The farther she drove, the better she felt.

Distance was strange like that.

She glanced at the clock and frowned. She'd been gone nearly two hours.

She slowed her speed further as she approached the city limits of a small town. Her stomach rumbled, reminding her she hadn't eaten in a while. She had been in such a hurry to get away that she'd forgotten her purse.

Perfect.

She pulled into a small gas station and opened the console, hoping to find a piece of gum.

The tiny light in bottom of the console illuminated something green. She reached in and pulled out two crisp twenty-dollar bills.

"I'm so going to kiss Solomon when I get home."

Taking a twenty, she headed inside the gas station for some food.

With a soda in the crook of her arm and her hand shoved inside a bag of cheesy chips, she stepped out of the gas station.

She looked over at her car and jerked to a stop. Three teenage guys leaned against the hood of her car.

"Nice car," the guy with the blond hair, letterman jacket, and gleaming white smile called out to her.

"Thanks." She walked around to the driver's door and gritted her teeth. They clearly had no manners, leaning against someone else's car.

Before she could get her door open, one guy slid between her and the car.

"I'm Mike, and these are my friends, Chris and Jared."

"Did you just scoot your butt across the door of my new car?" she gritted out between her teeth and glanced at his studded jeans pockets. If there was even just one scratch on her car, she was going to lose it on him.

Mike smiled. "You know, I'm the starting quarterback for our high school football team."

"Yeah, well, I'm pregnant and hungry." She poked him in the chest with her finger, leaving an orange dot on his white shirt.

"Pregnant? Wow, you still look hot for a pregnant chick." Mike whistled.

She clutched her Cheetos close to her chest, "Look, kid, I don't know what's wrong with you, but if you don't get away from my car I'm going to knock you out."

"Oh yeah?" Mike wagged his eyebrows. "With your plastic Coke bottle?"

"No, with my fist."

"A girl who likes the rough stuff." Mike's eyes glazed over. "That's hot."

"Are you on drugs, or just delusional." No guy in high school had even given her a second glance and now, obviously pregnant, she couldn't get away from them. She was definitely living in a parallel universe.

"If you don't get away from my wife, I'm going to reach down your throat and rip out your kidneys."

She spun around. Eric stood there, his eyes flashing with rage and his muscles tensing through his black shirt.

The three boys took one look at him and scrambled into a black Jeep. Seconds later they tore out of the parking lot, tires squealing.

"Did they hurt you?" He glared at her.

She gave him a droll look. "Hurt me? With what? Their idiot skills?" She popped a chip in her mouth.

"You were going to hit him." Eric crossed his arms. "Really, Celeste?"

"Get me angry enough and you'll be surprised at what I can do." She frowned. "How did you find me anyway?"

"I followed you with the tracking device."

"There's a tracking device on my car?" Her voice went low.

"Before you get your panties in a twist, you need to know that tracking devices are on all my cars."

Of course. He probably had over a million dollars in inventory alone. It wasn't like he was trying to keep track of her. It wasn't like she was special.

"You didn't tell anyone where you were going." He took a step toward her.

"I needed to get away for a while. I needed some breathing room." Her appetite now gone, she rolled up the bag.

"Breathing room from your parents? Or from me?"

"Both." She reached for the door handle.

He put his hand on the door, preventing her from opening it. "I didn't know you were going to the doctor by yourself. I assumed you had asked

Andrea Leigh to go with you."

She snorted. "That wouldn't be very smart."

"Why not?"

"She would want to know why you weren't going with me and I didn't feel like lying to her. It was simpler if I went alone."

"I didn't think you wanted me to go." He shoved his hand through his blond hair.

"Why wouldn't I want you to go? You're the father." Despite wanting to hold onto her hurt and anger, she couldn't help but feel some compassion for him.

"Really?" His eyes brightened.

"Yes."

"I'll be there at the next appointment." He moved his hand from her door and she slid inside. He waited until she started her engine before walking back to his car.

She sucked in a deep breath, wondering what had just happened between them.

It seemed like just when she thought she had him figured out, Eric Nordstrom confused her. And that was something she didn't need.

She needed to get through this arranged marriage with her heart intact.

CHAPTER TWENTY-SEVEN

"HOW'S THE BABY?" ERIC ASKED Dr. Sevalus as he helped Celeste up to a sitting position on the exam table.

"Everything looks normal. But I want Celeste to start eating more, especially now that the morning sickness has passed. Tell Solomon to bring you cheeseburgers instead of ginger ale and vanilla wafers, okay?" Dr. Sevalus grinned and scribbled in the chart before leaving the room.

Eric helped her down after the door closed.

"Why was Solomon bringing you ginger ale and vanilla wafers?"

"I had really bad morning sickness after my first doctor visit. Solomon had to pull over at a gas station. He bought me ginger ale and vanilla wafers to settle my stomach. Ever since then he has kept them in the car."

"That should have been me." His stomach curled into a tight ball. Solomon had taken care of her when she was sick. That was supposed to be his job, not his driver's.

"What?" She slipped her foot into her shoe and

looked up at him.

"I should have been the one taking you to the doctor. Not Solomon." He rubbed the back of his neck and studied the floor.

"It's fine. I know you have more important things to do." Her tone was light but he knew if he looked into her gaze there would be a heavy-hearted sadness hiding behind her emerald eyes.

"No. It's not fine." He hated that he'd been obtuse.

"You were busy." She shrugged and turned away to gather her purse.

"I will not be that kind of father to my child." He grabbed her arm. Her eyes wide as she gaped at him.

"What do you mean?"

"I will not be that kind of father who's always too busy to be there for my child. I want to see him take his first steps and hear his first words, and be at all his baseball games."

"Is that what your father did?"

"No. He did the opposite." He couldn't remember his father coming to any games or school events. Hell, his father hadn't even shown up for his graduation.

Her slender hand rested against his chest. "You will not be like your father, Eric. You will be a loving and attentive father."

The icy wall he'd built around his heart splintered and fell into a million pieces. In that moment, he knew he was fighting losing battle trying to stay away from her. And he knew why.

He was falling in love with her.

He took her hands between his. "Celeste, I …"

The door swung opened and the nurse walked in.

He stepped away, his heart pounding in his chest.

The nurse handed her a slip of paper. "Okay, Mrs. Nordstrom. Here's your appointment for next time."

Was it possible she meant what she'd said, that she believed in him? Or was she like the rest, willing to say anything in order to obtain his trust and get what she wanted?

Only time would tell.

"WHERE IS EVERYONE?" CELESTE WALKED into the kitchen and put her purse on the counter. Her mom sat at the kitchen island sipping a hot cup of tea and reading a book.

"Donovan and your father are going into the forest to do some investigating. And I think Mrs. Gambil is upstairs cleaning." Her mom frowned. "Where's Eric?"

"Had to go back to work." She gave her mom a reassuring smile. "The doctor said the baby is developing well. My next appointment is in a month."

"That's great, honey. Do you feel like a cup of tea?"

"No. But I would like to go for a walk. I need some fresh air."

"I'll go with you. I haven't seen the garden yet." Her mother washed out her cup and set it in the sink.

They strolled in silence and admired the last burst of color from the summer flowers.

"I have some questions." She wasn't ready to

entirely disregard everything her parents had told her, but something inside her struggled for the truth.

"Yes, dear?"

"I thought fairies had wings."

"We used to. But that trait died out when fairies intermarried with humans."

She blinked. "Well, I also thought that fairies were magical."

"All fairies have their own gifts." Her mother smiled.

"So we don't have magic powers?"

"All fairies are strong." Her mother turned. "We are excellent fighters and are very fast. Those are our gifts. But we all have individual powers specific to our character as well."

"Really?" Her heart drummed with excitement. "What's your power?"

"I have the ability to control the elements. I'm an elemental fairy."

"You mean like those superhero cartoons I used to watch?"

"Kind of, but I don't wear a cape." Her mother laughed. "When you were a child, did you notice how our land always was lush and green? And how we always grew an abundance of vegetables?"

"Yes."

"That's because I always made sure our land was given the right elements to flourish. I can make it rain, or make the sun shine or …"

"Make a ten-year-old's wish come true." Her heart tripped in her chest as a memory skipped across her brain.

The downside of living in the South was that it

never snowed. She remembered how she had complained to her mother that she wished it would snow, just once. The next week there had been a freak blizzard that had canceled school for a whole week.

It had been a childhood memory she always cherished.

"That was you?"

"That was me." Her mother smiled.

She had so many questions. Her mind raced with impossibilities.

"So what's Dad's power?"

"Your father can communicate with animals."

"You mean like Dr. Doolittle?"

"I think we let you watch too much television when you were growing up." Her mother shook her head. "But yes, he can talk to animals. Although he says that squirrels are kind of hard to understand. They don't ever finish a complete thought. Your father says it's very irritating."

"What about Donovan?"

"Donovan is another story." Her mother's expression tightened, her smile not quite gone but hidden under the surface. "He tends to keep things hidden from us, but we do know that he is very good with the ladies. It's almost like they can't control themselves."

"Definitely too much information." She shuddered.

"Remember, he is not your cousin, Celeste. And he has always been very fond of you, so just be careful where he is concerned." Her mother's sharp eyes landed on her.

"Believe me, you don't have anything to worry

about." She cringed. "So if all you guys have these powers ..."

"Gifts," her mother corrected.

"Okay, gifts. If you guys have these gifts, then why don't I?"

"You do have a gift." Her mother continued down the garden path. "Do you remember when you were young and you had a dream about a neighbor of ours?"

Celeste's throat tightened. "Yes. I dreamed he was killed in a farming accident. Then the following week it happened."

She had cried hysterically when she had told her mother. She remembered how terrified she had been, afraid something was wrong with her, afraid she was evil.

"It was then, Celeste, that I knew that your gift was prophecy. I didn't tell you. You were just a little girl and so very frightened."

She closed her eyes, letting the weight she'd carried all these years melt off her shoulders.

"You have no idea how relieved I am. I kept thinking in the back of my mind that something was wrong with me. That I was evil." Her eyes snapped open. "Wait. I remember praying never to dream again. And then the dreams stopped, like they dried up."

"Prophesying. They weren't just dreams, you see."

"Okay, I stopped prophesying." Celeste frowned. "And on my twenty-third birthday I started dreaming gain. And since I've been pregnant I've been dreaming a lot." And the dreams were terrifying.

"Pregnancy can intensify our gifts and make them more powerful. Now is the time for you to learn to control your gift."

"Do you think I'll be able to control it? It only happens when I'm asleep."

"You can learn to prophesy when you are awake. All it takes is some time and patience." Her mother smiled. "We can try today if you feel up to it."

"I'd like that." She twisted her wedding band on her finger and looked away. It both frightened and excited her.

She needed to know more about her dreams. Maybe if she could control her prophesies, then she could change the future and she wouldn't have to tell Eric about the horrific things she'd seen.

"Let's do it then."

Her mother led her to the bench off the garden path and she sat.

"Close your eyes and concentrate." Her mother said.

After a few failed attempts, Celeste finally quit.

"Nothing. All I got was a headache." She frowned and rubbed her temple.

"It's normal. We just need to work on it every day." Her mother's reassuring tone did nothing for her ego.

"Why don't you rest while I go see what your father is up to?" Her mother gave her a hug before heading back to the house.

She felt a smidge of guilt for not telling her mother about her horrible nightmares. She couldn't. Not yet.

Until she figured out why she was dreaming such horrible things, she planned on keeping her dreams a secret.

CHAPTER TWENTY-EIGHT

ERIC LOOKED UP FROM HIS desk. He had been trying for the past hour to focus on his paperwork instead of stealing glances at his wife while she pored over that damn book that Ben had taken. He hadn't called Uncle Stephen and let him know that the book had been stolen. He figured since his uncle hadn't mentioned it being gone, there was no point in bringing it up.

It was just a book about fairytales anyway.

"Where did you get this book?" Celeste held up the leather-bound book and tugged the cream colored shawl around her shoulders more tightly.

"Your father gave it to me." He glanced at the fireplace and wondered if he should put another log.

"My father had it?" Her brows drew together in confusion and her eyes sparkled like emeralds.

He didn't think it was possible, but she grew more beautiful every passing day.

"Your father got it from Uncle Stephen." He wasn't going to lie to her.

"So this book was in the house the night the

night we… met?"

"Met? We did more than just meet." He grinned.

She blushed and glanced away.

Even her shyness was sexy.

"Yes. It was in my uncle's house the night we met. Why do you ask?"

"No reason." She licked her lips. "Have you read it?"

"I have." He'd stayed up most of the night reading it after Ben had given it to him. Once he'd started, he couldn't put it down.

She set the book on the coffee table and thrust her chest out and rubbed the small of her back. Her full breasts strained against the thin material of her shirt.

His body tightened and his mouth watered. Thoughts of his mouth on her nipples had his pants getting tighter.

"It has a lot of stories about fairies." He was shocked at his hoarse voice. Probably from lack of blood, as all of it seemed to have headed south of his zipper.

"But it's not all about fairies. It talks about vampires, werewolves, and witches a lot. Did you read where it said that werewolves were divided into packs and each pack controlled their state?"

"I saw that. I believe, according to the book that vampires are rare and not as common as other creatures." He added. He had to admit the book was very captivating.

"It also has a lot about pixies in here too. It says they are mischievous and like to play pranks," she added.

"Fits Donovan to a T." Even though he didn't

believe the whole fairy business, one thing he was certain of. The more he was around Donovan, the more he didn't trust the bastard.

"It also says they are known to steal things. They prefer stealing horses because they like speed." She looked up and frowned. "If pixies like speed, wouldn't a modern-day pixie like to steal a car instead of a horse?"

"You're right." He picked up the phone and hit the button for his garage. "Solomon, make sure from now on to lock the keys up every time you leave the garage."

He didn't think Donovan was a pixie, but he wouldn't put it past the guy to take something that didn't belong to him.

He pushed back from his desk and crossed the library to where she sat. He took her hand in his and pulled her to her feet.

"What are you doing?" Her brows creased and she looked at him.

"Your back hurts. Let me help." He sat on the couch and pulled her down in front of him, placing her back into his chest.

"Stretch your legs out on the couch." She obeyed and he slid his hands down her lower back. Slowly he began to massage her sore muscles.

She moaned.

The sound shot straight to his dick.

"Feel better?" His raspy voice sounded like he'd run a marathon. He closed his eyes and inhaled her scent. God, he'd never wanted to make love so badly in his entire life.

"Yes," she whispered and leaned into his hands.

"Pick up your hair." He swallowed and tried to

keep his mind and his hands from wandering over her body.

She lifted her hair off her neck. He rubbed her slender shoulders. Every time he massaged a sore muscle, her breath caught in her throat.

"What else does the book say?" He shook his head, trying to distract his oxygen-deprived brain.

"Well, it says some pixies can shape-shift."

He snorted. "Maybe Donovan would shape-shift into a jackass. That wouldn't be so hard to believe."

A laugh bubbled out of her.

"Eric, why are you missing so much work?" She looked at him over her shoulders. "Is everything okay?"

"Everything's fine. I've shored up my commitments over the last few months, and I can take care of everything else from home."

"Oh."

"Why do you ask? Are you getting tired of me being around so much?"

"No. I just didn't want you to feel obligated to be around since my family is here. Before they arrived, you were gone a lot. I don't expect you to pretend to want to be here all the time while they are here."

His fingers froze.

Pretend to want to be here? Is that what she believed? Had he been gone that much?

Of course he had.

When he'd first brought her home, all he could think about was getting her into his bed. But he'd known it would have scared the hell out of her, so he'd quickly thrown himself into his work, trying to focus on anything but her.

"Did you really think I didn't want to be here?"

She stiffened in his arms and then stood. Pain flashed across her eyes.

"I should go." She turned and headed for the door.

She made it three steps before he grabbed her and swung her up in his arms.

"What are you doing? Put me down." She struggled in his arms. "I'm too heavy. You're going to hurt your back."

"You hardly weigh anything at all."

"What are you doing?" She narrowed her eyes at him.

"We need to talk. But not here." He needed privacy, without her parents or Donovan interrupting them.

He grabbed the shawl off the couch and headed out of the house and into the backyard.

Crisp fall air stung his lungs. The brilliant moon hung heavy and bright in the sky, signaling a change in season. Cold leaves crunched under his footsteps and his breath came out in a white puffs.

He carried her into the middle of the garden and settled her on the concrete bench. After he tucked the blanket around her legs, he stood.

"When I brought you here I knew it would be difficult, being away from your family, your friends, your work and the life you had in Atlanta. You gave up everything familiar and moved to an unknown place. I figured that in your resentment, you would find a way to make me miserable."

Her chin trembled and she dropped her head.

He sucked in a deep breath before continuing on. He had to. She had to hear everything. He hoped, in the end, she would understand.

"I thought you would be bitter and angry. In fact, I expected you to be. But at our first dinner date with my friends you were graceful and kind, even to Leslie. When Leslie verbally attacked you in our home, you said nothing. When it came to others, you stood up for them. You defended me to your own father when I didn't deserve it."

He had wanted to tell her all these things for weeks. He'd never opened himself up to anyone before, never made himself vulnerable. Until now.

He sank to his knees and placed his hands on either side of her legs, trapping her between his arms.

He looked down, struggling to compose himself.

"After the way I blackmailed you into marriage, how can you even show me the tiniest shred of kindness?" He swallowed hard and looked at the ground. "I don't deserve you."

"Eric. . ." Her voice was soft as she reached out and touched his cheek, lifting his gaze to hers.

He expected to see condemnation and resentment, but only gentleness shone in her eyes.

"Don't say anything. I need to finish this." He shook his head. "I stayed away from you because I can't be in the same room with you without wanting to make love with you. Seeing you day after day and not being able to touch my own wife has been torture, yet I knew I would never force you. I know how much you must hate me for forcing you into a marriage you never wanted."

"I don't hate you, Eric. I never did." She said softly.

He held his breath. She didn't hate him?

He stood and pulled her up into her arms. She

fit him perfectly. He'd known that the first night they made love.

He enveloped her slender body in his embrace and knew at that moment he would never let her go.

Her hands slid around his neck, and she pulled him down and kissed him deep. She opened her mouth under his, giving him access to her sweet mouth and clinging to him.

"I want you." He groaned against her mouth and then sucked her tongue.

Sliding his hands past her waist, he cupped her butt and pushed her back against the concrete garden wall.

"Here?" she whispered yet didn't let go. She ground against him, arching her body into his.

"Yes, here." He shoved down the neckline of her shirt and pressed his mouth against her flushed skin. She sighed. "If we go inside, that asshole Donovan will find a way to stop us. I'm not stopping tonight."

Her breath quickened with every kiss of his lips. She slipped her hand down the front of his jeans and grabbed his cock.

"Sweetheart…" Her touch felt so good.

Suddenly the silence of the night was broken by a growl. The sound, low and feral, echoed in the darkness. He stilled and then turned.

"Eric, what...?"

He held his fingers to her lips and looked around for the threat.

From out of nowhere something barreled into them and slammed them to the ground.

CHAPTER TWENTY-NINE

CELESTE LANDED HARD ON HER back, knocking the breath out of her lungs. She gasped and struggled to breathe as she frantically searched for Eric.

Her gaze locked on his motionless figure sprawled on the ground a few feet away.

The moonlight glinted off something metallic protruding out of his chest.

"Eric!" Panic pressed on her heart like truck tires on wet sand.

He didn't move.

Fear crawled into her throat, threatening to suffocate her.

Do something. Do something. Do something.

She forced her legs under her and stood. The same invisible force slammed into her again, shoving her back to the ground.

It held her to the ground as pain spread across her chest. Her first thought was that she was having a heart attack. But as she squinted into the darkness, she saw it.

Those eyes.

Evil eyes rimmed in yellow hovered above her.

"You shouldn't have disobeyed me in the woods." As it spoke, the body emerged and grew around the eyes, just as it had before.

The demon's putrid breath hit her and she swallowed back the overwhelming urge to vomit.

She tried to move, but the demon tightened his claw-like grip around her shoulders.

She was pinned to the ground like a bug on a display board.

The demon sneered, its pointed teeth more horrifying against the moonlight.

She was looking into the face of death.

Her death.

Something shiny swung through the air. It struck the demon across the head. The demon rolled off her and let out a horrendous howl.

Eric stood above her, holding a pipe.

She pushed herself off the ground.

"I want her!" The demon focused its gaze on her.

"Well, you can't have her." Eric pushed her behind him.

The demon lunged.

Eric swung the pipe and slashed the creature across the stomach. Black blood spurted out like a geyser. The demon screeched in pain.

A second growl, different and deeper, ricocheted through the night air.

Something sprang through the air and skidded to a stop in front of them.

It was the largest gray wolf she'd ever seen.

Trembling, she reached for Eric's hand.

The large wolf turned, threw them a glance, and then focused its attention on the demon.

The wolf opened its mouth and growled. The sound raised the hair on her neck.

The wolf paced back and forth, never taking its eyes off the demon as a steady humming growl rolled out of his mouth. Every time the demon tried to advance toward them, the wolf would block him.

The wolf was acting as a fence between them and the demon.

Eric tightened his grip on her hand. "Run."

She didn't need to be told twice.

They raced for the house.

Eric kept a death grip on her hand, refusing to let go as they ran for their lives. They made it to the back door and scrambled inside. He turned and locked it behind them.

She leaned against the wall and slid to the floor. She sucked air to her oxygen-starved lungs while tears streamed down her face.

"What happened?" Her father rushed into the room and squatted in front of her.

"It's back, in the garden." She cradled her stomach.

"Are you okay?" Her mother quickly knelt down.

"Yes. I'm fine." She leaned her head against the wall.

"Eric, were you there?" Her father looked over his shoulder at Eric's back.

"Yes," he answered, still staring out the window.

"How did you get away?" Her mother's hands were on her, assessing for damage.

"Eric hit it with a pipe." She pressed her hand over her racing heart.

"And then a wolf leaped through the bushes." Eric turned. Everyone's eyes went to him.

Her heart caught, skipped a beat, and then tumbled to her stomach.

"Oh my god."

Blood saturated the front of his shirt and dripped to the floor in a quickly growing puddle of red.

She ran to him.

Eric took a step toward her and stumbled. Her father caught him before he hit the floor and eased him into a chair.

"He must have been stabbed with the pipe he hit the demon with." She knelt and pushed his shirt off.

Hot tears slipped down her face and she forced back her horrified revulsion.

Blood pulsed from a large gaping hole in the middle of his chest. Tissue and muscle lay torn, jagged and flayed.

"Call 911!" She grabbed the nearest pillow and held it tightly against his chest. Blood seeped from his wound and soaked into the pillow. She pushed harder, trying to get the flow to stop.

"Don't just stand there. He needs help." She looked over her shoulder.

"They can't help him. He's going to die from the iron in the pipe if he doesn't bleed out first." Her mother's voice's tone was hard, unflinching.

"Iron? What the hell are you talking about?" She pressed the pillow harder against his wound.

"Iron is poisonous to fairies. That's what's going to kill him, not the wound itself."

"There's got to be some way to save him. We're

fucking fairies." Anger and fear filled her voice and her body. She'd never raised her voice to her parents in her life, let alone cursed at them. She had to make them see, make them understand.

"You'll have to do what I tell you or he's not going to make it." Her mother's voice was stern and harsh.

"What do I do?" Warm blood seeped through the pillow and squeezed out between her fingers. Eric's eyes drifted shut. The color drained from his face, giving his skin a gray pallor as his life slipped away.

"You need to kiss him, Celeste."

"Kiss him? How's kissing him going to help?" She shot back.

"It's one of your gifts. Healing. It's in your Fae blood," her mother said.

"He's dying, Celeste. You need to hurry," her father urged.

Prophesy was her gift. They had told her that. She glanced at Eric's face and knew the life was slipping from him. She was out of options.

She cupped his face between her hands and leaned down. The coppery smell of blood choked her.

What if it didn't work?

What if she couldn't save him?

Panic and fear wound like fingers around her heart and squeezed until she was almost dizzy.

She was running out of time.

She squeezed her eyes and brushed her lips against his, trying to ignore the taste of blood.

A tiny jolt shot through her body the second they touched. She pulled back and the sensation stopped. She pressed her mouth more firmly against his and tensed. The jolt grew stronger, surging through her body into his.

Blood rushed through her veins. A thrum, that same physical thrum she'd felt when Eric had first touched her, pulsed through her entire body.

She opened her mouth and kissed him deep.

Immense power poured like liquid from her body into Eric. Euphoria licked through her veins like pulses of lightning.

Eric moved his head.

Encouraged she kept her mouth on his, pouring her energy into him and willing him to live.

His eyes flew open. His blue eyes stared into hers.

She tried to pull away, but he cupped the back of her head and held her against him. He kissed her with the same passion he had shown her the night they'd made love. Wrapping his arms around her, he sat and pulled her into his lap. His erection pressed into her stomach and she quickly forgot the world around them.

Her father cleared his throat.

Startled, she pulled away and looked down at him. He stared up at her with a desire so intense she was afraid he was going to pull her panties down and have her right there in front of her parents.

"Let me see your chest." Breathing heavily, she pushed his shirt aside. She traced the healed area where the wound had been. There wasn't even a hint of a scar.

"That's impossible." She shook her head in disbelief.

"I knew it. I knew my girl was a healer." Her father's tone was both proud and astonished.

She kept her gaze glued to Eric.

His narrowed blue eyes locked on her and he cocked his head.

A chill ran down her spine. Did he think she was a freak now?

She climbed off him and they both stood.

White stars settled into her vision and she felt her strength leave her body.

Her legs buckled and she stumbled.

Eric's hands wrapped around her waist and steadied her.

"What's wrong with me?" She closed her eyes and tried to steady herself.

"You're weak, honey. Healing can do that." Her mother gave her an encouraging smile.

"I'm fine." She brushed Eric's hands away.

She reminded herself that it didn't matter what Eric thought of her.

He knew she was different. He knew what she was.

She'd never fit in before, so why should now be any different?

She stared into his suspicious eyes.

"What did you do to me, Celeste?"

CHAPTER THIRTY

AFTER THE ATTACK IN THE garden, Eric refused to leave Celeste alone. If he had to leave for urgent business, then he made sure her parents or Donovan stayed with her. He wasn't going to risk her safety.

As much as he hated the man, he knew Donovan would protect her.

Celeste was all that mattered.

She'd healed him, saved his life. No doubt about that. He just couldn't wrap his mind around how she'd done it.

His logical side warred with what his gut was telling him. He still hadn't made up his mind exactly what to believe.

He knew she was getting cabin fever so he decided to take her out for lunch.

He glanced at his watch.

He just needed to make one quick phone call while she was still getting ready.

Sarah and Ben had headed into town early that morning, and Mrs. Gambil was busy upstairs cleaning. The house was relatively quiet.

He entered the library and stopped short.

Donovan sat in his leather chair with his feet propped on the desk. He was staring intently on a framed photo in his hand.

It was their wedding photo.

"What the hell are you doing?" Anger boiled in his chest and his vision clouded.

"Just looking. No harm in just looking, is there?" Donovan placed the photo back on the desk.

"Just make sure looking is all you do." He clenched and unclenched his fists. "She's mine."

Donovan shot to his feet. "You're a fool if you honestly think you can keep her, Nordstrom. She was always meant to be mine."

Anger turned to possessive rage. "She is *my* wife. And if you ever so much as look at her wrong, I'll rip your fucking heart out."

"Is everything okay?" He turned at the sound of Celeste's voice coming from the doorway.

She stood, dressed in a velvet green dress that molded to her growing stomach. Her silky blond hair fell in waves across her shoulders.

She took his breath away.

"We were just talking, sweetheart." He kept his tone light and pulled her into his arms.

She smiled at him and then turned to Donovan. "Donovan, do you want to go eat with us? My parents left, so you'll be here alone otherwise."

Eric shot him a warning glare.

"No thanks, my love."

Eric flinched at the endearment.

"Maybe next time. Besides, I'm still working on my next battle strategy." He shot her a smile.

"To stop the demon?" Celeste asked.

Donovan aimed his gaze right at Eric. "Precisely. To stop the demon."

☾

ERIC'S ALTERCATION WITH DONOVAN HAD left him on his guard. If Donovan so much as put his hands on Celeste, he wouldn't hesitate to kill the bastard.

He ran his hands across his eyes. Hell, he hadn't even put his hands on Celeste, at least not in the way he wanted.

As much as he wanted to make love with her, he wanted to give her something more. He wanted to give her the romance and tenderness and love that she hadn't gotten the first time they were together.

She deserved better than hot, hard sex.

Sex. Just the thought of it made him stiff. It had been six months, one week, and four days since they'd had sex. He hadn't been with anyone since her.

He hadn't wanted anyone else.

He glanced across the bed at her as she moved in her sleep. She arched and stretched against him. Her full breasts rubbed against his arm. He fought back a groan, and his dick hardened to the point of pain.

She blinked and smiled. "Good morning."

"Good morning." He rolled to his side and traced his finger down her cheek to her shoulder.

Her pupils dilated at his touch.

His fingertip skipped down to the swell of her breast. He held her gaze, waiting for her to stop him.

She inhaled sharply and grabbed his hand while

gazing into his eyes. She pressed his hand to her breast and arched against his palm. A soft moan of pleasure drifted out between her parted lips.

"I want you, Celeste. I don't want to wait another minute."

Her eyes widened and she nodded.

He propped himself up against the headboard and lifted her until she straddled him.

With her gaze on him, she ran her fingers up his chest, exploring his body in detail.

He kissed her softly on each cheek. He wanted to go slow to make it good for her.

He brushed his lips across her chin and then her forehead.

He pulled back and saw the trust reflected in her eyes, it floored him.

He covered her lips with his. The taste of her, more delectable than anything he'd ever savored. He'd slept with a lot of women, but none had compared to her.

Her fingers tightened around his wrists, holding his hands where he gripped her hips.

She moaned under his lips as his tongue sought out hers, fueling an already out-of-control wildfire. Urgency to claim her body in every way possible crowded his mind as his hands slid down her chest.

He ran his thumbs across her full breasts, wanting to memorize every silky curve of her body.

She moaned and fisted her fingers in his hair.

His hands slid farther down her flesh to her thighs. He reached for the hem of her nightshirt. His fingertips brushed across soft satin skin, and she trembled.

He pulled her shirt over her head and tossed the

garment to the floor.

She sat before him in nothing but her pink panties.

She was fucking beautiful.

He clenched his jaw, holding back from taking her right then. He wanted to remember this moment, to take it all in.

His gaze traveled across her full breasts and rosy nipples and then farther down to her stomach.

"God, you're beautiful."

She reached for his hands and pressed the palms to her breasts. He sucked in a breath and fought to go slow.

He teased her nipple between his fingers until another low moan escaped her lips.

"Don't stop, Eric."

"There is no stopping this." He found her sweet mouth as he pulled her against his chest.

He gripped her hips and pressed his cock against her wet panties. He wanted every inch of that sexy body pressed against his. His lips trailed down her neck to her shoulder as she clung to him.

"I hope I'm not interrupting." Donovan's sharp voice echoed in the room.

She screamed and burrowed into his chest, trying to hide her nakedness.

Gritting his teeth, he glared at Donovan over her shoulder.

"What the fuck are you doing barging in here?" He wrapped his arms around her naked back, hiding her from her cousin's view. If she hadn't been on top of him, he would have jumped up and beaten Donovan to a bloody pulp.

"Sorry. Your guest said it was important." Donovan smirked.

"What guest?" He had no appointments today.

"An old flame of yours. She's downstairs and insists on talking to you. I think she said her name is Leslie." Donovan's smirk grew wider.

Celeste flinched against his chest.

In that moment, he wanted to kill Donovan.

"Donovan, get out of here," Celeste insisted.

"It's not like I haven't seen you without your clothes on." Donovan waggled his eyebrows.

Rage ignited in Eric's gut.

"I was five, you idiot." She glared at Donovan across her shoulder. "I need to get dressed. Do you mind?"

"I don't mind at all." Donovan picked up her nightshirt and rubbed the silky material between his fingers. He lifted it to his face and inhaled.

Blind rage flooded Eric's entire body. In one swift motion, he jerked the covers over Celeste and jumped out of bed. He was on Donovan in two steps.

He snatched her shirt out of Donovan's hand and tossed it back to her. He grabbed Donovan around the throat.

"My, my, so possessive." Donovan grimaced and pulled free. "Okay, fine, I'm leaving."

Eric waited until Donovan closed the door behind him. He snatched his robe off the chair. He couldn't even make love to his wife in his own damn house.

"This won't take long." He walked over to the bed and kissed her long and deep until he felt her body relax against him. Reluctantly, he pulled away. "Don't get dressed. I fully intend to finish what we started."

He tried to adjust himself so his erection wouldn't be so noticeable, but it was useless.

He had been walking around with a hard-on ever since she'd moved in. He should be used to the discomfort by now.

Five minutes later, he strode into the library. The second he saw Leslie, he lost his erection.

"Leslie. I'm surprised you have to nerve to show your face in my home." He sat down behind his desk and glared. He regretted not trying to get Leslie voted off the board.

"I know it's early, but I really need to talk to you." Leslie fingered the gold necklace hanging between her breasts. She eased into the chair across from him.

He wondered how she could breathe in her tight-fitting red sweater. She looked like a strangled sausage.

"I see that I woke you." She licked her lips. Her gaze drifted down his chest.

"Why are you here? As I recall, the last time you were in my house, you insulted my wife and disrespected me." His gaze flickered to the grandfather clock in the corner. He really wanted to head back upstairs and find Celeste in bed, naked and waiting for him.

"That's why I'm here. To apologize. I didn't realize you were so fond of the girl." She laughed nervously.

"The girl?" He arched his eyebrow. "Celeste is my wife and the mother of my child." He leaned back in the chair and inhaled deep. "Of course, I realize the age difference between the two of you is noticeable. Maybe that's why you refer to her as a girl."

Fury flashed in her eyes before she composed herself and fixed a contrite look on her face. It struck him as odd how someone who possessed so much beauty could be so emotionless, so cold, and so empty.

"I had too much to drink and I really didn't realize what I was saying. I just wanted you to know that I am truly sorry." She folded her hands in her lap and studied the floor.

He narrowed his eyes. He didn't trust her. He'd learned a long time ago that women like Leslie were always working an angle.

"I'm not the one you should be apologizing to."

"It's early and I don't want to wake her. I know she must need extra rest in her condition."

"She's not asleep. At least, she wasn't when I left her a minute ago." He didn't hide his smirk. He let her imagination run wild on that bit of information.

She cleared her throat and shifted in her seat, clearly uncomfortable with the visual.

"I'll ask her to come down." He picked up phone. The quicker Leslie apologized, the quicker he could get Celeste back in bed.

"Are you decent?" He kept his voice low. "Throw on your robe and meet me downstairs."

❦

"I HATE THAT BITCH." CELESTE THREW on her robe and checked her hair in the mirror. She had never really hated anyone until she'd met Leslie Andrews.

When Donovan had announced that Eric had a female visitor, she'd immediately known who it was. Her arch nemesis, Leslie.

Leslie was a beautiful woman.

And thin.

She ran her hand across her protruding belly as she walked down the stairs. She wanted to get dressed, but Eric had told her just to throw on a robe.

Any confidence she had flew right out the window when she entered the library and spotted Leslie dressed in skinny jeans and a red sweater stretched within an inch of its life across her pert breasts. The knee-high black boots put her at eye level with Eric.

Her self-esteem took a hard hit.

"Good morning, Leslie."

"Good morning." Leslie looked from her back to Eric.

Eric closed the distance and pulled her into his arms. He kissed her, hard and deep.

She hadn't meant to moan, but whenever he touched her she couldn't quite control her body.

When he pulled back he looked down at her, only at her.

"Leslie has something she wants to say." He cupped her cheek.

"I was hoping I could speak to Celeste alone, if you don't mind." There was a subtle tightness to Leslie's voice.

"It's okay." She smiled and nodded. His kiss had given her the confidence she needed to face Leslie on her own.

He hooked a finger in her robe and pulled. His

gaze dropped down to her breasts. She slapped his hand away.

"Just making sure you didn't put anything on." He grinned, and gave her another kiss before leaving the library.

The look of shock on Leslie's face gave her the surge of confidence she needed.

"Did you want to see me, Leslie?" She tied her robe tighter and sat on the couch.

Leslie immediately recovered her poker face. "Yes. I just want to tell you that I am very sorry for everything I said that night. I had too much to drink and I was out of place. I hope you can forgive me."

She didn't really think Leslie was sincere. She also didn't think that Leslie Andrews had ever apologized to anyone in her life.

"I accept your apology." She might forgive, but forgetting was an entirely different thing.

"You do?" Leslie blinked. "I mean, that is very generous of you."

An awkward silence settled between the two women. She was being a poor hostess by not offering Leslie anything to drink, but she didn't really want this woman in her house a minute longer than necessary.

"I know it must be hard to be married to someone you hardly know." Leslie smiled. "I've known Eric for quite a while. Did he ever tell you he modeled for Calvin Klein?"

"No." *What an odd thing to bring up.*

"It was when he was in his early twenties. He got tired of his father and did it just for spite. That's how I first met him. I was a model and we met at a runway show during fashion week in Paris. He was definitely in his element. He went through models like water. Once he got them in bed, he moved to the next one." Leslie laughed.

Celeste took a slow breath. She wasn't going to let Leslie get a reaction out of her. Eric's past was exactly that. The past. It had no bearing on their relationship now.

"He always said he would never get married. He said he didn't want the responsibility of taking care of someone else." Leslie cocked her head. "Did he ever tell you about the Elizabeth Humphries scandal where he almost lost his company?"

A wave of nausea washed over her. She knew Leslie was baiting her. She wasn't falling for it. She smiled. "I'm aware of what happened."

Leslie exhaled. "Well, then, you can understand why I thought he married you. I mean, after she claimed he raped her he was put on suspension."

"He never raped her. It was consensual." She narrowed her eyes.

"I know. But he was still on suspension after you guys married. The board was afraid he would continue to put the company in jeopardy if he didn't keep his pants zipped. I assumed he married you to prevent another scandal, especially with you being pregnant." Leslie shrugged. "I mean, you could have cried rape too. He could have lost everything."

Celeste tried to hold her smile in place. He hadn't mentioned anything to her about being on suspension.

Leslie waved her hand. "I'm sure he's told you all about it." Her face brightened. "I brought you something. I found these when I was cleaning out my closet, some old magazines he was in. He seemed so happy back then. Guess it was all the models." Leslie handed her a stack of glossy magazines that she pulled from her designer bag. "I wouldn't worry. I'm sure he's gotten all that out of his system by now."

Celeste's stomach plummeted.

Leslie stood up and grabbed her purse. "Well, I've got to run. I'm so glad we had this chance to talk, Celeste." Leslie made her way to the front door and let herself out.

Celeste sat alone with the magazines in her lap weighing her down like bricks. Why had he not told her about being on suspension?

She thought back to when he'd asked her to marry him.

He had said then that if he signed the documents to terminate his parental rights, it would give her all the control.

He said that she could come back and blackmail him with proof of him being the father.

Her chest squeezed.

Very carefully, she turned the first page. Halfway through the magazine she found the ad.

Eric, dressed in Calvin Klein underwear, was leaning against the mast of a yacht. He was shirtless and his body an ocean of ripped muscles, looking much the same as he did now. His arms were raised above his head and his face angled away from the camera, giving an amazing view of his square-cut jaw. Her stomach did little flips.

In the next magazine, he was on the cover, wearing jeans and a white unbuttoned shirt. He looked dead at the camera with his devastating grin.

A surge of lust shot through her body.

With a shaking hand, she flipped the pages until she came to the interview.

It started out with very basic questions about his family, his background, which companies his father owned, where he lived. Then the questions became more personal. He was asked who he was dating. He replied that he refused to tie himself down to exclusively one person.

Her mouth went dry.

The next question asked whether he would ever consider marriage. He answered he would never get married because he was incapable of being faithful to just one woman.

He could never be faithful to just one woman.

The magazine slipped out of her hand and rustled to the floor.

Her stomach bottomed.

He had married her to save his company, not to do right by their child.

Less than an hour ago, she'd been about to give her body to him, thinking that he cared about her.

He had stated himself in an interview that he could not and would never be faithful.

She'd been a fool to believe otherwise.

CHAPTER THIRTY-ONE

TEARS BURNED IN CELESTE'S EYES and slipped down her face.

She gathered up the magazines and hurried upstairs. She skidded to a stop just before bumping into Mrs. Gambil.

"I'm so sorry."

"It's my fault, Mrs. Celeste. I was coming in to tell you that Mr. Eric had to run over to the garage to check on something. He said to tell you he would be right back." Mrs. Gambil smiled brightly.

"Is everything okay?" She kept her head down, pretending to straighten the stack of magazines in her arms to hide the tears in her eyes.

"Solomon called and said that one of the motorcycles was missing. I think Donovan borrowed it. I could have sworn I passed him as I was headed in." Mrs. Gamble frowned and tapped her finger to her chin.

The older woman's gaze dropped to the stack of magazines in Celeste's. "What have you got there, dear?" She touched a finger to the magazine with Eric on the cover. "Oh, yes. I remember that. His father was worried to death, thinking he would never settle down. Mr. Eric sure had a thing for beautiful women."

Her heart tumbled in her chest like a rock rolling down a mountain. Mrs. Gamble's words solidified what she feared most. That Eric was still a womanizer.

"Excuse me, Mrs. Gambil. I've got to get dressed." She hurried up the stairs, away from the prying eyes of the housekeeper.

Once in the safety of her room, she locked the door. She turned on the closet light and hid the magazines in the bottom of her closet under a couple of shoeboxes and pulled out some clothes.

The weather was getting colder in Vermont, so she chose black jeans, a white sweater, and boots and quickly dressed. Grabbing her coat and purse, she headed outside.

She saw Eric walking out of the garage. She ducked behind a tree and held her breath. She couldn't face him right now. She didn't want to hear his lies.

He hurried toward the house. She guessed by the scowl etched across his face that Donovan had taken one of the motorcycles.

When the coast was clear, she ran to the garage and got into her car. She made it half a mile down the road before her cell phone rang.

"I was looking everywhere for you. Where are you?" Eric asked.

"I forgot that I promised to go over to Andrea Leigh's house today." She managed a chuckle. "She wanted me to come over for coffee. Since my parents have been here, I haven't had a lot of time to visit with her."

"I don't like you going alone. Why don't I meet you over there, just so I know you made it all right?"

"That's not necessary. I'll just call you when I get there." She swallowed back the tightness in her throat. "Look, Eric, I'm okay. And with all of you guys hovering over me, it's making me claustrophobic. Besides, it's nine o'clock in the morning. Nothing bad happens this early in the morning."

He sighed. "Okay. But you have to call me the minute you get there."

"I will."

"Celeste?" He hesitated. "Did Leslie say something to upset you?"

"I'll call you when I get there." She ended the call and threw the cell phone on the seat.

She was hurt, tired, and angry. She was hurt because Eric didn't love her and probably never would. She was tired of hearing about Eric's wild history with multitudes of women. Most of all she was angry with herself because now she was married to a man whom she had given up everything for.

She had sacrificed her independence, her dreams, and her identity.

She was so busy nursing her heartbreak that didn't notice the deer step out in front of her car. She jerked the wheel hard to the left and stomped on the brakes.

Tires squealed. The car fishtailed on the wet asphalt from last night's rain.

Thundering panic gripped her heart as she struggled to get control of the car. She didn't even have time to scream before the car slammed into a tree.

☾

"CELESTE, OPEN YOUR EYES."

White-hot pain shot through her chest down to her stomach.

She tried to lift her head. A jolt of pain wracked her body and she screamed.

"Celeste, open your eyes."

She forced her heavy eyes open. She was in her car, her head resting on the steering wheel. Thick white ash hung in the air.

She remembered the deer and losing control of the car. The rest was hazy.

She tried to focus in the dark. The sun was long gone. She must have been unconscious for quite a while.

She lifted her arms, checking for broken bones. She could move both limbs without pain.

Something warm trickled down her face. She touched her head and then held her hand in front of her eyes. There was just enough moonlight for her to see her blood-tinged fingers.

"Celeste."

"Donovan?"

"I'm going to get you out. The door won't open. I smashed the passenger window."

She lifted her head despite the pain and turned her head toward the passenger side. "I think the car is on fire. There's ash."

"No, that's just the stuff from the airbag."

"Donovan, I'm scared." A tear slid down her face and a sense of foreboding washed over her.

He reached in and gently wiped a tear with his

thumb. "It's okay. I'm here."

"I'm going to open the door now, so don't be afraid." He gripped the door where the window had once been and pulled. Metal groaned as he twisted the door completely off its hinges.

With inhuman strength, Donovan tossed the door over his shoulder.

"There's no way you just did that. I'm hallucinating."

"Trust me, you're not." Donovan gave her a sheepish grin.

"Donovan, you pulled my car door off," she whispered.

"Yeah."

"With your bare hands."

"I know. Are you mad about your door?" He leaned in and ran his fingers across her body, checking for injuries.

"A little. It was the first new car I'd ever had." Donovan touched a place on her stomach. She cried out as the pain shot through her.

"You're badly injured."

"Am I dying?" She already knew the answer. The pain receded as a bone-deep coldness took hold of her body.

"Yes." His voice cracked. "I have to move you so I can help you. Okay?"

She gazed at him. Childhood memories of them swimming in the pond and chasing lightning bugs flooded her mind.

"I have to move you, honey."

"It's going to hurt," she whispered.

"I'll try to be quick, okay?"

He slid his arms behind her back and under her

legs. He kept her head resting against his shoulder.

She took a breath and braced.

The unbearable pain sliced through her stomach and chest like a million knives.

She screamed.

He carried her away from the car and laid her beside a grove of trees. "You are bleeding internally."

"The baby?" She met his gaze. "What about the baby?"

He looked away, but not before she caught the pain in his eyes. She grabbed his arm refusing to let go.

"The truth. I'm tired of everyone lying to me." She forced out the words, each syllable enunciated with pain.

"With your blood loss, I don't see how the baby will make it."

She squeezed her eyes shut. Gut-wrenching despair gripped and twisted her heart.

He cupped her face. "Listen to me. You still have a chance. You can try to heal yourself."

"I can't." She barely had strength to talk. There was no way she could heal herself.

"Not on your own. I'll have to help you. I have a special gift. I have to ability to increase a fairy's power."

"I thought your fairy power was strength."

Donovan barked out a shaky laugh. "I have more than one talent."

Each second that passed, she could feel the pain ebbing away, taking with it her life.

"What do I need to do?"

"Kiss me." He leaned over her. "You need to

focus on the pain, that's where you need to heal."

He didn't give her time to answer. He bent his head and covered her lips with his.

She let her eyelids drift shut.

Drawing on what little strength she had, she focused. She visualized her heart beating rapidly to compensate for the blood loss. Right at the top of the heart, a tear that leaked blood with each squeeze of her heart.

She focused all her energy to that one area. Healing energy poured from her body into that area. Injured tissue and muscle began to weave itself back together with lightning speed. She focused harder until her heart was completely healed and beating strong.

Then she focused on her child.

His heartbeat slowed with each pulse.

Fear spilled through her, jagged and painful. She had to do more. She wouldn't let her child die.

She reached behind Donovan's neck and pulled him deeper into the kiss, merging their energy.

Energy sparked and arched between their bodies. She could see the energy trailing to her baby.

She examined the baby's body from head to toe to find the injury. When she reached the umbilical cord, she saw a small tear. With energy soaring through her veins, she focused. The tissue began to heal. Her baby began to move. She could literally feel his heartbeat increase.

The pain that had been so intense had now faded.

She pushed against Donovan's chest, but he didn't move.

She tore her mouth away, breaking the kiss. "Get off, Donovan."

The next minute Donovan went air born. He flew backward and slammed into a tree.

Eric stood above her, rage etched into his handsome face.

Donovan rushed Eric and knocked him to the ground. The sickening sound of fists pounding into flesh sounded in the dark. She stood and stared in disbelief.

By the light of the moon, she could see both men were bloodied, but neither seemed to be surrendering as they tore into each other. The harder they hit, the more pissed off they got.

"Stop it, both of you." She stepped closer. Donovan's fist missed Eric and contacted with her cheek. Blinding pain and stars shot across her face, and she fell to the ground.

"Damn, Celeste, I'm so sorry." Donovan knelt, his face contorted in regret and concern.

"You fucking asshole." Eric picked Donovan up over his head and threw him several yards away.

Eric dropped to his knees and cradled her face in his hands. "Are you okay?" His eyes shone with anger.

"I'm fine." The pain lessened and she could feel the tissue heal itself.

"Are you kidding me? You just wrapped your fucking car around a tree. You're certainly not fine." Eric pulled her tightly into his chest and buried his face in her neck.

"She's fine now." Donovan dusted off his clothes. "She and the baby were dying, but she healed herself."

"Is this true?" Eric searched her face for confirmation. It wasn't anger she'd seen in his face, it was fear.

"Yes. But I didn't heal on my own. Donovan helped." She cut her eyes at Donovan. "Although you seemed to be enjoying it a little too much."

"I do have to say, you are one hell of a kisser, Celeste." He touched his fingers to his lips and grinned.

Eric growled. She stepped in front of him, preventing him from lunging at Donovan.

He looked at her hand on his chest, raising them to her face. "The tracking device must have been damaged by the crash. It never sent a signal."

"How did you find me, Donovan?" She frowned.

"Let's just say that we are more connected than anyone thought." Donovan smirked.

"What the hell does that mean?" The muscle in Eric's cheek twitched.

"It means that I can smell Celeste." Donovan arched his eyebrow, his gaze locked on her.

She picked up a lock of hair and sniffed.

Donovan laughed. "Your blood, Celeste. I can smell your Fae blood."

"That's gross." She stood.

"Every fairy has their own unique smell. Some are sweet, some are bitter, some are floral. But your blood is very sensual."

"Again, very disturbing."

"Oh, it's quite the opposite." Donovan closed his eyes and inhaled. "The closest thing I could compare it to is an aphrodisiac." He opened his eyes. "And it's not just other fairies that can smell you. Sometimes humans can smell your blood too."

"So you're telling me that when you smell my wife, you want to…" Eric growled.

"Fuck her till I collapse." Donovan smiled brightly.

"You son of a bitch." Eric lunged but Donovan was quicker, and scurried up a tree like a squirrel.

"It's not like she's getting any from you." Donovan mocked him from his perch on a limb.

"Stop it. You two beating the hell out of each other isn't helping." She stepped in front of Eric.

"But it would certainly make me feel better." Eric glared.

Donovan flipped Eric the bird. Eric tried to move around her, but she wrapped her arms around his waist.

"Eric, please." The baby kicked against his stomach.

He glanced down. "Is the baby okay?"

"He is now." Despite her anger at him that morning, she couldn't help but soften at his obvious concern. "I'm tired. I just want to go home."

"Let's go. We'll call your parents on the way."

She walked back to her car, examining the horrific damage she'd just walked away from.

The front of the car was wrapped around the large oak tree, and the driver's-side door was gone. "Donovan had to take the door off." She bent to climb in the car.

Eric grabbed her arm. "What are you doing?"

"I need to get my purse."

"I don't want to see you in that car. I'll get it." He scowled and quickly retrieved her purse.

"How is Donovan getting home?"

"He can drive my motorcycle. The one he stole." He opened his car door and waited for her to get in.

For the majority of the ride home, she said nothing. She could feel his anger filling the car.

When she couldn't stand the silence anymore, she looked at him. "Look, I'm sorry about wrecking the car."

Eric pulled onto the shoulder of the road and killed the engine. He turned in his seat and stared at her. "I don't give a damn about the car."

"Then why are you so pissed off?" She narrowed her eyes.

"I couldn't find you for almost twelve hours. Andrea Leigh said she had no idea you were coming to her house. The tracking system was useless when you wrecked, and your cell phone went straight to voicemail every time I called. You probably have a hundred messages on it. And then Donovan calls and tells me he's found you. That was probably the second-worst thing that happened tonight." He ran his hand through his blond hair.

"What was the first?" She cocked her head. "You said seeing Donovan kiss me was the second-worst thing that happened tonight. Tell me what was the worst?

"Knowing you were dying. Knowing you were dying was the worst thing I've ever experienced." His strained voice cut her heart.

She wrapped her arms around herself, shivering at his words. She had always imagined death would be quick and painless. But what she'd experienced tonight was anything but painless.

"Did Donovan tell you I was dying when he called you?" She tucked a stray strand of hair behind her ear.

"No. He didn't need to. I felt it. I felt the pain

in my chest. And then I heard you scream in my head."

He stroked her face. "And now here you are, completely healed. As pissed as I am about Donovan kissing you, I'm grateful that you're alive."

Before she could say anything, Eric was out of the car. He opened her car door and pulled her out of the car and into his arms. He held her tight and kissed her hard. He pulled back and stared at her with an intensity that frightened her.

"God, Celeste, do you know what was running through my head? I will not lose you."

His lips descended on hers, hard and demanding. His tongue delved into her mouth, insistent and without tenderness.

She tightened her arms around his neck, needing to feel safe and protected.

An eighteen-wheeler whizzed passed them and blared its horn. Eric reluctantly broke the kiss, but his eyes held an emotion she'd never seen on him.

She saw a promise of hope.

CHAPTER THIRTY-TWO

"YOU CAN PUT ME DOWN." Celeste hid a yawn behind her hand while Eric carried her up the stairs to the front door of their mansion. She'd been so drained from healing herself and the baby that she'd fallen asleep on the way home.

"No. I want to carry you." Eric placed a kiss on her forehead.

"You never told me you were a Calvin Klein model." She rested her head against his shoulder.

He stopped and gave her an odd look. "How did you know that?" Realization flickered through his eyes and he gaze narrowed. "Leslie told you."

"She said you had a thing for models."

"Jesus." He blew out a hard breath and stopped walking. "Is this why you left? Because she said I screw everything that moves?"

"She said that you would never marry because you couldn't be faithful."

"Back then I couldn't be faithful." Regret slashed across his face. "Back then I used casual sex like alcohol, just something to numb the pain." His lips thinned. "I've not been that person for a very long time."

She nodded and tightened her arms around his neck while he shoved the front door open.

"Are you okay?" Her mother ran into the foyer, her face distraught. "Eric, what's wrong with her?"

"She was in an accident but healed herself and the baby. She's just tired."

"Are you sure you're okay, honey?" Her father cupped her cheek and looked at her with wide eyes.

"Yes, Daddy. I'm just exhausted." She laid her head on Eric's shoulder. He didn't give them time to ask any more questions. He climbed the stairs, taking them two at a time. She vaguely remembered Eric tucking her into bed before she fell asleep again.

That night, she dreamed.

Eric strode to the front door heading out to work. A limo waited outside to take him to the board meeting. A horrible foreboding washed over her as he walked out the door.

She ran after him and grabbed his arm, begging him to postpone his trip, but he wouldn't listen. He kissed her and whispered in her ear, "I'll be back before you can miss me." Turning, he got into the limo. The car made it half way down the driveway before the car exploded.

She woke and bolted upright in bed. Heart racing and drenched in sweat, she reached for Eric.

The bed was empty.

Déjà vu flooded her in a rush of heat.

With her heart in her throat, she scrambled out of bed and raced downstairs. Eric stood at the counter, dressed in one of his expensive suits and drinking a cup of coffee. His eyes warmed when he saw her.

"Good morning, Mrs. Celeste." Mrs. Gambil smiled.

"Good morning. How are you feeling?" Eric asked.

She ran and jumped into his arms, knocking the coffee cup out of his hands. It shattered against the marble floor. Mrs. Gambil frowned and reached for some paper towels.

"What's wrong?" he whispered against her ear as he held her tight.

"Eric, don't go to work today. Stay here," she pleaded.

His eyes softened. "I'm only going for a meeting."

Nausea washed over her.

"What's wrong?" He narrowed his eyes and placed his hand on her stomach. "Is it the baby?"

"Eric, please don't go." She tightened her arms around his neck, unable to stop the flow of tears.

"Why? What's wrong?"

Mrs. Gambil quietly excused herself.

"Eric, I dreamed you died." She pulled back. her eyes pained and sad.

"Sweetheart, don't worry. It was just a nightmare." He cupped her face and kissed her. "I'll be back before you miss me."

Her head swam and she got dizzy. He caught her before she hit the floor. "I've got you." He swung her up in his arms and walked into the living room. He gently placed her on the sofa.

She dug her fingers in his suit when he tried to stand. She couldn't let him go. She had to make him understand. She had to make him stay.

The doorbell rang and she jumped.

"Mr. Eric, the limo is waiting for you." Mrs. Gambil announced from the doorway.

"The meeting is not until ten o'clock. How about I wait a little longer and drive myself? Would that make you feel better?" He spoke softly, his voice near her ear.

"Just don't go."

He kissed both cheeks then unwound her hands from his suit. He stood up and walked back into the kitchen.

She scrambled to her feet and followed.

Her parents stood at the counter, chatting. They stopped when they saw her face.

"What's wrong?"

"Celeste had a bad dream. She doesn't want me to go to work today."

"Then don't go." The tone of her father's voice sent chills up and down her back.

"If you care anything about Celeste, don't go." Her mother touched Eric's arm.

The doorbell rang again.

Eric walked to the door.

She followed on his heels, ready to pounce on him if he tried to leave.

He opened the door. "I'm sorry to inconvenience you, but I don't need a limo today." He pulled out his wallet and handed the driver a few hundred-dollar bills. "For your trouble."

She wrapped her arms around Eric's waist and sagged against him before he could even close the door.

"Why did you hire a limo to drive you to work instead of Solomon?" She kept her gaze on the limo as it drove away.

"I would feel better if Solomon were here to drive you. He's a bodyguard too, in case there was another attack. He's had some military training." He smiled down at her. "So what exactly was supposed to happen if I had gotten into the limo?"

A loud explosion vibrated the windows as the vehicle exploded into a fiery ball of flames.

"That. That's what I dreamed."

ERIC FINISHED ANSWERING QUESTIONS FROM the police. They had spent the better part of the day cleaning up the debris and when the cops left they were calling it a terrorist attack against his company.

He knew better but didn't bother correcting them.

The family congregated in the library trying to sort this thing out.

"My dream came true." Celeste rubbed her hands up and down her arm and studied the floor.

"It wasn't a dream, Celeste. It was a vision." Ben paced in front of the fireplace of the library. He rubbed his chin, his eyebrows drawn together.

"Prophecy. I thought you were a healer?" Eric narrowed his eyes.

She cringed and lifted her gaze to his. "When I was a little girl, I had dreams that came true. It scared me. I thought something was wrong with me, that I was evil. I didn't want to be different. I just wanted to fit in."

She licked her lips. "The dreams stopped before I turned thirteen. For years I didn't have another dream until a few weeks before the Cryptic party. I had a recurring dream about a book inside your uncle's house that was supposed to explain what I was." She pointed at the leather-bound book on his desk. "That book."

"That's why you were at the party." He sucked in a hard breath. "That's why you were so intent on going to the library."

She nodded.

His stomach twisted. "I guess that night was a big disappointment then. You didn't get the book."

"It's not like that, Eric." She reached for him.

"Then what is it like?" His words came out more sharply than he intended. He knew it was stupid, but it stung his ego.

"I went there to find out what I was. I had no idea you were there. I didn't have a dream about that part."

Her mother spoke up. "That's because Eric is Fae too. You wouldn't have been able to see him unless you had better control over your visions."

"So you just went with me on the chance that I could lead you to the book faster." He scowled.

"You have no idea what it's like to never be invited to a sleepover in elementary school or to never be asked out on a date or even go to senior prom. I needed to know what was wrong with me."

"That's our fault." Sarah said softly.

"What do you mean?" asked Celeste.

"The prophecy you had about our neighbor dying scared you so much. You were so terrified, so we made the decision to wait until you were older to tell you about having Fae blood." Her mother's slender shoulders slumped.

"But you never did."

"By the time we thought you would be ready, I was busy fighting off all the damn boys who were trying to take out my little girl," Ben groused.

"What are you talking about? I never had a boyfriend. No one ever asked me out, not even once." She looked from her mother to her father.

Donovan spoke up from his corner of the library while he flipped through a book. "That would totally be your parents' fault, Celeste, not yours."

"What are you talking about?" Celeste leveled her gaze at him.

Ben cleared his throat. "Well, honey, you see, when you turned sixteen, boys started calling the house."

"No they didn't. They didn't even know I was alive."

"They were very much aware of you. If Uncle Ben hadn't put that veiling spell on you, I would have had to kill quite a few guys." Donovan scowled and slammed the book shut.

Eric bristled.

"I'm sorry, honey, it's just there were so many of them, and Ben did try to talk to them about leaving you alone, but it did no good. They were fearless. We even caught a few of them trying to get into the house after dark." Sarah sighed.

"Why were they trying to get into the house?" Eric demanded.

"They were trying to get into Celeste's room." Donovan's harsh voice matched the look in his eyes.

"Are you kidding?" Celeste's eyes widened.

"You never could see your own beauty, Celeste. Why do you think all those girls were so cruel to you in school? They were jealous." Sarah's gentle voice hung heavy with guilt.

"We veiled your beauty from boys. The girls still knew how beautiful you were, how beautiful you still are." Ben looked at her with pain in his eyes.

"So you made me invisible?" She stood and straightened her shoulders.

He couldn't imagine the torture she'd gone through as a teenager as she grew more beautiful every year, yet she never realized it.

"We were trying to protect you from getting pregnant. From bearing the curse."

"What about Donovan?" She narrowed her eyes at her mother.

"What do you mean?"

"How did Donovan help me heal that night of the accident?"

Eric had wondered the same thing.

"I can increase a fairy's natural power a hundred times. Kind of like a booster shot." Donovan smirked.

"But that's not all you can do, right?" Celeste gave Donovan a pointed look.

"As a pixie, I do a number of things quite well."

"Look, Donovan, do you shape-shift or not?" Celeste asked.

"Yes. And it's usually animals. Humans are too hard to do—too many emotions." Donovan held his hands up and backed away with a shudder.

"You were the wolf in the garden." Eric had suspected as much since reading that book.

"Yes." He rubbed the back of his neck. "But

don't let that get out. There are some wolves that aren't fond of me shifting into their kind."

"You were also the black cat." Celeste arched her eyebrow.

"Correct again." Donovan walked to the desk. "But I'm guessing we need to get back on track versus discussing my many talents."

"We need to figure out who put that bomb in the limo." Ben rubbed the back of his neck.

"In my dream, the bomb was meant for Eric. But that doesn't make sense. I thought the demon was after my baby." She put a protective hand over her stomach.

Sarah stopped pacing. "The demon does want the baby. But apparently the demon underestimated Eric's strength. It believes the only way to get to you is if Eric is out of the way."

Celeste looked at him, her face pale.

"Don't worry. Nothing is going to happen," Eric reassured her.

"How can you tell me not to worry?" Her gaze darted around the room. "The demon knows where we live. It attacked us in our own backyard and you were almost killed. So don't tell me not to worry when there's a whole lot I need to worry about."

"I promise nothing is going to happen to you or our baby." He would lay down his life to protect his family.

"You don't know that. It seems to know our every move. How can we fight against that?" Her eyes shone with unshed tears.

"I've been giving that some thought myself." Ben's gaze rested on the sword hanging on the wall over the library's fireplace. It was an antique broadsword Eric's father had picked up in an antique shop in England. "I believe after today we will have the advantage."

"How?"

"Our advantage is Celeste." Ben smiled.

"Me?" She blinked.

"You have the gift of prophecy, daughter. You'll see what's coming for us."

"I only have visions when I'm sleeping. It's not something I can control." She shook her head.

"Not yet. But with practice you will be able to. We can teach you."

"Let's say I can predict what's going to happen next. Then what? Do we live our lives avoiding limos and not going outside?"

"No. We fight." Ben leaped up on the desk and grabbed the sword off the wall. With lightning speed, he began a series of complicated sword movements. The sword was nothing but a flash of silver cutting through the air.

"Quit showing off, dear," Sarah chided.

"You are forgetting that fighting is what fairies do best. We might be a little rusty." Ben shrugged and jumped off the desk. "So I suggest we start practicing."

"And we need to let the rest of the family what's going on. If anyone knows anything about this demon, it would be Aunt Agatha." Sarah grabbed a pen and a piece of paper off his desk.

He couldn't deny it anymore. He had been attacked and had seen the demon with his own eyes. He'd even felt Celeste's healing power as it had coursed through her to heal him.

He couldn't explain it. Maybe he never would.

He looked down at her. "I know you love your independence, Celeste, but there are going to be some new rules. You will under no circumstances go outside this house without one of us with you. Do you understand?"

"Now, wait a minute."

"No. That bomb was too close today. What if you had been out in the driveway when it blew? You could have been hurt or even worse. You will not leave this house without one of us. Do you understand?" She might hate him now, but at least she'd be alive to forgive him later.

Hopefully.

She smiled tightly and nodded.

"Starting tomorrow I'm giving the staff time off, including Mrs. Gambil, so we can start training and preparing. We don't need to have anyone else around. It could put them in danger."

Ben nodded in agreement.

"And since you're the expert, you are in charge of everyone's training." Eric looked directly at his father-in-law.

"Sounds like a plan." Ben's eyes glinted with excitement.

"Do you feel up to working on your gift?" Eric turned back to Celeste.

"I can try."

"I read that a fairy's gift is sometimes more pronounced when they are pregnant. Has something to do with the hormones." There was a ton of information in that book.

Her mouth fell open.

"So let's take advantage of that while we can."

He grinned.

God knew they were up against something that was more powerful than he'd ever imagined.

They were going to need all the prophecy they could get.

CHAPTER THIRTY-THREE

"IS HERE OKAY? I THOUGHT the bedroom would be a quiet place to work." Celeste walked into her bedroom and glanced over her shoulder at her mother.

"This is perfect." Her mother spread out a throw on her bedroom floor and they both sat.

"In order to control your visions, you must be able to block out every distraction and focus. Don't be discouraged if nothing happens at first. It may take a while."

"What do I do?"

"Close your eyes and relax. Take a deep breath."

She followed her mother's instructions.

"As you feel your body relaxing, start blocking everything out: sounds, emotions, thoughts, all of it. It is only when you are at a place of complete peace that you will be able to see a vision."

She rubbed her palms on her knees and closed her eyes. She tried clearing her mind.

She separated the sounds around her, a door shutting, a vacuum running, an airplane flying over. She pushed back the sounds until she was surrounded by perfect stillness.

She repeated the process with emotions and thoughts, pushing them away until there was nothing in front of her, until there was nothing but white blank canvas.

A flash of an image flickered like a movie reel. Then suddenly it was gone.

She poured her energy and concentration into bringing back the image. Her heart rate sped up as she tried to pull the image into focus. It was impossible, like catching a firefly.

Warm, strong fingers intertwined with hers.

"Now try," Donovan whispered. "Concentrate."

She focused on that image that seemed to evade her. Only this time, when she concentrated it came into focus and a scene unfolded before her.

Everyone was in the living room. Donovan sat by the fireplace roasting a marshmallow. When he pulled it out of the fire, the marshmallow dripped on the floor.

"Clean up your mess," Eric demanded.

"I'll do it later." Donovan smirked.

Celeste frowned as the argument grew more heated.

"It's snowing," her father announced from his position at the window. Everyone went to the window to look out. Celeste grabbed her coat and headed out the door, but Eric stopped her.

"You can't go outside by yourself. What if that thing is out there?"

Everyone rushed past them, headed out to enjoy the first snowfall of the season.

"Eric, please?" She looked up at him and pouted.

Eric pulled his own coat out of the hall closet. "Stay by me, okay?"

She flashed him a smile and stretched up on tiptoes to

kiss him.

In her excitement, she practically pulled Eric out the door. They stepped outside together. A fine dusting of snow covered the ground.

Donovan tilted his head back, catching snowflakes on his tongue.

Sarah and Ben held hands and smiled as snowflakes stuck to their hair.

She walked into the driveway and held out her hand, watching the wet flakes melt on her glove. The snow picked up, and the flurries came down faster and harder.

Celeste looked over at Donovan, who was attempting to make a snow angel despite the fact that there wasn't much snow on the ground. She laughed. Eric covered her mouth with his and kissed her.

Something barreled out of the woods and knocked them down. She landed on the concrete. Her head bounced off the surface. Blood seeped from her scalp, and pain curled around her head. Eric hurried over to where she was lying.

She shivered, feeling the coldness on her face, her back, her limbs.

"Celeste."

White-hot pain licked at her head until she lost consciousness.

"Celeste. Are you okay?"

She opened her eyes and looked around. She was still in her bedroom but was lying on the floor with Donovan leaning over her. "What happened?"

"Sarah left when I came in. She wanted me to try to increase your ability to concentrate and focus. I'm guessing that it worked."

"It did."

"How do you feel?" He pulled her to her feet.

"Weak."

"That's normal. Once you can control your visions, you won't have any residual effects at all. In fact, you may feel more energized."

She nodded.

"Did you have a vision?"

"Yeah." She caught the look of surprise that skittered across Donovan's face. "Is that normal? I thought it would take more time for me to develop my gift."

"It just means you're stronger than we thought."

"Really?"

"What did you see?"

"Should I say? Or will that change the future?" She hesitated.

"Don't tell me anything specific. Just tell me the date and time if you know it."

"Well it happened at night and it was snowing. Still seems vague. I didn't know it that helps any."

"I'll check the weather and see if we are expected to have snow within the next week." He pulled out his phone and then looked up. "From the look on your face, I take it that this wasn't a happy vision."

"No, it wasn't." It was anything but.

☾

ERIC SLID INTO BED NEXT to Celeste. She'd gone to bed not long after dinner. He knew she was exhausted and needed her sleep and he didn't want to wake her.

The moonlight cast its light through the window and illuminated her delicate features.

How could she grow up thinking she wasn't desirable? Hell, every time he even thought about her, he got hard.

A twinge of guilt slid across his gut. Deep down, he was glad her parents hid her beauty from the world. He was glad he'd been the only man to touch her.

Her blond hair spread over her pillow like gold satin. Thick, sooty lashes lay across her cheeks. Her full lips were parted as if begging him to kiss her.

His body hardened. Images of kissing her from her soft lips down her body to between her thighs had him strangling the sheets.

She hadn't gone to the cocktail party to seek him out. Thinking back, he realized she'd been trying to get away from him until he'd mentioned giving her a tour. But he knew from her body's response to that first kiss there hadn't been anything else on her mind at that point but getting him naked.

Their attraction had been too strong.

Maybe she hadn't used him after all.

Maybe they'd been brought together by something he couldn't explain.

Whatever the reason, she was his now. And he intended to keep her.

☾

"FUCK." ERIC GLANCED AT THE clock. Three a.m. He'd not been able to sleep since he'd gotten in bed. Too many worries on his mind.

Namely Celeste.

Celeste rolled to her side and mumbled.

He leaned closer but realized she was talking in her sleep.

Whatever she was saying definitely wasn't English. It sounded like an Irish dialect.

Wracking his brain, he searched all the languages he had been taught growing up. His mother had been adamant that he become multilingual, even learning dead languages as well.

His heart picked up speed. She was speaking Gaelic.

"*Gra.*" She kicked off the remaining covers and clasped her hands across her stomach.

Despite the cold weather, she wore a pink tank top and boy shorts. Her body was still slender, the only extra weight in her stomach. From behind she didn't even look pregnant.

She jerked and then tensed.

"Celeste?"

Her body moved upward off the bed. At first it was only an inch, then three inches, until she was levitating two feet off the bed.

He froze. *What the fuck?*

"Celeste?"

She didn't respond. He found himself wondering whether he should wake her.

He had always heard never to wake a sleepwalker. Perhaps this information applied to pregnant levitating fairies as well.

He shook his head. Who was he kidding? This was so totally out there, even he didn't know where to begin.

"*Bhais.*"

He grabbed a pen and paper out of the drawer of the nightstand. He scribbled down as best he could the two words she'd spoken in Gaelic.

She moaned and slowly drifted back down to the bed, until she sank into the mattress.

He leaned over her and searched for any evidence that she was awake.

She never opened her eyes.

☾

"I NEED TO SPEAK TO YOU." Eric cornered Ben once they were alone in the dining room.

"Is something wrong?" His father-in-law frowned.

"You tell me." He murmured and glanced around, making sure they were alone.

"Can it wait? Sarah and Celeste are waiting for me to drive them into the city."

"This does concern Celeste."

Ben nodded and silently motioned him outside. The older man looked around, making sure they had privacy. "Okay, what's going on?"

He rubbed his neck. "Have you noticed Celeste acting weird?"

"I did catch her eating a grilled-cheese sandwich with ice cream on top." He shrugged. "Other than that, no."

"Not weird food cravings." He leaned closer. "Weird as in talking in her sleep."

"Lots of people do that."

"While levitating in the air." He deadpanned.

"Oh. That." Ben gave him a sheepish grin and rubbed the back of his neck.

"That's not normal. It's evil."

"Don't associate us with being evil." Ben lifted his chin. "We were labeled evil when one human happened to see something they could not explain. And now levitating has become associated with the devil."

"So this is normal?"

"When Sarah was pregnant, she used to levitate all the time."

"Really?"

"Yeah. The first time, it scared the hell out of me."

"What did she say about it?"

"Sarah didn't remember doing it when I asked her about it." Ben frowned. "I take it Celeste isn't aware she can do this?"

He shook his head.

"I wouldn't ask her. It would only embarrass her. She has enough to deal with."

He couldn't argue with that.

"Is there anything else you were wondering about?"

He crossed his arms. "Yes, there is. You said you stole that book from my Uncle Stephen's library."

"Yes?"

"How did you know it was there?"

Ben crossed his arms and gave him a long look. "When I found out that Celeste had gone to the company party, I became very concerned."

"Why?"

"Parties are out of her comfort zone."

"Parties were out of her comfort zone, thanks to you and your wife making her believe she was an outcast. Did she tell you she hosted a beautiful party in our home and did a wonderful job?"

"We were trying to protect her," Ben hissed.

"However noble your intentions were, they backfired."

With a long sigh, Ben dropped his gaze to the ground. "We never meant to hurt her."

"I know that." He felt for the guy. If he had a

daughter as beautiful as Celeste, he'd kill any man who so much as looked at her.

"I don't think she does." Ben shook his head.

"She does. Even if she doesn't agree with how you handled this, she won't hold it against you forever. Now stop trying to change the subject. Get back to the book."

Ben lifted his head. "I knew that there was something very important that made her go to that party. That alone made me suspicious. When we were having that meeting in the library at Stephen's house, I noticed the book sitting on the shelf. I was afraid that Celeste would see it, too. I knew she wasn't ready to learn about her background, so that's when I started that argument with you." Ben winced.

Eric arched his eyebrow. "So you weren't really upset with me?"

"Oh, yeah. I hated your guts. But Celeste had warned me before we even went in to sit there and not say a word. She said if I didn't, she would never talk to me again. She didn't even want us to go with her."

His heart warmed. So she hadn't been hiding behind her parents.

"Anyway, after the wedding, I went to see your Uncle Stephen. While we were in the library, I asked him about the book. He said it had belonged to your mother. Apparently she had picked it up on a trip to Ireland. I asked if I could borrow it."

"I thought you said you stole it."

"Well I don't intend to give it back." Ben gave him a "duh" look. "Anything else you want to know?"

"Do you know what bhais means?"

Ben's eyes widened. "It's Gaelic. It means 'death.'"

CHAPTER THIRTY-FOUR

CELESTE RUBBED THE SMALL OF her back and let out a sigh. She'd been working with Donovan for almost two hours straight, and she hadn't seen a vision yet.

"You're not focusing." Donovan's brows slammed together. "What is it? Thinking about what to cook for dinner, or are you worrying about what the decorator is doing downstairs?"

Since Mrs. Gambil had been given a forced vacation, Celeste had taken over cooking duty. With Thanksgiving approaching, a decorator had been called in to make the house festive.

"I already prepped lasagna for tonight, so all I have to do is pop it into the oven." She waved her hand. "I peeked downstairs and the decorator is doing a beautiful job. She should be finishing up."

Orange pumpkins and red and white chrysanthemums decorated the entrance to the mansion. A huge wreath in the same color scheme and an autumn-themed garland hung against the massive front door.

Inside, the decorations were even more elaborate.

Smaller pumpkins and floral arrangements in fall colors were tucked in every available space.

"So what's got you worried?"

"I don't know." She averted her gaze.

"Yes, you do. What's wrong?"

She stared at him for several seconds. "Donovan, can I ask you something?"

"You can ask me anything."

"I've been reading that book about fairies." It had no title, so everyone in the house had started referring to it as "that book."

"And, well, it says that some fairies can levitate."

"And?"

She leaned in and whispered, "I thought levitating was something the devil did, you know, like in the movies."

He burst out laughing.

"I knew better than to ask you." She glared.

Donovan smothered his laughter. "Are you asking if you're evil because you can levitate?"

"You mean, it's true? I can levitate?"

"Yes. You are probably doing it in your sleep and don't remember. And to answer that other question that keeps rattling around in your brain, no, you are not evil."

Her shoulders sagged with relief. She had been worrying about that since she'd read it. She hadn't told Eric. He'd already threatened to hide that book if she didn't stop freaking out over everything she read.

"Are fairies good or evil?"

"Honey, fairies were created by God. And as with any living thing, God gives us all free will, free will to choose what path in life we will follow."

"So I'm not bad."

Donovan grinned. "Not unless you want to be."

☾

"FUCK IT." ERIC COULDN'T REMEMBER when he had been in a worse mood. He was exhausted, irritated, and worried.

He continued to work even with everything going on. Since he had been taken off suspension, he'd made every effort to keep his company profitable, which meant longer hours. After work he would train with Ben. Every day, the cars were driven out from the garage so they could practice fighting inside.

He hated having to put up with Donovan. He knew Celeste needed him to help her hone her gift of prophecy, but he resented the time they spent together.

He worried about another attack on Celeste. When he wasn't training or working, he made sure Celeste was by his side.

Celeste.

Every time he thought about her, he couldn't help but smile. She was the only thing he thought about—at work, at home, or in his dreams. Every time he tried to sneak in some time alone with her, Donovan always interrupted.

Sexually frustrated didn't even begin to cover how he felt.

The other day, he'd pulled Celeste into the pantry and kissed her senseless. Just when he'd managed to slip his hand under her shirt, Donovan had burst in, saying he was looking for a snack. Embarrassed and angry, Celeste had fled into another part of the house, leaving him standing with an erection the size of the Empire State Building in his pants.

It had taken all Eric's restraint not to plow his fist into Donovan's satisfied smirk.

He sighed and glanced across the bed. They were finally alone.

And Celeste was sound asleep.

He punched his pillow and plopped onto his back.

The only way he was going to have Celeste tonight was in his dreams.

HE SWIPED HIS HAND ACROSS his cheek at the tickling sensation and cracked open his eyes.

His heart nearly froze in mid-beat.

Celeste hovered above him in midair, her blonde hair brushing against his face.

Keeping his eyes on her, he reached for the lamp and turned the light on.

Her arms rested on her stomach and her eyes were closed. Without thinking, he raised his hand up to her cheek. Just as his fingers made contact, her eyes fluttered opened.

"Celeste?"

She stared down at him with a cautious look in her eye. Her full lips slid into a smile. She mumbled something in Gaelic.

"Celeste, I don't understand what you're saying."

She floated downward. She straddled his stomach, leaned over, and placed her hands on either side of his head. Her face was inches from his face.

"Celeste?" He tried to ignore the fire burning in

his stomach.

"Yes." Her words held an Irish lilt. Her eyes raked over him boldly.

"Celeste, do you know who I am?"

She lowered her face and for a second he thought she was going to kiss him.

Instead she buried her face in his neck. Pressing her nose against his skin, she inhaled deep.

His cock jerked to life.

"Yes, I know you." She lifted her face. "You are the father of my child." She narrowed her eyes. "Yet you have not marked me. Not since putting your seed within my body."

Holy fuck.

His body strained toward her. He slid his hands across her thighs to her hips.

"It's your blood that runs through my child. I can smell it. You're the father of the one I carry, yet you have not made me your mate." She lifted her chin and stared down her nose at him.

"You're my wife, so that means you're my mate." His voice was as hard as his dick. And why was she speaking like that?

"Tell me, what do I smell like to you?" She drew her hair away from her shoulders.

He wanted nothing more than to pull her panties down and bury himself in her tight body. He closed his eyes and inhaled.

"I smell perfume."

"No. What does my blood smell like?" She arched her neck against his lips and pressed her groin into his.

He grabbed her neck and held it against his face.

Her scent hit him. He remembered Donovan

saying that Celeste's blood was like an aphrodisiac to him.

It was ten times better. His erection grew impossibly harder.

"You smell wonderful." He pressed his lips to her neck. His heart thudded in his head and his blood raced through his veins.

She tried to lift her face, but he couldn't let her go. He pressed his face into her neck and groaned.

With incredible strength, she grabbed his hands and pinned them above his head. He expected to see anger in her eyes, but what he found confused him.

"Does my blood arouse you?" She arched her brow.

"God, yes."

"So if my blood is so appealing to you, why haven't we had sex?" Her green eyes narrowed.

"What?"

"My blood is intoxicating to many, but to my mate it would be impossible to resist me. And since you've not touched me, it makes me wonder. Maybe I'm not your mate? Maybe you have another as your mate?"

"No. Of course not." If she scooted down a fraction of an inch, she would feel how much he wanted her. "I've not wanted another woman since I met you. You have no idea how much I've wanted to touch you."

She released his hands. A grin spread across her face. She ran a finger down his chest and flicked his nipple.

In an instant, his arms were around her back, pulling her down on top of him. He devoured her in a kiss.

She moved back and smiled. "Ah. You don't seem so cold toward me after all."

His mouth never left her skin. "I've wanted to make love to you every night that you've been in my bed. But . . ."

"Perhaps it is because I am with child that your lust has cooled?"

"I want you more because you are carrying my child."

Her expression softened. "Are you scared you will hurt the baby?"

"That's part of it."

"What else?"

"I'm scared I'm going to hurt you." His voice was a hoarse whisper.

"Then perhaps it is best if I do everything." She slid his body down until her face was even with his stomach. She looked up and grinned as she pressed her lips to his abs.

He hissed at the hellish pleasure. Her wet tongue traced tiny circles across his skin. He didn't think he had ever felt anything so good. And she hadn't even reached his dick yet.

He grabbed her by the arms and eased her up his body. "Keep that up and you're going to make me come before I get inside you."

"But I've not taken you in my mouth yet."

"You're killing me sweetheart." He pulled her up and kissed her deep. He swallowed every moan she made and wanted more.

How could he ever get enough of her?

She rubbed her body against his and he dragged her nightshirt down her shoulder. He flicked his tongue across her bare shoulder, tasting her sweet flesh.

She tensed.

"What's wrong?" He stilled. Had he hurt her?

She grabbed his face between her hands. Her eyes glazed.

"*Cogadh.*"

Without warning, she began to levitate. She positioned her hands across her stomach while her body straightened like a board. Her eyes closed. She floated to her side of the bed and then drifted downward until she sank into the mattress.

He sat up and leaned over her, studying her face to see whether she was awake.

She was sound asleep.

His hard-on begged him to wake her up and coerce her into making love.

He ran a hand over his face.

She was obviously exhausted.

And he was a total bastard for even entertaining the idea.

He threw off the covers and stomped off to the bathroom in search of a frigid shower.

CHAPTER THIRTY-FIVE

"SHE SAID *COGADH*." ERIC LOOKED at Ben over his coffee cup. The women had already left the kitchen and were going upstairs to the nursery to continue to decorate.

Ben's expression turned grim. "*Cogadh* means war. It must be a warning for what lies ahead. Perhaps the Queen is preparing to go to war with us. But the Queen doesn't know that Celeste is our element of surprise. With Celeste's gift of prophecy we can defeat her."

"I hope you're right."

"I'm always right." The older man had a gleam in his eye. "Then you two lovebirds can get on with it."

"What are you talking about?"

"For a CEO, you're not very bright." Ben gave him a look of disbelief. "I can tell by the way you two look at each other that you're in love. Hell, even Donovan gets sick of Celeste talking about you all the time."

"Did Celeste say she's in love with me?" A surge of hope welled up in his chest.

"If you bother to listen to what she says or how she acts when you walk into a room, you could see that the girl is clearly in love with you." He narrowed his eyes. "Don't tell me you haven't told her you love her."

He looked away. He was the biggest fool in the world.

"Maybe you don't feel the same way."

Clenching his teeth, he met his father-in-law's eyes. "You know I love Celeste."

"Why are you telling me? You should be saying it to her."

He thought back to the many times he had seen the look in her eyes when she caught him staring at her. He remembered the gentle way her slender hand slid down his suit jacket before he headed out for work. He'd even seen it in her smile when he complimented her. She cared for him, it was obvious.

But did she love him?

"I've got to find her." He hurried toward the house, trying to keep his frantic heart from beating out of his chest. He needed to find her.

Rounding the corner to their bedroom, he slammed into her. He reached out and steadied her. "Are you all right?"

"I'm fine. I thought you would be outside training with my parents." She stepped out of his embrace.

"Why do you look like you just got out of bed? Are you feeling okay?"

"Just some lower back pain. Mom says it's normal." She smoothed down her hair. "I need to fix my hair."

"You're beautiful."

She laughed. "Right."

"Just because you can't see it doesn't mean it's not true." He eased into the chair and patted his knee. "Sit with me."

"I'm too heavy."

"No, you're not." He scooped her up and placed her on his lap.

She relaxed against him. His hand slid down her back and began to knead her muscles.

"That feels wonderful." She sighed.

He rubbed his lips against her silky hair. He inhaled her scent and tried to rein in his lust.

He rested his other hand on her stomach. The baby kicked against his palm. "No wonder your back hurts. He kicks like a soccer player."

"You should tell him to stop kicking so hard. He certainly doesn't listen to me."

He shifted her, leaned down, and put his mouth to her stomach. "Son, I know you are anxious to come out, but you need to be gentle with your mother. Boys aren't supposed to kick girls."

She laughed.

The melodic sound shot straight to his heart. In that moment, every brick around his heart tumbled, leaving his heart wide open and vulnerable.

He placed her hand on his cheek. Turning his face, he planted his lips against her palm.

"I can see why your parents hid your beauty. I'm glad your father did it—otherwise I would have had to kill the man you would have married."

He'd seen her face twist with pain the night her parents had revealed what they had done to mask her beauty. Her adolescent years must have been a living hell.

She traced his lips with her fingertip. His heart slammed into his chest.

He needed to feel her underneath him now. He bent and took her lips in a blazing kiss.

She locked her fingers around his neck and pulled him closer.

It was all the encouragement he needed.

He scooped her up and laid her on the bed.

"It's still daylight." She said breathlessly.

"Yes, it is." He leaned over her. "I want to see you. All of you."

He pressed his body into hers and pulled her arms above her head, threading his fingers with hers.

He kissed her slow and deep, taking his time.

He tugged her shirt over her head and tossed it on the floor.

"Beautiful," he murmured as he kissed from her neck down to her stomach.

She threaded her fingers in his hair.

He unhooked her bra with blinding speed, then took her nipple into his wet mouth. She groaned as he swirled his tongue around the sweet peak.

"Eric, that feels so good." She clung to him as he continued his delicious assault.

He licked his way to her other breast and sucked her nipple. She pressed his face closer, gasping for another breath.

He was going to burn her alive.

As if sensing her desperation, he positioned himself between her thighs. She wrapped her legs around him.

Keeping one hand on her breast, fondling her

nipple, he kissed his way up to her mouth. "I could kiss you all day."

"I want more than just kissing." She tugged his shirt out of his jeans and slid her hand across the hardened ridges of his stomach. The muscles tensed under her fingertips setting off a wave of tremors in the pit of her own stomach.

He pulled away and tugged off her pants. His fingers were strong yet gentle as they brushed across the top of her panties.

He moved with deliberate slowness, caressing her through the lace material. She wanted to scream for him to hurry up and touch her, flesh to flesh, but her heaving lungs struggled to suck in enough air to form a coherent word.

He slipped his hand under her panties and swept his finger across her clit. She jerked at the delicious pleasure.

He brought his thumb against the hardened nub and moved in slow tantalizing circles.

"Oh, god," she moaned against his shoulder.

"Like that, sweetheart?"

"Yes. That feels so good."

"I love hearing those sounds you make." He slipped a finger inside her. It was all she could do to keep from crying out in pleasure.

She dug her fingers into his broad shoulders, pressing herself against his hand while her heart thudded in her ears. He continued the measured movements on her clit while his finger slid in and out of her.

"Eric."

"Let go, sweetheart. I want to see your beautiful face as you come."

She arched, her body shaking as the orgasm racked her body with a series of brilliant explosions of ecstasy. She lay there trembling in the aftermath, unable to move.

He stood and stripped off the rest of his clothes.

Her gaze dropped to his cock. Her heart caught in her chest.

He climbed between her legs, careful to keep his weight off the baby.

Looking into his eyes, she reached between their bodies and grasped his hard cock.

"Damn, sweetheart." He panted as she squeezed up and down.

Sweat broke out across his forehead and he moved her hand away and positioned himself at her wet entrance.

He pushed, straining to go slow, letting her body stretch to accommodate his size.

"Hurry." She panted and pulled at his shoulders. She wanted to feel all of him inside her now.

He looked at her. "You're really tight, sweetheart. I don't want to hurt you."

She wrapped her legs around his waist and dug her heels in. She buried herself on his cock in a burning sweet motion.

"Keep that up and you're going to make me come too quick." He buried his face in her neck.

She brought his mouth down across hers, sucking his tongue inside. She held him close as his thrusts grew deeper and more urgent.

Grasping her hips, he powered deep in her body. Each thrust inside her body, each teasing motion with his tongue had her breathless and clinging to him. Their bodies, slick with sweat, moved together as one, like they were always made to find each other, always made to be together.

Liquid pleasure shot through her body like mercury, and she cried out his name as her second orgasm hit her.

"Fuck." He groaned.

She held him tight as he moved faster, his breathing becoming more erratic. He thrust deep and hard as he found his own release inside her body.

Breathless and boneless, she nuzzled his hand as he stroked her cheek. She wasn't sure if it was the effects of the orgasm she'd just had or the feel of his hands, but the words spilled out of her mouth before she could stop them.

"I love you."

Eric blinked. Surprise flashed through his eyes.

"I love you, Celeste. You are my life." He brushed her cheek with his knuckles.

She flinched and pulled back, careful not to touch him.

"Don't say it if you don't mean it." She'd never said those words to a man before. She didn't use those words lightly.

Eric cupped her face with both hands. Emotion welled in his chest. He wasn't going to let her run away from him. Not again.

"Do you think I'm a liar?"

"No. I never said you were." Her eyes widened at his accusation.

"Good. Then you should know I don't say words I don't mean. Ever."

Doubt registered in her eyes, and he knew she was going to argue his feeling for her.

"I think you need a little more convincing." He

grinned before he brought his lips down across hers. She didn't protest as he slipped his tongue inside her mouth. He would claim every inch of her body as his before the day was done.

He reluctantly broke the kiss and pulled her into his arms and snuggled her against his chest. She sighed and trailed lazy circles across his nipple with her fingertip as he trailed his hand down her arm.

He rested a hand on her belly, curving it against the baby. He didn't hide his grin when a tiny kick pushed against his hand. "I think we have our son's approval."

"I think he is trying to tell us to cut it out so he could sleep." She chortled.

"Does it hurt?"

"When he kicks? No." She frowned. "Though I wonder . . ."

"Wonder what?"

"I wonder about the labor."

"You have the best doctor in the Northeast. I'm sure everything will go well."

"I'm worried about the pain." She shrugged.

He kissed her head and held her close. "Sweetheart, they'll give you an epidural and pain meds to help with the pain. You won't feel a thing. I'll be in the room with you and your parents will be there as well." He stroked her hair.

"I wanted to talk to you about that." She looked up at him and bit her lip. "I wanted it to just be us in the room."

His eyes widened. "You don't want your mom in there?"

"It was just us when we made the baby. I want it to be us at the delivery."

Euphoria spread through his chest, warm and tingling. He didn't think he'd ever felt so perfectly at peace than in that moment with her.

"I think that will be perfect." He pulled her into a kiss before they made love again.

CHAPTER THIRTY-SIX

THANKSGIVING DAY ARRIVED IN A flurry of colored leaves, pumpkin pies, and turkey. Despite the danger, Celeste wanted to make the holiday special. It was her first holiday as a married woman and she wanted to impress both her parents and Eric as well as make it memorable.

With the table set and the silver polished, everyone helped load the massive amounts of food onto the dining room table.

Once seated around the table, each person reflected on his or her blessings over the past year. It was a tradition she had grown up with and her father insisted they continue.

"Eric, it's your turn. What is your biggest blessing this year?" Her father asked.

"I think it's pretty evident." Eric looked straight at her. "My biggest blessing is Celeste and our baby."

She thought her heart would burst with love.

She had never thought her one night with him so many months ago would have led her here. To have a husband she was madly in love with and a baby on the way. She was a fairy with the gift of healing and prophesies. She was different, and Eric didn't seem to mind.

More importantly, she had accepted herself.

After Thanksgiving dinner, everyone gathered in the living room by the fire. Her mother sat in one of the oversized chairs and worked on a baby quilt while her father read a book from Eric's library.

She snuggled closer to Eric on the couch while he checked his messages from work on his phone.

Donovan sprawled by the fire, staring thoughtfully at the flames dancing in the fireplace.

It was as picture perfect as one could get.

"Do we have any marshmallows?" Donovan looked over his shoulder.

"In the pantry." She hid a yawn and closed her eyes. Between the turkey and the warm room, she could barely keep her eyes open.

"Found them." Donovan came back from the kitchen with a bag of marshmallows and plopped down in front of the fireplace.

She watched him slide two large marshmallows onto a skewer and hold them over the flames.

She frowned. A sense of uneasiness swept through her.

Donovan pulled the marshmallows off the fire. A thick gooey stream dripped onto the hardwood floor.

"Damn it, Donovan. Be careful." Eric's voice carried through the room.

Donovan ignored Eric and ate the burned marshmallow directly off the skewer. He put another marshmallow on the skewer and held it over the orange flame.

Eric got up and stormed into the kitchen. When he came back, he had a roll of paper towels and cleaner.

"What?" Donovan looked up at Eric looming over him.

"Clean up your mess." Eric thundered.

"I'll do it when I'm finished."

"You'll do it now."

"Why don't you fuck off?" Donovan stood.

"You lazy son of a bitch." Eric spat out, all the good humor of the day now gone.

Paralyzed by fear, she couldn't speak. An overwhelming feeling of impending doom swept over her, leaving her nauseated.

She stood. "Donovan."

"What?" Donovan cut his eyes at her. His narrowed gaze went wide-eyed. "Celeste. What's wrong?"

"It's happening." She tried to keep her voice from shaking.

"What's happening?" Eric hurried to her side and reached out to steady her. "Is it the baby?"

"No. It's my vision."

"She had a vision a few weeks back." Donovan's voice was strangely calm.

"I saw this. I saw you and Donovan arguing." She looked into Eric's face and broke out in a cold sweat.

"Donovan and I argue all the time. That's nothing new." Eric shrugged.

"But never over marshmallows."

"What happens next?" Her mother dropped the forgotten quilt and moved closer.

"Dad, see if it's snowing." Celeste pressed a hand

to her stomach.

Her father walked to the window and peered outside. "She's right. It's snowing."

The room grew heavy with choking silence.

"Is something bad supposed to happen tonight?" Her father looked at her.

"Yes."

Her father let out a slow breath. "Another attack?"

"Yes. Once we go outside."

"Who does it attack?" Eric's voice sounded gravely and low.

"Me." She swayed on her feet and leaned into Eric. He held her steady.

"Okay. Let's take this nice and slow. I want you to tell me what happens when everyone goes outside." Her father's voice took on a calming tone.

"Everyone goes outside. When I grab a coat, Eric tells me I can't go." She tried to swallow but her mouth was too dry. "We argue, and he finally agrees to let me go, but I have to stay close to him."

"What else?" her father urged.

"The snow starts coming down. I'm amazed at how fast it's covering everything. I look over at Donovan, and he's trying to catch snowflakes on his tongue. You and Mom are standing together in the middle of the yard holding hands, just enjoying the snow. By this time I've walked over to the side of the house with Eric. He leans down to kiss me when …"

"When what?" Her mother and father spoke in unison.

"When the demon comes rushing out of the woods. It happens so fast. None of us sees it until it's too late. It knocks me and Eric apart, and we fall to the ground. I hit my head on the walkway and I start to bleed." She stopped, aware that every eye was on her. "And that's when the perception of what I see changes."

"What do you mean?" her mother asked.

"Before I get hurt it's like I'm physically there, like I'm living it, feeling it. But as soon as I hit the ground, the view is different. It's like I'm watching it from above. But the weird thing is I can still feel what's going on."

"What do you feel?"

"I feel the pain from where I hit my head. And I feel the wet snowflakes hit my face as I'm lying on the ground." She looked at her father. "Does that mean anything?"

Her father nodded.

"Tell me."

Her parents avoided her gaze.

She knew it was bad. But she had to know. She didn't want to be lied to anymore, even if they thought they were protecting her.

She looked at Donovan. He would tell her. He always told her the truth no matter how painful. "Donovan, tell me."

"You were looking at yourself as you were dying." Donovan looked away.

Nauseating fear rose in her throat.

"That's not going to happen, Celeste." Eric held her too close.

"Okay. Let's calm down and think about this." Donovan looked out the window. After a few agonizing seconds, he faced everyone. "Do you remember exactly where the demon was when it attacked you?"

"Yes." She pulled away from Eric, and despite her trembling hands, gave him a reassuring smile before walking over to the window.

"There. It breaks through the tree line." She pointed to the dense patch of trees that sat a few feet from the house. It wasn't as lit up as the front of the house. The perfect place for a demon to lie in wait.

"Donovan, go to the closet. There are two swords I hid behind the coats. Go get them," Eric said.

Donovan quickly retrieved the swords. He walked back into the room, careful to keep away from the windows. He handed Eric a broadsword. "I didn't know you had these, Nordstrom. I see you've been holding out on me."

"I hid them because I know you have a habit of stealing." Eric narrowed his gaze.

Donavan snorted.

She shook her head. One minute they were ready to tear each other's hearts out, but give them weapons and they became best friends. Typical men.

"I had these delivered a week ago. I put them in the closet in case we needed a weapon fast and didn't have time to go to the safe room. Can you use it?" Eric had shown them the safe room in the library some weeks ago. Since then, they began storing weapons.

"All fairies know how to use swords, Nordstrom." Donovan snorted.

"Yeah, but you're a pixie."

"Smartass." Donovan turned his attention back to the window.

Her father walked to the closet and returned with two coats. Her parents slid them on. Her father reached inside his coat pocket and withdrew two ornate daggers.

"Here, put this up your coat sleeve." He handed one to her mother. Her mother obeyed and concealed her dagger in the sleeve of her coat.

Eric turned his attention to her. He looked even bigger and sexier holding the sword.

"Donovan, I need you to guard the back of the house. The minute you see the demon, you attack it from the behind. If you miss, I'll get it from the front. Sarah and Ben, get ready to back us up. Now that we know how it's going to attack, we can stop it."

Everyone nodded and moved into the foyer. Her parents opened the door and walked out while Donovan eased out the back door.

She grabbed her coat.

"You are not going out there." Eric grabbed her arm.

"I have to."

"No. You are going to stay right here in this house where it's safe."

She glared. "What if it attacks me in the house while everyone is outside? Did you think about that?" She couldn't let Eric face that danger by himself.

The reaction on his face clearly showed he hadn't thought about that scenario.

"If anything happens to you, I won't be able to live with myself." He shook his head.

She pushed up on her toes and kissed him long and hard. "You're not going to lose me."

He reached into the back of the closet and pulled out a short-handled scythe. "If we all miss, I want you to cut off his goddamn head."

She nodded and took the scary-looking weapon.

"Stay beside me," he ordered.

His grip was painful, but she didn't say anything. She found the bruising hold oddly reassuring.

She tried to focus on the task at hand. Being distracted by fear would only hinder them. Any mistakes they made this time might be their last.

She let Eric lead her in the direction of where the attack happened in her vision. When he stopped, she realized they were still close enough to the front door that they could be inside within seconds.

Complete silence filled the night, the snow blanketing any noise.

She took deep breaths to calm herself, but it was useless.

Her parents stood ten feet away. Her mother had her eyes closed with her arms by her sides with her palms up, as if she were catching snowflakes. Though her lips were moving, Celeste couldn't make out what she was saying.

Her father walked slowly, scanning the tree line for any movement.

She knew Donovan was around but couldn't see him, which hopefully meant their enemy couldn't see him either.

Eric stood between the woods and her, keeping a firm grip on her hand and his keen gaze on their surroundings.

Choking fear welled up in her chest. She had the overwhelming desire to go inside. Something wasn't right.

A sharp pain ripped through her abdomen. Putting her hand to her stomach, she bit her lip to keep from crying out.

"What's wrong?" Eric whispered.

"It's the baby. He's kicking. Hard."

He placed his hand on her stomach just as the baby kicked. His hand was knocked away by the force.

She doubled over and sucked in a breath. He stuck the sword in his belt and picked her up.

"We're going inside now," Eric announced.

She didn't argue. They managed one step when a piercing cry echoed around them, shattering the silence.

CHAPTER THIRTY-SEVEN

THE DEMON BARRELED TOWARD THEM, screaming in rage. Its physical form far from human as Celeste had ever seen.

It had the body of a beast and a face resembling a dragon. Its teeth lengthened to razor sharp points as it ran toward them on four legs. Black blood poured from a deep gash in its side.

It was still alive. And pissed off as hell.

Eric put her down and picked up his sword. He swung. The demon dodged the blade and crashed into them, knocking them both down. The sword clanged and skittered across the frozen ground.

She landed on her shoulder with a thud, pain sweeping through her body.

Instinctively she reached for her stomach, making sure the baby was okay. Despite the pain, she almost laughed with relief as she felt the baby kicking against her fingers.

A hideous shriek echoed in the quiet night.

Eric was on the ground, the demon pinning him down. In a flash, the demon bared its teeth and lunged for his neck. He blocked the attack with his arm. The demon's pointed teeth sank into his flesh. Eric cried out.

She scrambled to her feet. Remembering her scythe, she reached inside her coat. An inexplicable warming sensation swept through her body as she tightened her grip on the weapon.

She moved behind the demon and swung with all her might, slashing the steel blade across its neck, separating the head from the body. The demon's body crumpled to the ground. The head rolled a few feet and stopped.

Its black blood seeped into the pristine snow.

Her knees buckled and she crumpled to the cold ground.

"Celeste," Eric moaned.

"Eric." Shaking she crawled to him. She winced against the sharp bite of the cold ground but kept going.

His eyes were closed and his face was pale. The demon had bitten though bone, mangling tissue and ripping muscle. His arm lay at an odd angle and was held together by ligament and torn muscle.

"Eric, open your eyes." She blinked back the tears. Her father gently pushed her out of the way and helped Eric inside the house and laid him on the couch.

She knelt beside him and placed her lips over his to heal him. An enormous rush of energy flooded her body like a white-hot heat. She concentrated on his wound and kissed him with more force, feeling the power rush into his body. It began to heal him and she concentrated harder to speed up the process. Within seconds, she pulled away and looked down into his eyes.

She glanced at his arm. Perfectly healed.

Eric leaped off the couch and grabbed her. He kissed her deep, every inch of his hard body pressed intimately against hers.

Apparently healing had affected other areas of his body as well.

She kissed him back, threading her fingers through his hair. His hands went to her butt and he pulled her tighter against him.

"Donovan." The fear in her mother's voice made her pull away from Eric's heated kiss.

Donovan stood in a puddle of his own blood. His lips were white and pressed together. When her eyes dipped lower, she stifled a gag.

His hands gripped his lower stomach. He'd been cut so deep his intestines were trying to escape between his fingers.

He was literally holding himself together.

Her father eased him on the smaller sofa. He cried out in agony.

She was shocked Donovan was even conscious.

"I have to help him." She looked over her shoulder at Eric. It wasn't a request but a statement. No matter how much her husband hated the man, she couldn't let Donovan die.

He nodded. "Do it."

She prayed she wasn't too late.

She kissed Donovan gently on the lips. His mouth was cold and she could barely feel his heart beating.

She closed her eyes and put all her focus on his wound, straining to help his body mend itself, to bring him back from the path to death.

A sudden energy pulled at her, like her body was being sucked away from this reality and into another.

She broke the contact and opened her eyes. Instead of being in her home, they were alone and standing in a swath of warm white light.

"Donovan, where are we?"

"We are between the mortal realm and the eternal realm."

"Why?" Grief gripped her heart like a hand.

"Because I'm dying."

"No, you're not. I can help you. I can heal you, Donovan. Help me heal you."

"You don't need me here. You have Eric now."

"Of course I need you. You are part of my family. I don't want you to leave." She reached out for him, but he stepped back.

"You can't heal me because you don't love me enough."

"What? Of course I love you."

"Do you? Do you love me like family? Or is it deeper?" He raised his hand to her cheek and smiled weakly. "Celeste, I will always love you." He dropped his hand and turned away.

"Donovan, don't go. Please."

He walked toward her until his face was inches from hers. "How bad do you want me to stay?"

He didn't give her time to answer but pulled her against him and covered her lips with his.

She should have been shocked when he kissed her, but she wasn't. He pulled her up against his body while his tongue swept inside her mouth. His kiss was different from Eric's, more urgent and more aggressive. She fell backward, and then everything went black.

She struggled to open her eyes, but she was so very tired. Pushing through the utter exhaustion, she managed to open her eyes.

She was back in her house. And Donovan was kissing her.

She shoved at him, but it was like trying to push against an elephant. He held her tight, one arm around her back while the other clamped down hard on her ass.

"Let go of her." Eric ripped Donovan's hands away and swung her up into his arms. Her head lolled against his shoulder. She didn't even have the energy to wrap her arms around his neck.

"Are you okay?" he whispered against her ear.

"Yes," she breathed.

"Thank you, Celeste. That was amazing." Donovan snickered.

She felt Eric's muscles tense under her. She turned her head to catch the arrogant grin spreading across her cousin's face. He certainly didn't look close to death now.

"Everyone's fine. That's the important thing." She laid her head back on Eric's shoulder.

"Is he still kicking you?" Eric murmured.

"No. He stopped after the demon attacked." She caught the look of surprise on her mother's face and explained. "The baby started kicking when the demon came out from around the house."

"The baby was warning you," her mother whispered.

"Warning me?"

"The baby was warning you about the demon. The baby could sense the danger. Her mother and father exchanged a look.

"Of course. Why didn't I think of that?" Her father rubbed his hand across his mouth. "While you carry the child, he shares the gift of prophecy, as well."

"That's all well and good, but I want to know how you are feeling." Eric pulled her attention back to him.

"Sore and tired." She ran her fingers over her stomach. "You can put me down, Eric."

"We killed the demon. So this should be the end of it, right?" She looked to her parents.

"When you kill a demon, another can take its place." Her father looked out the window.

"Will another come back tonight?"

"I doubt it. Just in case, I'll stay up and keep watch. Donovan, you can relieve me at three."

Her father gave her an encouraging smile. "It won't get past us."

"Go on up and get ready for bed. I'll be up shortly." Eric caressed her cheek.

After a hot shower, she slid into one of Eric's t shirts. She didn't even bother turning on the bedroom lights but went straight to the bed and pulled down the covers.

"Are you going to tell him?"

She jumped at the sound of Donovan's voice.

"Donovan, you scared the shit out of me." She flipped on the lamp and glared at him as he sat in her chair.

"You didn't answer my question. Are you going to tell him?" He continued to watch her.

"What are you talking about?" God, she was so tired. All she wanted to do was sleep. Not stand here and go twenty questions with Donovan.

He stood and took a step toward her. "You know what I'm talking about. The fact that you love me. The fact that you are mine. The fact that we belong together. Have you told Eric that?"

Her mouth fell open. He couldn't be serious. "Have you lost your mind?" She took a step back when he stepped into the light. "Eric is my husband."

"And I am your soul mate." His words came out scorching and hot. His eyes were intense as they roamed across her body.

The back of her thighs brushed against the mattress as she took another step back. She had nowhere else to go. She was trapped.

She'd never been afraid of Donovan before, but now, looking into his eyes, she was seeing a different side of him.

The baby kicked. The force knocked a scream out of her and she doubled over and wrapped her arms around her stomach.

"Celeste?" Donovan grabbed her. The baby kicked again, sending white-hot pain through her stomach.

"Don't touch me," she hissed, but he didn't listen. He picked her up and laid her on the bed.

Eric ran into the room and shoved Donovan out of the way. "What the hell did you do to her?" Eric leaned over her and brushed her hair out of her eyes.

The kicking stopped.

She sucked in a deep breath.

"What happened?" Her mother and father ran into the room with daggers in hand.

"The baby started kicking when …" She clamped her mouth shut. She cut her eyes at Donovan. If she told him what Donovan had said, Eric would kill him.

A knowing look flashed across her mother's eyes. She turned to Donovan. "Leave the room, Donovan."

A brief glimmer of pain passed through his eyes before he looked at Celeste. "It seems like you have your own little sentry. But he will learn to love me, don't worry." Donovan stormed out of the room.

Eric sat on the bed next to her. "What did he mean, *sentry*?"

"Apparently, the baby has very strong emotions about who touches his mommy." Her mother smiled.

Heat rushed to her face. How did her mother know?

"Did Donovan hurt you?" Eric's expression hardened.

She shook her head.

"I'm sure the baby wouldn't have allowed him to. Your child is very possessive of his mother, even in the womb." Her mother looked at her.

She caught the subtle twitch in Eric's jaw. "If I catch that bastard anywhere near Celeste while she's alone I'll kill him."

"I wouldn't worry, Eric. I doubt that Donovan will try to touch her again, seeing how much pain he caused."

She closed her eyes and hoped her mother was right.

☾

ERIC UNDRESSED AND SLID INTO bed. He wrapped his arms around Celeste and pulled her close.

"Was Donovan trying to start trouble?" He tried to keep his voice calm.

She went still.

He got his answer.

"I'll ask him to leave tomorrow." He kissed her forehead.

"It wasn't entirely his fault." Her voice was quiet, unsure.

"What do you mean?" His chest constricted.

"When I was healing Donovan, we ended up in some kind of realm. He said he was dying because I didn't love him and it was time for him to go."

She took a breath. "I told him I did love him. He was my family and I didn't want him to die."

He gritted his teeth. "So he told you that he was going to die if you didn't tell him you loved him."

"Well, not exactly those words."

"But the same general idea." He gritted his jaw. Donovan was nothing but a manipulator.

Her eyebrows slowly slid together. Maybe her faith in good old Donovan was wavering.

God, he hoped so.

"He deceived you, Celeste. We all witnessed you healing him. He wasn't dying. In fact, he was grinning the whole time." He fought the image out of his mind. That was the last thing he wanted to be thinking about while lying in bed with his wife.

"Grinning." Celeste rose up on her elbow and looked down into his face. "You mean Donovan . . ."

"Lied. Deceived. Tricked you. He made you

believe he was going to die if you didn't tell him you loved him."

"That son of a bitch."

He grinned.

"It's not funny." She punched him in the shoulder.

"No, it's not." He quickly sobered. "But I'm glad that you see Donovan for who he is. You are too trusting. You believe there is good in everyone."

"I'm stupid. That's what I am." She lay back on the pillow and blew out a breath.

"Don't ever say that. You are gentle and kind and trusting. It's why I love you." He loved how she relaxed into his body and sighed. God, he loved those little sounds she made. And how she looked. And how . . .

He cleared his throat. "My son will protect you from Donovan any time I'm not around." He bent his head to her stomach. "Isn't that right?"

A small, gentle kick pressed against his lips.

The question was, who was going to protect Donovan from Eric?

CHAPTER THIRTY-EIGHT

IT TOOK CELESTE TWO DAYS to recover from the effects of healing both Eric and Donovan.

Whenever she woke, Eric was at the bedside, his eyes filled with worry. She tried to reassure him that she was just tired, but he still refused to go to work until she fully recovered.

On the third day, she was strong enough to get out of bed and head down to the kitchen.

"How are you feeling, honey?" Her mother set her coffee cup down and wrapped her arms around her.

"I'm sore from lying in bed for so long. You should have made me get up."

"You needed to rest. Healing takes a lot of energy." She motioned for her to sit.

"No kidding." She eased onto the bar stool.

"Are you hungry?"

"Starving."

"Good. What do you feel like? Everyone else has eaten. They are in the garage training with swords."

She placed her hand over her growling stomach. "How about a horse?"

"Fresh out of horses, but I can make you pancakes." Her mom grinned.

"Even better."

Half an hour later, after eating way too many pancakes, Celeste decided to take a walk.

Slipping on her on heavy winter coat, gloves, and hat, she walked out into the blinding light.

The scene was so different from that of a few nights ago. The sun shone bright in the cloudless sky. The snow had melted, leaving the ground mushy and damp. If not for the cold wind, it would seem more like an autumn day than a winter one.

She inhaled deep and let the winter air sting her lungs while she shielded her eyes with her hand. She should have brought her sunglasses. She was going to get crow's feet from all the squinting against the brightness.

She walked around the back of the house and stopped. Her gaze ran along the ground. This was where Donovan had been attacked, yet there were no signs of a struggle. The melting snow had erased any traces of blood that had been spilled that night.

She trudged around to the front of the house and stopped at the tree line. Nothing had changed. Everything was in the same place. She wondered why everything seemed so much scarier at night, but she already knew the answer.

It was because no one could see the evil coming. If the attack had happened during the day, she could have seen it coming, been prepared. But night was different. The night hid the evil's secrets.

Maybe she was like the day. Her family's light, their hope in the darkness. Everyone was counting on her ability to see the evil that was coming so they could stop it.

What if she couldn't? What if she failed? What if next time someone died?

She shivered and closed her eyes.

"What are you doing?"

She opened her eyes. Eric stood in front of her wearing jeans and a black tee shirt, holding the largest sword she'd ever seen.

"Aren't you cold? You're not even wearing a coat." Her belly went all warm and gooey, and she wanted nothing more than to lick the sweat off his neck.

A grin spread across his gorgeous face, and she wondered if he had read her mind.

"I'm sweating from all the practicing. It feels pretty good out here." His hair, wet with sweat and clinging to his forehead, made him look like a model for a fitness magazine.

She let her gaze roam across his chest where his shirt clung, revealing defined pecs and a washboard stomach.

Her heart raced. A strong surge of lust ripped through her straight to her core.

"Are you feeling better?" He cupped her cheek.

She stepped closer and wrapped her arms around his narrow waist. She buried her face against his damp chest and smiled. He even smelled sexy.

"I can't believe I slept so much. You should have hauled me out of bed. I'm trying to walk off some of the soreness. And the pancakes I just ate."

His arms tightened across her back. "Your father said it's normal for you to be so tired. Not only did you heal me and Donovan, but you are helping the baby develop every day. He said that after the baby is born, you won't be tired at all. In fact, he said you will be even stronger."

"I wonder if I will be able to control my visions better too. You know, like knowing what the weather will be like the next day, or picking the winning lottery number."

He laughed.

"What?"

"Money is not something you will ever need, I can guarantee that."

She glanced at the garage. "What exactly do you guys do when you train?"

"Why don't you come and watch?" He took her hand and they walked into the garage. Walking past the line of cars parked outside, she stopped. Solomon stood on the other side of the Mercedes.

"Solomon, I didn't know you were back." Other than Mrs. Gambil, Eric had made sure to keep the other employees away.

"I got back a few days ago, Mrs. Celeste. Mr. Eric tried to talk me into taking a longer vacation, but I refused. I heard there had been trouble here, and I can't leave you unprotected. Even if that trouble is in the form of a demon." He flashed a grin.

Her mouth dropped.

"It's okay. Solomon knows all about us. Apparently he has had some experience fighting demons."

"Are you a . . ."

"A fairy? Yes, ma'am. My family came from the African fairy line. I've known Mr. Eric had Fae blood for a while. I was just waiting to see if he would accept his fate. And thanks to you, he has."

Solomon knelt, one arm bent across his chest as he cast his face to the ground. "On my honor, you have my fealty. I will protect you and this family with my life."

Humbled by the gesture, she blinked back tears. "Thank you, Solomon. I hope it doesn't come to that."

"Come on. Let's go check out the garage." Eric laced his fingers with hers.

The scent of oil and tires overwhelmed her as soon as she stepped inside. He carried a chair from the corner over so she could sit. After waving to her father and Donovan in the middle of the room, she settled back to watch them fight.

The men held identical broadswords and shields on their arms. They bowed and began delivering strikes with their swords. Their movements were intricate and specific and graceful.

Eric knelt by her side. "It's almost like they've been doing this for years. How did they get so good in such a short amount of time?" She couldn't take her eyes off them.

"Apparently it's in their blood."

"You mean our blood. You have the same blood running through your veins."

He nodded his head. "Yes, I suppose you're right. I'm amazed at how fast I picked up the moves. And the feeling, it's like an adrenaline rush."

"So you believe in what you are now?"

"I don't think I could deny it, even if I wanted to." His gaze bore into hers. "I looked back at my family tree and I am the descendent of Naddoddr." He looked away, lost in thought. "Having Fae blood in my veins would explain something in my past I couldn't."

"What is that?"

"My strength. When my parents and I were in a car accident, I managed to get out. The car was upside down and I managed to turn it right side up. With my bare hands." He gazed at her. "I often wondered how I had been able to do that. Now I know."

"So are you as good as they are?" She nodded toward the men.

"Your father says I'm better." He smiled. "It's been there all along, buried deep. My fighting ability didn't disappear, just got a little rusty. It only took me a couple of days to catch on and after that I was fighting as well as your father."

"So if it's in your blood, does this mean I can learn to fight as well?" She wanted to kick some ass, too.

"Absolutely not." Eric scowled.

"I need to know how." She needed to be able to defend herself and the baby if the need ever arose. The last thing she needed was Eric getting all parental on her.

"I don't want you fighting, and that's the end of it." Eric growled.

As much as she loved him, she really wanted to punch him in the mouth.

"Hey Celeste, did you come to watch me in action?" Donovan strutted over, but his smirk quickly faded when he saw her face.

"What's wrong?" Her father walked up and looked uneasily between her and Eric.

"I don't see why I can't learn to fight too." She crossed her arms.

Donovan looked at her like she had admitted to eating puppies for breakfast. "Don't be ridiculous.

You can't fight. You're almost nine months pregnant."

"But . . ."

Her father nodded. "He's right, honey. It's just too dangerous."

"Why don't I walk you back to the house so you can lie down?" Eric took her arm to help her out of the chair.

She snatched her arm away. "I don't want to go lie down. I just got out of the bed. You are all treating me like I'm some ninety-year-old woman."

Donovan said, "But Celeste, in your delicate condition —"

"Forget it!" She turned on her heel and stomped out of the garage.

☾

SINCE SHE WASN'T ALLOWED TO fight, Celeste decided to spend her time in another worthy pursuit—volunteering at the food bank. She remembered as a child how her parents had taken her every holiday season to feed the hungry.

Eric agreed that she could go as long as she took Solomon with her.

At night, they discussed how families were having trouble keeping food on the table. He listened patiently, not saying anything. On her last day of volunteering, she found out he had written a generous check in her honor.

That night she went home and cried. That night, not being allowed to fight didn't seem like a big deal after all.

CHAPTER THIRTY-NINE

"I COULD LIVE LIKE THIS ALL year. Wrapping presents and sipping hot chocolate." Celeste sighed and took another sip.

Her mother laughed and finished tying a red bow to a shimmering green present.

Celeste stared at the dancing flames in the fireplace and took a sip of hot chocolate from the steaming mug. She sat on the Persian rug with her mother in the library among a sea of colored wrapping paper and glistening bows. Bing Crosby crooned "White Christmas" over the speakers.

She fought back a grin when she glanced over at the chair pushed up against the door. Donovan had tried to snoop and see his gifts. But her mom had run him out of the room and placed a chair under the doorknob to make sure he didn't get back in.

She secured the end of the foil paper on the shirt box and sighed.

"Are you tired? I can finish these if you want to go to bed." Her mother tied a perfect bow on a square box.

"It's not that." She cut her eyes at her mother.

"How long after you had me did you get back in shape?"

"About three months." Her mother cut a long strip of burgundy wrapping paper and positioned a square box in the middle of it.

"Three months! I can't wait three months!"

Her mother laughed. "Well, it took nine months to put on the weight, so I thought I was doing pretty good to take it off in three."

"Yeah, but you weren't married to one of the hottest men in America. No offense." She looked down at her enormous belly. She'd hoped she would lose a lot of her weight quickly after the baby came.

"Honey, Eric loves you. He'll love you no matter what size you are."

That didn't make her feel any better. She wanted to look good for him. Sometimes she felt like the ugly duckling.

"I wouldn't worry. With your healing ability you'll be back to your slim size surprisingly quickly."

"Really?" She hadn't thought of that. She glanced at her mother, wondering if now was the right time to bring up another topic.

"Is there something else on your mind?"

"The men won't let me fight." She stopped folding wrapping paper and looked at her mother.

"I know. Your father told me. He said you were pretty upset about it too."

"What do you think?" She held her breath. Maybe her mother would be on her side.

"I agree."

She blew out her breath. Or maybe not.

"You shouldn't be fighting while you're pregnant."

"That's so not fair."

"But after you have the baby, I think you should learn."

"Really?" She jerked her head up.

"Yes, really."

"I doubt the guys are going to agree to teach me." She rolled her eyes.

"They don't have to. I can teach you."

"You know how to fight?"

"Of course."

Celeste met her mother's gaze and grinned.

"You'll be an excellent fighter, just like the rest of the family."

☾

CELESTE COULDN'T HAVE WISHED FOR a more perfect Christmas Eve. It snowed all day, layering the ground in a perfect pristine blanket. The house, decorated to perfection once again by professional decorators, shone with silver and blue.

Mrs. Gambil was still away on vacation, so she and her mother had spent the better part of the day preparing Christmas Eve dinner and casseroles for Christmas Day.

With an hour until dinner, she tossed her apron aside. Her back had ached all day, and the thought of a warm bath had her hurrying up the stairs to her bedroom.

Stripping off her clothes, she stepped into the bubble-filled tub.

"Perfect." She sighed and sank deeper into the water. Closing her eyes, she rested her head against the back of the tub.

Her life had certainly changed within the span of a year. She had never envisioned the life she had now. Now that she had it, she was eternally grateful.

A smile crossed her lips. When she first arrived she had given up hope of ever having anything but a doomed marriage with Eric.

So much had changed. Including her feelings toward him.

A bloodcurdling scream rang out. She bolted upright, sloshing water onto the tiled floor.

It was her mother.

She reached for her robe with trembling hands and struggled to get it on. When she reached the top of the staircase, she leaned over.

"Mom. Are you okay?" Peering over the banister, she held her breath.

Dead silence floated around her.

Grabbing the banister in a death grip, she descended the stairs. Icy panic curled in her chest.

When she was halfway down, the lights flickered.

She froze, her heart pounding in her chest.

The lights blinked out. She was surrounded by complete darkness.

She gripped the banister with both hands, bracing herself, expecting the demon to push her down the stairs. She waited, counting off the seconds, her own ragged breath echoing in her ears.

Nothing.

She needed to move, needed to find out where her family was.

She felt for the next step with her foot while keeping a solid grip on the banister. She kept expecting the next step to be her last. When it wasn't, she forced herself not to speed down the stairs but to take the steps slow and easy.

When her bare foot touched the cool marble of the foyer floor, she wanted to cry with relief at the small victory. She didn't have time. She had to keep moving. She had to find her mother.

She ran her hand along the wall, searching for the light switch. Her fingers brushed against the smooth wall plate and she flipped the switch.

No lights.

She sagged against the wall. Everything was quiet. It reminded her of the silence just before the attack in the forest.

It dawned on her that the scream came from outside.

The baby moved and then kicked hard. Pain gripped and spread across her tight stomach. She doubled over clutched her abdomen.

When the pain finally eased, she straightened and scanned the pitch black. It was no use. She couldn't even see her hand in front of her face.

Keeping her hand on the wall, she eased forward until she found the doorway to the living room. Her hopes of finding the fireplace still lit dwindled when she didn't see any light coming from that room.

Her fears were confirmed when she stepped through the doorway.

In the blinding darkness, she felt her way into the room, palms sliding against the walls. Her leg grazed the arm of an overstuffed chair and she stopped. She eased into the chair and curled into a protective ball.

Heart pounding in her throat and tears welling up behind her eyes, she expected any minute the demon would grab her with thick claws and rip the skin from her flesh.

Terrified and paralyzed, she waited.

After several minutes, she forced herself to uncurl her body. She couldn't just sit there and wait for an attack. She knew what she needed to do. She needed to calm down and focus.

She inhaled and forced her fear away.

She needed to find the others.

Straining against the inky darkness, she tried to listen for the others.

Everyone else had been out in the garage.

Eric would know the lights were out. He would come searching for her. He would be coming through the door any second now.

Seconds ticked into minutes, and the only sound she heard was her own heartbeat thudding in her ears.

No one called her name, no footsteps of her family entering the house, and no one tore through the house looking for her.

Nothing.

If they were under attack, then she should at least hear the fighting, the sound of metal against metal, or even the sounds of the wounded and dying.

Something was wrong.

She rubbed her hand across her heart, trying to ease the ache.

What if they were all hurt?

Or worse?

What if . . .?

She couldn't bring herself to even say the words.

Seizing upon the single thread of courage she had, she bolted in the vicinity of the front door with outstretched arms. Her hip slammed into the table in the foyer. She stumbled but managed to keep her balance.

"Damn." She rubbed her hip but continued toward the front door.

Her fingertips brushed against the metal doorknob. She took a deep breath and flung open the door.

Instead of a demon, darkness. Instead of noise, quiet.

It was strange that it was just as black outside as inside. Even the moon and stars seemed to be swallowed up.

She shivered as the cutting winter wind whipped at the bottom of her robe. She regretted not grabbing her coat and shoes. No matter. She wouldn't be able to find them in the darkness.

If she was lucky, maybe she would freeze to death before being attacked.

She tried to slow down her breathing while her thoughts tumbled wildly in her head.

Maybe it was a county-wide power outage.

Maybe someone had gotten hurt while they were practicing in the garage.

Maybe that's why her mother had screamed.

It would explain why she hadn't seen anyone in the house. Everyone was probably out in the garage trying to find the breaker.

She kept her hand on the rough brick and stone of the exterior of the house and inched her way toward the garage.

"Shit." The shrubbery stabbed her skin, and the

cold ground crunched painfully under her bare feet.

She felt like a freaking pin cushion.

Her fingertips found the sharp corner of the house. She'd have to find her way to the garage blindly.

She took a step.

"Ouch!" Something sharp bit into the bottom of her foot.

Bending down, she touched something cold and pointy. A rake.

Her fingers closed around the wooden handle. At least now she had some kind of weapon.

She continued picking her way across the yard. Her progress was slow, but she couldn't stop now. She had to keep going.

Her rake stuck something solid.

She had made it to the garage. Relief poured through her like warm oil.

Sharp hot pain rippled through her stomach. She screamed and doubled over.

This pain was different. It was intense and grew stronger. Unable to stand under the pain, she slumped to the ground, her hands clutching her stomach, her screams filling the darkness.

"There you are. I've been looking for you all night."

CHAPTER FORTY

A BREATH-STEALING WAVE OF PAIN SPREAD across her stomach in claw-like tentacles. She screamed.

It felt as if her stomach were being ripped open from the inside. After a few seconds, the pain eased. She forced her jelly legs under her, stood, and glanced around. She was no longer outside the garage, but in some sort of cave.

Torches hung on the walls, and yellow flames flickered against the shadows on the bumpy stone wall. The cave was enormous with stalagmites protruding up from the floor. The constant drip of water trickling down the walls left behind a musty odor from years of seepage.

"How the hell did I get here?" Her whisper echoed along the bleak cave walls.

She glanced around the room and her gaze landed in the center of the cave where a rough stone altar rested. In the center there was a black X.

She shivered and crossed her arms. Her fingers brushed against silky smooth material.

She no longer wore her terry cloth bathrobe, but

a white sleeveless tunic that hung to the ground.

Whoever had brought her here had changed her clothing.

Before she had the chance to feel embarrassment and anger at a stranger seeing her naked, another tight pain ripped through her abdomen.

Sweat broke out across her forehead and panic kicked up her heartbeat.

Something was terribly wrong.

The baby wasn't kicking.

Was she . . . oh god . . . in labor?

After an excruciating minute, the pain eased. She glanced around for an exit. She needed to get out of this place. She needed to get home.

"Where do you think you are going?" Icy breath brushed her shoulder.

She froze, her feet paralyzed to the cold ground. She sucked in shallow gasps of air and her heart drummed fast. She couldn't stop shaking.

She knew that voice. It was the voice of the demon that had attacked her. The one they had killed.

Don't turn around. Don't turn around. If she turned around, it would be real.

"Look at me, Celeste."

She pressed her hands to her stomach and turned.

She had expected the same demon from the forest. But this one looked different. Instead of dark features, this demon had blond hair and fair skin.

Yet one thing remained the same. The same soulless eyes, rimmed in yellow, stared back at her.

She gagged, choked by the evil pouring off his body.

"Who are you?" She couldn't keep the tremor

out of her voice.

"I have many names." It grinned. "But you can call me Lust. I believe you have met my brother Wrath."

Her heart dropped. "Wrath and Lust? Two of the seven deadly sins?"

"So you have heard of me." He smiled. "That's good. That's very, very good."

She stepped back and sucked in a harsh breath. "Are you sure you and your brother didn't get each other's names mixed up?" There had been no question in her mind that Wrath was going to rape her in the woods.

"I do apologize for his behavior. He never was one to know how to act in the presence of a beautiful lady." The demon grinned, revealing two rows of pointed shark-like teeth.

"You see, people get us mixed up all the time. Wrath likes sex just as much as I do. He just likes it with a bit of pain."

"Where is my family?" She needed to keep talking, to buy some time. Eric had to be looking for her by now.

Lust ran his cold fingertips across her mouth. His pale lips stretched into a grotesque grin.

"Your family is very annoying. Like mosquitos. When we were sent to find you, we didn't expect so much trouble. We thought you would be easy to capture."

"The Queen sent you?" She fought the urge to slap his hand away, knowing it would only anger him. "The Queen of the Fairies, the one from Ireland?"

"Yes. That's her." Lust waved his hand impatiently,

apparently bored with the conversation.

"She's still alive?"

"Of course. She's immortal."

"I thought fairies were mortal since The Fall." Donovan never said anything about fairies becoming immortal.

"When the Pixie king failed to kill Naddorddr's children, the Queen made a deal with the devil. She pledged fealty to the devil in exchange for a child born to the linage of Isa and Naddoddr."

"Why didn't The Queen kill the children herself?"

"Because Isa veiled them so the Queen couldn't find them. After they grew up, Isa separated them. Her daughter went to Ireland and her son …."

"Stayed in Sweden." She swallowed. "Isa thought if she put her children on different continents there would be no chance of their offspring ever meeting and . . ."

"Fucking." His lips curled over his vile teeth.

Thick ice sliced through her veins.

"We've been watching you for a while. I had to slip that invitation into your box at work to get you into that party."

"It wasn't an accident?" He hadn't mentioned her visions. It was a great possibility that the Queen didn't know she had the gift of prophecy.

"There are no accidents in life." Lust grinned. "The Queen needed to get you and Eric together so he could put his seed in you." His evil gaze slid between her legs.

Her flesh ached as if a thousand spiders were clinging to her skin.

"We thought we were going to have to step in

and hurry things along between you and Eric. He seemed to have grown a conscience between the time he stuck his cock in you and the time he found out you were a sweet little virgin." Lust growled.

"What do you mean?" She fought not to cover herself.

"We thought he might pull out and that just wouldn't do. The Queen needs the child."

"And if he had changed his mind?"

"Well, then I would have had to possess him. And it would have been me fucking you, instead." Lust laughed. "We met the night of the party. Don't you remember?" The demon shifted into the matronly old lady from the Cryptic party.

A terrified moan slipped past Celeste's lips. She clamped her hand across her mouth.

"Fairies can be possessed." She had never come across that in her research. Her brain struggled to find something else to keep him talking.

"Only if you are poisoned." Lust gave her a knowing smile. "In this case, Wolfberry."

"You poisoned Eric?"

"I didn't get the chance." Lust frowned. "Someone slipped something else in his drink first."

"Who?"

"I don't know. Some bitch." He narrowed his gaze.

"What was it?" Her mind raced back to the night of the party. They had both drank the same thing. Had she been affected as well?

"Viagra."

"We both drank champagne and I wasn't affected." She swallowed. Is that why he'd slept with her? Because he had a raging hard-on?

"Think, Celeste. What else did he drink besides the champagne?"

Her stomach dropped. "The scotch." He'd even said it tasted different.

"So you do remember. Very good." Lust circled her like she was his prey. "It doesn't really matter at this point. You must know no one can help you now."

"I suppose you can't keep the Queen waiting much longer. She must be very irritated at having nothing to do but wait all these years."

"Oh, she occupied her time in other ways. In fact, she was responsible for that nasty little disease in Europe. Ever heard of the black plague? Her handiwork. She got upset when a baron didn't return her advances. 'Hell hath no fury like a woman scorned' She coined the phrase."

Her gaze flickered from the cave walls back to the demon. "Where are we?"

"We are practically in your backyard."

"I think I would have noticed if there were a cave-in my own backyard." She fought to keep her voice from cracking.

"It's because you were not looking closely enough."

"Where is my family?"

"They are being taken care of as we speak. If you were planning on screaming for help, don't waste your breath. There will be no one left to hear you." Lust took a step toward her.

She stepped back.

Something moved at the far side of the cave, catching her eye. She jerked her head in that direction.

Eric stood in the doorway, his gaze on her. He had come for her.

"Eric." She sucked in a relieved breath.

A sparkling light emerged from beside him, growing bigger and brighter until a woman materialized, statuesque in height with long red hair and familiar green eyes. She was quite possibly the most beautiful woman Celeste had ever seen.

Celeste immediately knew who she was.

The Queen of the Fairies.

"Eric?" Why was he just standing there?

"I don't think he's interested in you anymore, Celeste." Lust smirked.

Eric turned his attention to the beautiful woman. He reached out and pulled the Queen into his arms and kissed her.

Horrified, she watched, unable to look away. Hope drained out of her soul and her heart shattered in her chest.

"See, he cares nothing for you, or that thing growing inside your belly."

She barely heard the words the demon uttered before he pushed her, sending her flying through the air. She landed hard on the stone table.

Pain rippled across her back, stealing her breath.

Lust pounced and landed on top of her, vulgarly shoving her legs apart.

She screamed and scraped her nails across his face.

Lust punched her in the face. She heard the cartilage break in her nose. Pain exploded and spread across her face. Tears and blood ran down her cheeks as she cupped her face.

He wasted no time. He wrapped his fingers around her throat.

The last thing she remembered were claw-like hands squeezing her neck before darkness surrounded her.

CHAPTER FORTY-ONE

One hour earlier . . .

ERIC WALKED INTO THE GARAGE humming a Christmas carol. It was the same Christmas song Celeste had been singing as she'd hung the stockings on the mantel of the fireplace for Santa an hour ago. Her face, bright with excitement, had been almost too beautiful to look at.

His life had changed over the last eight months. He realized that he had never been content until Celeste had turned his life upside down. He had found the unconditional love that he had missed his whole life.

She loved him, not his money.

He was determined to make her happy. He didn't want her to ever regret marrying him.

He stopped at the last car. Solomon had done a great job putting the huge red bow on her new black BMW. He knew she was getting tired of Solomon driving her around, and she needed a new car, since hers had been wrecked. He couldn't wait to give it to her tomorrow morning.

He cut the light and locked the door behind him.

"Eric!" Sarah hurried toward him.

"What's wrong? Is it Celeste?" His gut clenched.

"They're here." Donovan and Ben emerged from the direction of the woods.

"The demons?" His heart stilled.

"No. The Fae. They're patrolling the woods. They caught the scent of a demon and are tracking it to the woods. That's not all. Aunt Agatha said that they sensed something is going to happen tonight."

"But how can that be? Celeste didn't have a vision."

"Celeste can't see the Queen coming. No fairy can." Sarah's face paled. "She's too powerful."

He sprinted toward the house, his only thought to make sure Celeste was okay. He reached the front door.

Sarah screamed. He turned and saw his mother-in-law lying on the ground by the tree.

In the illumination of the security lights around the house, two demons emerged from the tree line at frightening speed.

Ben knelt beside Sarah, his face contorted with rage.

Ben jumped to his feet and unsheathed his sword at his waist and faced the first demon.

Donovan, with daggers in his both hands, approached the second demon. He swung and missed. "Cut the lights!" Ben yelled.

The demon was quick and slashed his claw across Donovan's shoulder. Donovan howled as blood seeped down his shoulder.

"How will we see them in the dark?" Eric questioned.

"Just do it!" Ben answered.

Eric hesitated for a second and then bolted for the side of the house. He found the breaker switch and flipped it, throwing everyone into complete darkness.

Something began to happen. His vision began to change. Green images against a black background appeared. Those green images were Sarah, Ben, and Donovan along with the two demons. It was like he was looking through night-vision goggles.

"What the hell?"

The demons groped blindly for their target. But every time a demon got close to Donovan or Ben, the men would stab them and jump out of their reach.

Eric grabbed one of Donovan's daggers. He sprinted to the demon nearest to Ben. Just as the demon grabbed Ben, Eric ran his dagger through the demon's chest.

It shrieked. Its body turned to rotting flesh and then disintegrated into ash. The ashes disappeared on a gust of winter wind.

Donovan slashed his dagger down across the second demon's throat. It howled in pain and anger before it, too, turned to dust.

"Is she okay?" Eric's heart had stopped when he had seen Sarah lying on the ground. Memories of his parents' deaths came flooding back.

"I'm fine." Sarah stood with Ben's help. Her eyes widened as she looked beyond them.

He followed her gaze to the tree line. The lights were still off. A bright light grew in the darkness, and a beautiful woman with long red hair dressed in an elaborate gown of gold appeared.

He knew immediately she was the Queen.

"You people go to so much trouble protecting such an insignificant thing."

"She is more important than you will ever be." Eric stepped forward, but Ben grabbed him.

"Now is that any way to greet your Queen?" she sneered.

"You're not my fucking Queen," Eric said.

The Queen's smile grew slow and snakelike. "You must be her husband."

"I am," Eric snarled.

"So tell me, where is your little wife?"

"I'm not telling you a fucking thing. I won't let you get within a hundred feet of her." He clenched his fists. The only way that bitch was getting to Celeste was over his dead body.

The Queen let out a deep laugh. "We'll see about that."

With a flick of her wrist, six more demons slunk out of the shadows of the trees. Unlike the previous demons, which had appeared in human form, these demons were in creature form. Their bodies were the shape of abnormally large wolves, but instead of paws, they had hoofs. Their faces resembled distorted pigs, with elongated teeth that easily measured four inches long.

Four of them held up a hoof. A long needle, like an antenna, slid out from each wrist. They took aim directly at Eric and the others. Apparently, these demons had no trouble seeing in darkness.

"This won't hurt. Much." The Queen's shrill laugh made the hair on the back of his neck stand up.

A stream of fire erupted out of the demons'

hoofs, hitting them in the chest. The force knocked them to the ground.

Pain wrapped around his heart and squeezed. He tried to scream but couldn't move. He couldn't even open his mouth. Whatever he'd been hit with had paralyzed him.

He listened for the others. He heard nothing.

A demon slunk over to Eric and snarled. It bit down on his shoulder, sinking its teeth in all the way to the bone. Lava-hot pain raced around his shoulder. His heartbeat sped up to an incredible pace. As much as he wanted to yell, scream, cry out, he couldn't.

With its teeth still in his shoulder, the demon dragged him into the woods. With every pull, his shoulder burned with pain. Another demon dragged Donovan by the neck while the other two demons carried Ben and Sarah.

The Queen barked out an order. "Bring me the girl."

He tried to open his mouth to warn Celeste, but he still couldn't move. He was utterly helpless.

The only thing left to do was pray. He prayed like he had never prayed before and hoped this time God was listening.

☾

THE DEMON DRAGGING ERIC STOPPED in front a large tree deep in the woods. It placed its hoof on a fallen tree trunk. Immediately, the wood began to expand and contort until a large portal appeared.

The demons stepped through the portal. They were carried farther and farther into what appeared to be a cave. Enormous uneven stone walls glinted with areas of water trickling down the side, giving off a musty odor and dropping the temperature a good ten degrees.

The demon tossed Eric into an empty chamber. He landed on his wounded shoulder, scraping dirt and gravel into the injured tissue. He watched helplessly as the rest of his family was thrown in the same way. The demons rolled a large boulder in front of the entrance, effectively sealing them in.

The numbness in his extremities began to fade until he could move them. Whatever drug they had been given wasn't permanent.

"Is everyone okay?" He pushed himself up to his knees.

"Yeah. The poison they hit us with should wear off fairly quickly." Donovan sat up and rubbed his hands on his legs.

"Poison?" He didn't even want to imagine them using that shit on Celeste.

"Yeah. It's deadly to humans. Thankfully, it only stuns fairies."

"We've got to get out of here. They're going after Celeste." He glared at his in-laws. "I thought you said the fairies were in the woods."

"They are. They are probably making their way to us now."

"Or maybe Aunt Agatha was overpowered." Donovan frowned. "Maybe they've already been captured."

"Or maybe we can't trust them." Eric added.

"We don't betray each other, Eric." Ben stepped away from Sarah.

"Really? Then why is the Queen of the Fairies

trying to kill her own??" He knew what would happen to Celeste if they captured her.

"The Queen chose the evil path the day she plotted to spill innocent blood. She is no longer one of us." Sarah maneuvered her way between him and Ben. "Now is not the time to argue. We've got to get out and find Celeste."

Protecting his family was all that mattered.

He stepped in front of the boulder and shoved as hard as he could. It didn't budge.

"You're not going to move it. It's too heavy." Donovan sank onto a smaller rock. "Whatever superhuman strength you had doesn't work in this realm. You're in her territory now."

"Get your ass over here and help me. I can't just sit around and do nothing. Celeste is in danger."

"I have an idea." Ben looked at his wife. "Sarah, we're going to need your help."

"Ben, I can manipulate the elements, not lift a boulder."

"What if you used the element of wind to roll it out of the way?"

"I thought you said our powers don't work in her realm," Eric spat out through gritted teeth.

"Yours won't. You just accepted your Fae destiny. But Sarah, she has lived her whole life as Fae. She has honed her powers every day. Our powers still might work."

"I've never used that amount of force with wind." Sarah lifted her hands at her side and raised her palms up. "But I'll try. Everyone stand back."

She closed her eyes and began to speak. Eric recognized the language as Gaelic, the same language Celeste had spoken in her sleep.

Without warning, the air began to swirl around her like a tornado. She pushed her palms outward and the tornado left her and engulfed the boulder. When she moved her hands to the right, the rock trembled and began to move. The farther her hands moved to the right, the more the boulder rolled. A few seconds passed before the exit was open.

He raced toward the opening, but Donovan grabbed his arm.

"You can't just go running out there. We need a plan."

"I can't sit here and do nothing while they take her." He had to do something.

Donovan lifted his head and sniffed. "They already have her."

"Is she hurt?" His heart stilled.

"I can't tell. She's in the chamber down the hall to the left."

"I doubt they've left her unguarded, so we're going to need a distraction." Ben turned to Donovan. "Do you think you can handle that?"

"Of course." Donovan sneered. "Distraction is what I do best."

"Good. We'll let Donovan go ahead of us. Even if the Queen or any of her minions catch him, we'll still have a chance to get to Celeste. Sarah, you follow Donovan from a distance, in case they capture him. Eric, I saw some swords at the entrance to the cave when we were being dragged in. We're going to need those since our weapons are in the garage."

Sarah wrapped her arms around Ben's neck.

"Everyone please be careful," Sarah whispered. "Remember, good will always overcome evil."

He hoped so. God, did he hope so.

CHAPTER FORTY-TWO

ERIC FOLLOWED BEN BACK TO the entrance to the cave where they found the weapons.

He picked up a broadsword and a cutlass while Ben grabbed a dagger and two swords. With his adrenaline in overdrive he felt like he could lift a fucking Mercedes.

They crept back into the bowels of the cave.

The longer he was away from Celeste, the more danger she would be in. They were running out of time.

Deep voices ricocheted off the walls. They pressed their bodies against the wall and held their breath.

He recognized the voices as belonging to the demons.

"Why the fuck do we have to go back out there?" One demon snarled.

"The Queen wants us to search the woods. She thinks there may be some more family members trying to protect the girl. She said if we find anyone we are to destroy them."

As soon as the demons were out of hearing range,

Ben shot him a look. "I told you they would not betray us."

He nodded. "I'm sorry. I just don't want anything to happen to her."

"I know." Ben's voice was husky. "Let's quit wasting time and go find my girl."

"No. Let's go find my wife." He met his father-in-law's gaze.

Ben nodded. "Let's go get your wife."

They hurried farther into the cave, keeping to the shadows and staying as quiet as possible. They didn't have to go far.

Donovan stood twenty feet ahead of them. Eric started forward, but Ben stopped him.

"We need to make sure no one is following him. Stay in the shadows."

☾

DONOVAN EASED HIS WAY TO where Celeste was being held. The second he stepped into the room of the cave, he knew *she* was behind him.

The Queen.

"What are you doing out?"

Her icy breath chilled his neck. The evil radiating off her was like a fucking category five hurricane.

Donovan gritted his teeth. Thank god he'd shifted before entering the room. Forcing a seductive smile onto his face, he turned. He knew the torch would illuminate his now ice-blue eyes and blond hair. He hoped the farce would work.

☾

ERIC'S MOUTH DROPPED OPEN. "THAT mother fucker. He shifted into me."

"Damn, that's good. Looks just like you too," Ben said.

He narrowed his eyes. Donovan better not pulled that shit with Celeste. If he had, he was going to have to kill him.

☾

"MY QUEEN. I WAS LOOKING for you." Donovan grinned.

Suspicion shone in the Queen's narrowed eyes. "I thought you would be looking for your wife."

"I can't seem to help myself. Your beauty has bewitched me." Donovan let his eyes drop to her mouth before dragging them back up to her green eyes. He hoped his interest seemed real enough. The longer he stood in her presence, the more he wanted to vomit.

Her lips curled up. "Come with me. Then we will see who you will choose." She led him deeper into the chamber.

The Queen disappeared. What was she up to now?

He looked around. His gaze landed on Celeste.

"Eric?"

His first impulse was to run to her. But he knew the Queen was watching his reaction. If he tried to intervene, she would kill Celeste.

The Queen materialized beside him. He forced his gaze from Celeste and turned to the Queen. He didn't miss the delighted look on the Queen's face.

He needed to distract her so Eric and Ben could

get into the chamber.

Donovan bent and kissed the Queen.

The kiss wasn't what he expected. Though she was beautiful, her skin was cold as ice. It was like kissing a corpse. He fought with himself not to pull away and retch.

Squinting, Donovan tried to imagine he was kissing Celeste. But all he kept visualizing in his mind was Aunt Agatha.

He thought back to the time he had spied on Celeste when she went skinny dipping.

He had stayed hidden behind a tree while she stripped down to nothing. She's dived in when she thought she was alone. Yet this time in his mind when she came up for air it wasn't Celeste's face he saw.

It was fat old Aunt Agatha.

The Queen broke the kiss and smirked at Celeste. "How ironic that you will meet your death on the fairy stone altar." She laughed. "Oh, I forgot, you just found out about being a fairy, so you wouldn't know what a fairy stone is."

Celeste's face paled.

"You see, the fairy stone was created after the fairies received news of the crucifixion of Christ. The tears they shed formed what is known as a fairy stone. That's why there is a cross in the center of it."

The Queen gritted her teeth. "Those fucking fairies never cried for me when I lost my sister. And I am their Queen."

"Yeah, well maybe if you weren't such a bitch, they would have cared," Celeste said.

"I will take your child and use him to bring my

sister back."

"You can't bring someone back from the dead." She cupped her hands around her stomach.

"It is only possible if you give a sacrifice of innocent blood from the right bloodline." The Queen grinned. "You and Eric have given me a gift no one else can. The right blood."

"No. You can't do that. I won't let you." Celeste's eyes shot to him.

Donovan fisted his hands. It was all he could do not to run to her.

The Queen looked at the demon. "I want that child now!"

The demon kept his attention on Celeste as he spoke. "Her contractions seem to be getting stronger. But labor can go on and on for hours before the child is delivered."

The Queen smiled. "Then cut it out."

The demon shrieked with delight.

Donovan's stomach clenched. Eric and Ben were close. All they needed was time.

The Queen looked up at him and clearly trying to gauge his reaction to her hideous request.

Never once did he flinch. Instead, he bent his head and kissed her again. He prayed that the footsteps he heard in the hallway belonged to Eric.

☾

CELESTE INHALED AND THEN COUGHED violently. Her throat burned with each breath.

She'd only lost consciousness for a few seconds. As much as she'd prayed for death, it hadn't come.

Lust pinned her hands under his knees. She bucked under his burdensome weight but didn't budge him.

Her gaze locked on the glint of a blade poised above her stomach.

He was going to kill her baby to raise the dead.

"No!" She screamed and struggled under the demon. "Eric, help me!"

Her senses were alive in that long moment. The shriek of the demon. The swish of the dagger as it cut through the air. The sickening sound as the dagger cut into her stomach.

The excruciating pain of the blade cutting her flesh was unbearable. The knife cut downward, slicing her stomach apart. She screamed.

Her muscle and tissues made a wet ripping sound. Her blood gurgled up, the sound mingling with her hoarse screams.

How could she be alive still?

Why hadn't she passed out?

Her pleas and screams went unanswered.

She managed to slip one hand free. Thrashing underneath the demon, she reached out for Eric.

But he didn't see her. He was kissing the Queen.

There was pressure and more pain as the demon pulled the baby from her womb.

Coldness seeped into her body. She strained to hear the cries of her baby. She heard nothing.

Everything was gone. Her baby. Her parents were probably dead too. And Eric, he was dead to her as well.

Nothing bound her to this earth anymore. There was no reason for her to stay.

"*You shall know the bite of betrayal and your heart will splinter within your very soul. There shall be no respite from your loneliness and no end to your heartache. You shall watch as your blood runs like a red stream until you sleep in the grave."*

She took one last shallow breath and finally let the darkness take her.

☾

ERIC TORE DOWN THE DIMLY lit passage and into the chamber at the sound of Celeste's horrific screams. The second he entered the chamber his heart stopped at the unbelievable bloody scene.

He bolted forward, vaguely aware of Donovan yelling at him to hurry.

☾

THE QUEEN PULLED AWAY THE second Eric entered the chamber. She scowled as she looked from him to Eric.

"What are you? You smell like Fae, but fairies can't shift."

"Fairies can't shift. But pixies can." Donovan shifted back into himself. He tightened his grip on the Queen.

She screamed and pushed Donovan away. She conjured up a knife in her hand. She stabbed at him, but Donovan blocked the lethal blow aimed for his heart. The knife sliced into his arm. He shoved her to the ground.

"Try again, bitch." He reached into the back of his jeans and pulled out a dagger.

He swiped at her, but she disappeared into thin air.

Donovan cradled his arm and glanced toward the entrance of the chamber while the sound of voices drew closer.

CHAPTER FORTY-THREE

ERIC REACHED CELESTE AND FELL to his knees. She lay on the stone altar, her young body flayed opened and bleeding like a sacrificial animal. Her beautiful green eyes stared lifelessly back at him. His whole reason for living had been snatched from him.

The demon straddling Celeste held their baby by its tiny feet and laughed victoriously.

The baby, like his mother, didn't move or whimper.

Eric knew that like his mother, their child was dead.

Anguish washed over him hard and quick, like an ocean wave. He had promised to protect his family.

Once again he had failed.

Echoes of Sarah and Ben's anguished cries seemed a thousand miles away. They had lost their only child and their only grandchild.

His fingers brushed the handle of the weapon at his side. He tightened his palm around the handle of the broadsword until it was an extension of his arm. Rage and grief filled him until he was trembling.

He got to his feet. He had but one purpose. To kill. To kill everyone who'd had a part in his wife's death.

An evil smile stretched across the demon's face. "You're too late, human. Your whore and your bastard are dead."

"Ben, what happens when you kill a demon?" He didn't take his gaze off the demon.

"They are locked in hell until the Last Judgment." Ben said.

Eric turned his attention to the demon. "Enjoy hell then."

A moment of surprise flickered across the demon's eyes before Eric lifted his sword. In one swift motion he swung and sliced across the demon's stomach. It took a couple of seconds for the demon's body to thunk to the floor in two separate pieces.

He dived and caught his lifeless baby before he could hit the ground. He nestled the child in his arms. His heart squeezed with a pain so sharp he thought it might stop beating.

He was beautiful. He had Celeste's mouth and nose, and he could still see a part of himself in his boy, too.

He swallowed back his grief as Sarah came up behind him. He turned and handed the baby to her.

He needed to see Celeste again. He needed to see his wife.

Kneeling beside her, he touched her face with his fingertips. He lifted her bloodied hand to his lips. He kissed each cool fingertip, grief and pain so acute he thought his heart would stop.

He wished it would. He had no reason to live anymore.

She was dead because of him.

She was dead because he hadn't protected her.

He didn't bother wiping the tears that slid down his face in a waterfall of grief. He didn't care. Everything that ever meant anything to him was gone.

Evil laughter echoed off the cave walls.

He looked up.

"Don't look so sad. I intend to kill you, as well. You can join your little bitch in death."The Queen smirked. A stream of demons poured in behind her, filling the cave.

A low, deep growl rolled out of his throat. He stood. "I intend to join her. But not before I kill you."

Ben moved to stand on his right side while Donovan flanked his left. "We're with you." Ben's voice was low.

Eric raised his broadsword and closed his eyes. Images of Celeste filled his head: her laughter, her smile, her face when they made love. He let all the memories wash over him until all he registered was rage at what would never be again. All he wanted was blood.

"Are you ready for hell?" He slowly turned back to the Queen and let his lips curl into a psychotic smile.

The Queen flinched. "Kill them all." She stepped back out of the line of attack.

He swung at everything in his path. He decapitated two demons and continued forward. Wielding his blade, he advanced to the next target, striking with deadly accuracy.

Shrieks and screams filled the cave, mingling with the sounds of clashing steel.

One thing he knew for sure: it would all be over very soon.

☾

SARAH SLUNK TO THE CORNER of the cave with the lifeless baby in her arms and tears streaming down her face. She wrapped the infant in her coat.

"Come on, sweetheart. Please breathe." She rubbed his chest with her hands.

She flicked the baby's tiny blue feet to get a response.

She turned him on his stomach and rubbed his back.

Clinging to a thin thread of hope, she bent down and covered his mouth with hers and gave him two quick breaths.

The baby's chest moved.

"Come on." She blew two more breaths.

A small wail escaped his lips. Her heart tripped in her chest as the small wail grew louder until it was a full cry.

The infant's color turned from blue to pink within seconds. Sarah nestled him close to her chest and sobbed.

If only Celeste could hear her child. If only Celeste were alive.

She swiped at her tears and looked around at the bloody battle around her.

It seemed every time one of the men killed a

demon, another one would appear to take its place.

She needed to get the baby far away from here before the Queen realized he was alive. Inching her way along the wall, she edged closer to the exit.

The Queen materialized in front of her, blocking her path. "Give me the child."

"No. I won't let you have him." She hugged the child to her chest and reached for the dagger at her waist with her free hand.

She felt nothing. She must have dropped her dagger when she took the baby from Eric.

The Queen narrowed her beautifully evil eyes. "I'll just kill you and take the child."

A knife materialized in the Queen's hand. Before she could run, the Queen threw the knife.

Sarah turned her body to shield the baby. Pain spiked in the middle of her back, stealing her breath. Numbness spread up her legs, and she crumbled to the floor. She tried to stand but her legs wouldn't obey.

She'd known immediately that when the knife hit had her it had severed her spinal cord. She had no control over her legs. Even her arms were growing numb.

She watched helplessly as the Queen plucked the crying baby out of her arms. "I'll kill you later, after you watch the rest of your family die."

The baby's cries went from a whimper to a high-pitched shrill.

Snarling, the Queen covered its mouth with her hand. The cry grew even louder. The Queen shoved him into the hands of the nearest demon.

The demon snarled and gave her a disgusted glare.

She glanced across the chamber at Ben. She opened her mouth to call out to him but caught herself. Any distraction from her might end his life. And she couldn't have that.

She had no more hope. Their last hope was the baby. Soon he too would be dead, like the rest of them.

Her head lolled against the wall. Her gaze moved to the table where Celeste lay. Her only child.

She wouldn't even be given a chance to grieve for her beautiful daughter who now looked like a scene out of a horror film.

A tiny light hovered above Celeste's body. It was bright white and continued to grow in size. The light drifted down and touched Celeste's chest. The light enveloped Celeste's body until she began to glow.

Blinded by the light, Sarah had to look away.

She glanced down. Tiny rocks on the cave floor began to bounce like jumping beans. The ground rumbled under her fingertips.

Was it an earthquake? Was it a cave-in? Was hell about to open up and swallow them all?

The light began to dim. She cautiously turned her gaze back to the stone.

Standing on the altar, dressed in shimmering white and holding a sword, was Celeste.

CHAPTER FORTY-FOUR

THE MOURNFUL CRIES OF HER baby struck Celeste's heart like a blade. It had been those very cries that had called to her from the other side. It was those cries that had brought her back from death.

The moment the Queen had touched her child, her baby called out to her. Despite death, the bond between mother and child could not be severed.

She stood on the altar where she'd been slaughtered. Her blood rushed through her veins in a thrum of power and unimaginable strength.

She scanned the battle inside the cave. Her gaze settled on the demon standing in the back holding her child. Her hand tightened on the sword. She ached to kill all those who stood between her and her baby.

Anger burned through her like wildfire.

"I. Want. My. Baby."

ERIC HEARD HIS WIFE'S VOICE and figured he must be dead.

Maybe he'd been killed so quickly his body hadn't even registered the pain.

He looked around. He was still standing in that hell hole of a cave, so he couldn't possibly be dead yet.

The cave grew eerily quiet. Everyone including the demons had stopped fighting. They were all looking at something behind him. He followed their gaze.

Celeste stood on the altar wearing all white. She wore what appeared to be a white leather breastplate that ended just below her breasts, a white skirt that ended a few inches above her knees, and white boots. He revealing outfit showed off her beautiful skin. She didn't even bear a scar showing where she had been so viciously cut open.

She was absolutely perfect.

And she was absolutely alive.

"Celeste," he called out, but she didn't acknowledge him. All her attention was trained on the back of the cave. Following her gaze, he saw his child screaming wildly as a demon held him. It took a second for his brain to register that both Celeste and his baby were alive.

"Give me my child, and I will kill you all quickly." Celeste's voice echoed in the cave.

"Don't you mean 'give me my child and I won't kill you'?" The Queen smirked.

"No. You are all going to die regardless. You can either die quickly or slowly. Your choice." Her eyes sparkled with anger.

"Yeah? You and what army?"

"This army."

Eric turned.

Aunt Agatha and her followers poured into the cave along with Solomon and a very large black wolf. The fairies were carrying the weapons from his house.

"Sorry we took so long. I tried to communicate with Donovan mentally, but I couldn't seem to get through. Apparently he had his mind on other things." Aunt Agatha cast a glance at Donovan. "Seriously, Donovan? Skinny dipping?"

Donovan looked both horrified and nauseated at the same time.

He turned his attention back to Celeste.

Her gaze never faltered as she glared at the Queen, the intensity of her anger burning from her emerald green eyes.

"Kill that bitch," the Queen ordered.

"No!" Eric shoved his way through the throng of fairies and demons fighting. His heart raced with fear. He needed to reach Celeste before it was too late.

He wouldn't fail her again.

Celeste jumped off the altar into a backflip and landed on her feet. She brandished the sword like an expert, slicing through the first two demons that approached her. Their heads rolled on the floor like a couple of bowling balls.

She immersed herself in the fight, leaving smoldering demons in her wake. Gone was any gentleness or uncertainty.

It was as if she had been fighting all her life. She was a demon-killing machine.

"Duck!" Ben yelled.

He obeyed and crouched. His neck barely missed the swipe of a demon's scythe.

Eric turned, met the demon's gaze, and shoved his sword into the demon's stomach. His body immediately turned to smoking ash.

His gaze searched the cave and he realized there were now more fairies than demons. The tide was turning in their favor.

They could win this.

ONLY A FEW MORE DEMONS stood between her and her child.

Celeste hurried forward. She stopped when movement caught the corner of her eye.

Her mother lay crumpled in a heap against the wall. Her breathing was erratic and her lips pale.

Celeste lifted her palm toward her. The energy shot from her body into her mother.

"Walk." She spoke softly.

Her mother blinked and stood. Her body healed.

"Celeste?" Her mother blinked.

She didn't have time to talk. She needed to reach her baby.

She cut through five more demons standing between her and her child and advanced forward.

She stood a few feet away from the demon holding her child. Every molecule in her body screamed out in rage at the audacity of something so vile daring to touch what was hers.

Never again.

She raised her sword and pointed it at his neck. Before he could turn, she tossed the sword through the air like a spear. It entered his throat and exited out the back of his neck, effectively separating the body from the head. She caught her child with one hand while the demon's body fell to the ground. She gathered her sword looked down into the face of her son.

He stopped crying.

He stared back at her with those familiar blue eyes and a slight smile playing upon his tiny lips. He was the most beautiful thing she'd ever seen.

"I will have that bastard's blood." The Queen's icy breath hit her neck.

She shielded her child with her body and tightened her grip on her sword.

Sensing the knife near her neck, Celeste ducked. The knife sliced through empty air.

Turning, she brought her sword up and back and plunged it into the Queen's chest.

The Queen screamed.

"You don't touch what is mine." Celeste hissed as she twisted the sword in the Queen's chest.

The Queen screamed, almost rattling the cave walls.

Everyone stopped fighting and covered their ears.

All except Eric.

He pushed everyone aside, grabbed the Queen's hair, and jerked her neck back. "I hope you rot in hell for all eternity." Eric raised his knife and slit her throat, decapitating her. Black blood poured out like a fountain.

Celeste stuck her booted foot on the Queen's chest and pushed her off her sword.

The Queen slid to the ground in a heap. Demons, realizing their leader was dead, vanished, leaving only the Fae.

☾

ERIC'S HEART STUTTERED IN HIS chest. He hardly believed what he was seeing. He couldn't take his eyes off Celeste as she cradled their son in her arms.

Their son. Just the sound of that made his heart sing.

He needed to touch her to make sure she was real and that this wasn't a dream.

"Celeste."

She glanced up.

"Stop." A booming voice shook the cave. Everyone fell to their knees and cast their eyes to the floor.

Unable to control himself, Eric fell to his knees. He didn't want to kneel, yet his body wasn't listening to him. It was like he was being pushed down.

A man stood on the altar where Celeste had died. He was easily seven feet tall and bigger than any human Eric had ever seen. He was dressed in white and had enormous wings spanning all the way to the floor. His hair was jet black and he had a sword similar to Celeste's strapped to his side.

He knew this was no man but an angel.

"You must not touch Celeste. She carries the presence of heaven." Every time the angel spoke, the cave trembled.

Eric noticed no one except him dared to look at the angel. In fact, they all looked terrified.

"Stand." The angel commanded.

Once again, everyone obeyed and got to their feet.

"Celeste, come forward."

She fearlessly walked up to him. She stopped only inches from him and smiled.

"Thank you, Michael." She handed him the sword and wrapped both arms around their child.

Michael? Michael the Archangel?

"Try to stay out of trouble." Michael tilted his head and gave her a stern look. Celeste grinned.

"What will the child be called?" Michael's voice grew louder.

"I haven't decided."

Michael looked directly at him. "Father of the child, come forward.

He stepped closer and held Michael's gaze.

"You are the one called Eric, are you not?" Michael frowned.

"That's right. I'm Celeste's husband." He needed to make sure Mr. Butterfly Wings knew who the fuck he was. Wasn't there some law in the Bible against coveting someone's wife?

Michael narrowed his blazing eyes.

Had the angel read his thoughts?

"How about Eric Christian?" Celeste spoke up.

His gaze drifted to her and his heart caught in his chest.

Michael nodded. "A fitting name for a warrior."

He looked at Michael. "You said I must not touch her. Why?"

"Celeste has been in heaven, and anything earthly that touches her will cause her great pain."

"But Christian has been in heaven too." He stared at his baby.

Michael nodded. "Yes, but that was before he was born. You can touch the child."

He fisted his hands. He wanted to hold Celeste

so bad he couldn't breathe.

"Don't worry. You can touch her after a few days." Michael stated.

He glared at Michael. Okay, maybe the angel was reading his mind.

Michael turned to the crowd of fairies. "Today you have fought well. Good conquered evil in this battle."

Victory cries and shouts reverberated throughout the cave. Light sparkled around Michael, and then a loud boom shook the cave.

As suddenly as he'd appeared, Michael was gone.

Eric turned to speak to Celeste but she was already making her way toward the exit of the cave.

CHAPTER FORTY-FIVE

CELESTE KEPT HER EYES ON her baby as she walked toward the exit of the cave. She didn't want to talk to anyone.

She didn't even want to be around anyone.

Glancing up, she spotted Donovan holding his bloodied arm. Frowning, she held her palm up in his direction. Immediately he was healed.

As soon as everyone realized she could heal, they began pushing the wounded closer to her. One by one, she healed them until there were no more wounded.

She knew that Eric was following close behind. She could feel him, sense him, and smell him. She couldn't bring herself to look at him.

He'd betrayed her with another woman and left her to die. Not just any woman, but the Queen who'd wanted to kill their child.

That was one thing she couldn't forgive.

Everything he'd ever told her was a lie.

She smiled down at her baby. Despite her breaking heart, a surge of unconditional love swept through her for her child. She was shocked at how much she loved a baby she'd just met.

The mouth of the cave exited into the woods. She sighed. Only a few more feet and she would be home. She was dirty and exhausted and needed solitude.

"I'll get the door." Eric spoke behind her.

She braced herself as Eric turned the knob and pushed the door open.

It was the first time he had spoken to her, further evidence of his infidelity. Perhaps he was ashamed of what he had done or maybe he was just distancing himself from her.

Any words he spoke to her were all lies. Now that the baby was here, he didn't need her anymore. He could carry on with previous life.

Indescribable pain squeezed her heart.

Without looking back, she walked up the stairs to her bedroom.

Everything looked different now as she gazed around her bedroom. Instead of peace and contentment and love, it carried a sense of sadness and broken promises and lies.

She froze.

Making a half-turn, she stared at her reflection in the full-length mirror. Her white clothes were smeared in black demon blood. Her face was splattered where she had struck down several demons that had stood in her way. Her matted hair looked like she had shampooed it with mud.

She looked at Christian. "And here I thought you were the one who needed to be cleaned up."

"I'll take care of the baby so you can get a shower." Eric said behind her.

She turned.

He stood in the doorway, staring at her strangely. She really couldn't blame him. How attractive could a woman be who was covered in demon blood?

Not that it mattered now.

"No, I need to clean Christian up first."

"Why don't I clean him up while you and Eric go shower?" Her mother walked up to Celeste and held out her hands.

She hesitated.

"I'll take good care of him, Celeste."

"I know you will." She carefully placed the baby in her mother's arms without letting her skin make contact.

Her mother talked to the baby as she walked out the door.

"I turned the shower on, so the water should be hot." Eric said.

For the first time since she'd been killed, she turned and looked at him. He was as bloody if not bloodier than she. A deep wound ran down his shoulder. She held up her hand to heal him.

He shook his head. "If it makes you weak, don't heal me."

"You're hurt badly."

"It will heal on its own. You've healed enough people tonight."

"What difference will one more make?" She head up her hand and power shot out into his wound. He gritted his teeth as the flesh knit back together.

"Thank you." He glanced down at his shoulder and then back at her.

"Why don't you shower first? You've not had a

chance to hold your son yet." She averted her eyes.

"Why don't we both get in the shower?"

Her head snapped up.

"There are four shower heads and enough room for both of us."

The quicker she showered, the quicker she could get back to her baby.

"I promise not to touch you."

Her heart cinched.

Yes, one thing was for sure. Eric Nordstrom would never touch her again.

ERIC STRIPPED OFF HIS CLOTHES and stepped in the shower first. He wasn't sure if Celeste was being emotionally distant because of coming back from the dead or if she was still in pain.

He stepped into the far side of the shower and turned his back.

The splatters of water tensed every muscle in his body. He wanted to turn around and hold her. But he remembered the angel's warning.

He gritted his teeth and restrained himself.

"Are you hurting?" He glanced over his shoulder.

She looked up, her eyes lingering at his back before speaking. "No." She looked down at her stomach.

He turned. His breath caught in his throat.

Her body was unmarked and unscarred from the attack. In fact, she looked as if she had never been pregnant at all. The only difference was in her breasts. They were noticeably fuller.

His hardened cock twitched. For the life of him, he couldn't stop staring at her breasts.

"You look amazing."

She burned him with a glare and turned her back.

☾

SHE LINGERED IN THE SHOWER after Eric got out. When she couldn't hear him in the bathroom, she stepped out and slipped on her robe. After brushing her teeth and quickly drying her hair, she walked back into the bedroom.

He held Christian in his arms and smiled. Her heart broke at the tender sight.

Her mother smiled. "I've bathed him and put his night clothes on. He's already had a wet diaper."

"Thank you."

"I'm going to check on Ben and Donovan. I'll come back and show you how to breastfeed him if you still want to try. Or we can give him a bottle tonight if you're too tired."

"No. I want to try."

She walked to the armoire and pulled out some silk pajamas. As she finished buttoning her top, Christian let out a pitiful wail.

"I think he's hungry." Eric rocked him in his arms.

She glanced at the empty doorway, wondering how much longer her mom was going to be.

"Here, why don't you sit in the chair and I'll hand him to you so you can nurse him." Christian's cries grew more insistent.

She eased into the chair. Eric placed Christian in her arms, careful not to touch her.

"What's wrong?" He knelt beside the chair.

"I'm not sure how to do this."

"Well, you might want to unbutton your shirt first."

Right. That would be a good start.

She cradled Christian in one arm while managing to unbutton her shirt with her hand. The baby turned his tiny head and began to root at her chest. When he latched on to her nipple, she gasped.

"You okay?"

"Yeah. I'm just a little sore, and he's quite aggressive."

She gazed at her son while he nursed. His small hand curled into a fist and kneaded against her breast. His wide eyes stared up at her as he grunted.

"He's so alert. His eyes are open and everything." Eric's voice held a sense of wonder.

"Babies are usually born with their eyes open. They're not like puppies."

He chuckled. "I've never been around babies before."

Her heart tugged. She'd been an only child too, but at least she had grown up with Donovan. Eric didn't have anyone.

She pushed away lingering guilt at Eric's past and focused on the future. It still didn't change the fact that he'd betrayed her.

Eric held out his hand. The baby's fingers curled around his long finger. Eric's face lit up. She was glad at how much Eric cared for his son. Even if they didn't stay together, at least the baby would always have a father who loved him.

"He has my eyes," he whispered.

"Yes, he does." She smiled at Christian sleeping

at her breast. She put him to her shoulder and patted his back.

"Has he eaten already?" Her mother slipped quietly into the room.

"He didn't want to wait." She looked at her mother.

"Did you have any problems?"

"Celeste was wonderful. She knew exactly what to do." Eric offered.

She shook her head. "I think the baby knew more about what to do than me."

Her mother chuckled. "Babies have a wonderful instinct. It's one of those mysteries of the universe."

"How is Dad? I didn't see him when we were walking back to the house."

"He's fine. He and Donovan are having a drink downstairs. Hope you don't mind, Eric. They dipped into your liquor cabinet."

"Not at all. Tonight seems to be a night of celebration for more than one reason." His gaze was locked on her. She looked away.

"Do you want me to put the baby in the nursery? Or would you rather bring the bassinet in here for tonight? That way you could get a little more sleep and have him at your side the entire night."

"I'd rather him be with me." She kissed the top of Christian's head and inhaled his sweet scent.

"I'll set it up while you both get ready for bed."

After checking on Christian in the bassinet, she climbed into bed and fell asleep.

❧

CELESTE'S EYELIDS FLEW OPEN AT the hungry cries of a baby.

Her baby.

It was still dark when she pulled Christian out of the bassinet and nuzzled his neck before sitting. While he nursed, she explored his tiny toes and fingers, counting to make sure he had the right number.

Guilt pooled in her stomach. That was something mothers did right after their babies were born, not six hours later.

Then again, most mothers hadn't died and been raised from the dead. And most mothers hadn't battled an army of demons to get their children back.

Once she had fed and changed him, she glanced at the clock.

Five a.m.

"Just a few more hours." She crawled back into bed and snuggled under the covers.

"SHOULD I BE WORRIED THAT Celeste is missing Christmas?" Eric scrubbed his fingers through his hair and stared at his mother-in-law.

"I think we need to let her rest. You know how exhausted Celeste is after healing just one person. Last night she had to heal at least thirty people." Sarah handed him a cup of coffee.

"Not to mention she had to come back from the dead," Donovan added.

It didn't feel right for Celeste to be missing the one holiday she'd been so excited about. Especially now, since they should be celebrating with their child.

"I think we should just postpone celebrating Christmas until she can be here."

"I think that's a wonderful idea." Sarah hugged him. "Just give her time to recover, and she'll be back to normal. You'll see."

He certainly hoped so.

CHAPTER FORTY-SIX

CELESTE STRUGGLED TO OPEN HER eyes. She reached her arms over her head and stretched. Her whole body ached like never before. She flung off the covers and went to the bassinet.

Blinking up at her were a pair of bright blue eyes in the prettiest face she'd ever seen. A surge of love shot through her heart as she picked up her baby.

She settled into the chair just as he started to fuss. Quickly unbuttoning her top, she put the hungry baby to her breast. As she fed him, she was amazed by how much she loved this little person already.

Christian would be her life now. He was all she needed.

"How are you feeling?" Eric walked through the doorway, his face set in a grim line.

"Fine." She brushed away the escaped tear.

"You're crying."

"I'm just amazed at how quickly you can fall in love with someone you just met." She brushed a finger gently down the baby's cheek. Christian made tiny grunting noises as he nursed.

"That's exactly what I thought."

She lifted her eyes. Her heart broke a little more every time she looked at him. She was glad he loved their baby, but she also knew he didn't love her. He had proved that.

That was not a life she could live anymore.

She needed more.

And this time, she wasn't backing down until she got it.

☾

WHILE CELESTE CONTEMPLATED HER FUTURE, her family contemplated her eating habits. Her appetite hadn't returned, and she only nibbled at the food Mrs. Gambil brought up to her room.

Her parents tried to coax her to eat more, but it only irritated her. Eric brought her oatmeal cookies to tempt her, but even that didn't seem to work. She told everyone that she would eat when she got hungry. And she would.

Since the baby was getting plenty of milk, they didn't push the subject.

A week passed and she hadn't left the bedroom. She kept the curtains closed and had no desire to see anyone. She told everyone she needed time to heal.

She could see the worried look in her parents' eyes. Even Eric hadn't gone back to work. She was too tired to care or to try to make them understand she had no desire to eat. Despite her emotional battle raging inside her, she constantly cared for her child, waking up to feed, bathe, and hold him.

She was doing fine. She just wished everyone else could see that.

"I'M WORRIED ABOUT CELESTE." ERIC cornered Sarah in the kitchen as she was fixing a sandwich for Ben. "She's still not eating much and she hasn't left the bedroom since the baby was born. Do you think we need to call her Dr. Sevalus?"

"And tell him what? That Celeste was captured by a demon, the baby was cut from her body, and she died for about twenty minutes— then she was miraculously resurrected?" Donovan bit into a fresh-baked oatmeal cookie.

Eric gave him the finger.

"Donovan is right. We can't tell the doctor anything about this. He is still wondering why we didn't call him when Celeste went into labor. And he's upset that we didn't call him until a couple of days later. When he saw Celeste, he said he had never seen a woman get her figure back so fast."

"Do you know how long it will be until I can touch her? I feel like I'm walking on eggshells, trying not to even bump against her. Hell, I can't even sleep in the same bed with her." He ran his hand through his hair. "Tell me what I need to do to help her."

"I'm not sure myself. I've never seen anyone come back from the dead."

"But the baby came back too, and he's doesn't feel pain when you touch him." He fired back.

"I know, but it's different. He was born without breathing. Celeste, on the other hand, left this world for heaven and then was brought back. You've got to understand that heaven is perfect and there is no pain. And she was brought back into this world, where pain and sorrow run rampant. Her body has to make the adjustment."

"Do you think she regrets coming back?" He held his breath.

Sarah shook her head. "No. If she regretted coming back, she wouldn't care about anything, and you see how she is with Christian. She is a great mother. I think she just needs a little more time." Sarah squeezed his arm and gave him a smile.

It did nothing to reassure him.

If not touching Celeste when they'd first gotten married had been difficult, he was officially in hell now.

Every time she walked into the bedroom from the nursery, he had to fight every instinct not to take her in his arms and kiss her senseless. She made him insane with lust. But that was nothing to what he experienced at night.

When he slept, which wasn't for very long since he had taken to the couch in their bedroom, he would have the most sensual dreams about Celeste. And when he woke up, he would have to take a cold shower to relieve some of the ache from his body.

He reminded himself that she just had their son. It was perfectly normal for women to have to wait six to eight weeks before they could have sex again.

But most men didn't have a fairy wife who was sexy as hell.

A WEEK PASSED, AND CELESTE NOTICED Eric acting strange. Every time she got up to do something like change a diaper, he was right there, standing over her shoulder. And every time she got up to feed the baby at night, he got up as well.

It was as if he didn't trust her with her own son. Her suspicions were further aroused when she walked in the nursery and found him in deep conversation with her mother. They immediately stopped talking when they saw her.

Though he monitored her every move, he went out of his way not to touch her. He even slept on the couch now instead of in their bed.

Maybe that's how life's going to be from now on.

He would carry on his life as he had before he met her, and she would quietly stay out of his way until he needed his wife to make an appearance at a dinner meeting.

She shivered and wrapped her arms around herself. She glanced around her elaborately decorated bedroom, noticing for the first time how close the walls seemed to be getting. She felt smothered.

She needed to get away and think without Eric hovering over her.

She grabbed the phone and called the only person who might understand.

☾

ANDREA LEIGH PICKED HER AND Christian up that very afternoon. Through a river of tears, she told her friend about seeing Eric kiss another woman. She left out the part about dying and coming back to life.

Celeste didn't think Andrea Leigh was ready for that part.

Andrea Leigh managed to convince Sarah to let Celeste ride with her up to Boston for a couple of nights so she could get fitted for her wedding dress. Sloan had to work, so Celeste and the baby could keep her company.

Celeste said that Eric knew and that they would be back in a few days.

She lied.

She had to.

She knew there was no way Eric was going to let her take the baby, especially with the way he watched over everything she did.

Within the hour, the group was on the highway and headed for Boston.

"So is this Sloan's house?" Celeste stepped through the door of the beach house with the baby carrier on one arm and an overnight bag on the other. She glanced around at the hardwood floors and cozy beach décor.

"Nope. It's mine." Andrea Leigh smiled.

She arched an eyebrow.

"Don't look so surprised. I bought it not long after I moved up north with Sloan. I was missing the beaches around Charleston. I came into some money after my grandmother died, so I made an investment." Andrea Leigh shrugged.

"Wow." It would be nice to have some assets of her own.

"Go on upstairs and get the baby settled in while I grab the bags out of the car."

"Thanks."

She chose the smaller of the bedrooms and settled down to feed Christian. She wasn't sure how long she'd been in the room when Andrea Leigh knocked.

"I'll be right down." She put Christian in the bassinet.

After changing into her pajamas, she padded downstairs into the living room.

She was a little surprised to see multiple boxes of Chinese takeout set up on the coffee table.

"I grabbed some food while you were busy with the baby."

"It smells good." For the first time in weeks, she was hungry.

"Good. Sit down and eat. You're getting too thin. It's hard to believe you gave birth a few weeks ago. Look at you. You truly need to gain weight, not lose any. If you were not my friend, I would so hate you right now." Andrea Leigh passed her a plate laden with fried rice, sweet and sour chicken, and wontons.

"I've not had much of an appetite lately." She popped a piece of chicken in her mouth, savoring the taste.

"Because of Eric?"

She nodded.

And just like that, her appetite was gone.

Thinking of Eric hurt her stomach. She tucked her feet underneath her and absently moved the food around on her plate with her fork.

"Thank you for doing this."

"For what? For being your friend?" Andrea Leigh raised an eyebrow.

"Yeah. I know I'm taking you away from Sloan and all your responsibilities at home. There must be a million things you still need to be doing with the upcoming wedding."

"Thankfully, my wedding planner has taken care of everything. There's nothing else I need to be doing. Besides, I didn't exactly lie to your mom. I really needed to come to Boston for my fitting. And as far as Sloan is concerned, being apart will do him good. What is that saying? Absence makes the heart grow fonder?"

Jealous and self-pity sucker-punched her right in the gut. Maybe she just wasn't meant to have that kind of love.

"Oh, Celeste. I'm so sorry. I wasn't thinking." Andrea Leigh looked pained.

"Don't you dare apologize for having someone who loves you like Sloan. You deserve every happiness in the world."

She nibbled on a wonton and hoped Andrea Leigh would change the subject.

"You know, when you told me about Eric, I couldn't believe it. I mean, I've seen the way he looks at you, and as long as I've known him, he's never looked at a woman the way he looks at you."

Celeste sighed and put her plate down. "Andrea Leigh, Eric married me because I was pregnant, not because he loved me. We spent only one night together, and I found out shortly after that I was pregnant."

There it was—the truth, hanging in the air. She should have just stopped with that, but for some reason, she caught a case of diarrhea of the mouth.

"When we came to Vermont, I thought maybe at least we could be friends. And as the months went by, I begin to fall in love with him. He was caring and kind. And then one day he told me he loved me. And I believed him. Until I saw him with that other woman."

Andrea Leigh looked at her and frowned. "Are you sure it was him?"

She narrowed her eyes.

"Okay. Okay. Well, was he drunk?"

"I know what I saw. Stop making excuses for him."

Andrea Leigh put down her plate and wrapped her arms around Celeste. "Sorry, sweetie. You know I'm totally on your side, right? I could just kill him for what he did."

"Thanks." She pulled back and looked at her friend. "Andrea Leigh?"

"Yeah?"

"What did you do when your ex-boyfriend cheated on you?" Andrea Leigh had told her once over the phone that she had been cheated on by an old boyfriend. She'd even gone into detail about how she'd found out. But what Celeste needed to know was how to get over it.

"I was furious. I got a can of red spray paint and painted 'I am a cheating bastard' on the side of his white BMW. Asshole called the cops on me." Andrea Leigh pouted.

"Did you get arrested?"

"Yep. But there's an upside."

"What's that?" She couldn't imagine anything good coming out of that situation.

"The cop's girlfriend and the woman my boyfriend was sleeping with were one and the same."

Celeste's mouth dropped opened.

"The cop asked me out, and we ended up getting it on at his apartment." She raised her eyebrows suggestively and then grinned. "His ex-girlfriend caught us."

For the first time in a long time, Celeste laughed.

CHAPTER FORTY-SEVEN

WHEN ERIC FIRST DISCOVERED CELESTE had left, he had been out of his mind with worry. His fear quickly turned to anger when Sarah told him she'd left with Andrea Leigh. She'd said that she'd thought he knew about the trip.

He tried reaching Celeste by phone, but it kept going to voicemail. He later found her phone upstairs in the bedroom, a clear indication that she didn't want to be found. After getting the address from Sloan, he had jumped in his car and driven like a bat out of hell.

She had another thing coming if she thought she could leave and take his son away from him.

He'd reached Boston after midnight. Finding the beach house hadn't been too difficult. As he sat in front of the darkened house, he contemplated his next move. If he rang the doorbell at this hour, it would wake the baby.

He started the car. He'd have to wait until morning.

IT WAS STILL DARK WHEN Celeste peeked in the bassinette. Christian was sleeping hard. His little fist tucked under his chin made him look like the sculpture of *The Thinker*, only cuter.

She pulled on some thick socks and headed to the kitchen. She made a pot of coffee and grabbed a quilt. She opened the back door to the porch and settled into a weathered white wicker rocker.

The cold wind bit into her skin, and she hugged the quilt around her body.

Despite the winter wind, she had never seen a more beautiful scene. The sun crept just above the ocean and she could taste the salty sea on the breeze.

She'd slept without dreaming and for the first time in weeks, she'd awakened refreshed. She let her thoughts wash over her like the waves lapping over the sand.

She didn't want to be trapped in a loveless marriage with a man who didn't care whether she lived or died. She had believed Eric when he told her he loved her.

She had been living a lie.

She refused to live it any longer.

One thing was for certain. She couldn't stay with Eric.

She would move to the city and find a job and raise Christian on her own. Eric would have visiting rights, of course. She would never try to keep him from seeing his own son.

She'd stuck to their agreement, and now it was time for him to honor his side of the bargain.

She knew he had an opening in a division of Cryptic in Burlington. She already had experience working at the one based in Atlanta, and maybe he would be generous enough to give her a job at the Burlington location. If he refused, she would just look for something else. Finding a job shouldn't be too difficult for her, not with her experience.

Celeste would give herself a day to think about how she'd tell Eric and then call him tomorrow with her decision.

ERIC HADN'T BEEN ABLE TO fall asleep. His thoughts kept coming back to why Celeste had left him. Could she not forgive him for not saving her in time?

He sighed and finally gave up on the hope of getting any sleep. He rolled out of bed and headed for the shower. It was still too early for Celeste to be up, but he wanted to be sure he wouldn't miss her if she left the house.

Less than an hour later, he pulled up outside of Andrea Leigh's house and cut the lights. He settled in to wait for the first indication of someone moving around in the house.

Cold air seeped into the interior of the vehicle quickly. He bundled himself more tightly in his coat, regretting the decision to turn the car off. If he turned the car back on, it might wake her and she might refuse to come to the door. What he wanted was the element of surprise in order to get some honest answers.

The house sat off to itself on a couple of acres. It was a charming cedar-shingle cottage with gas lanterns hanging on either side of the door. Though it was small, it looked inviting and cozy, especially on this winter morning.

He glanced across the street as a neighbor walking his dog urged the tiny poodle to hurry and do its business. The man, dressed in his robe, hopped from one foot to the other, attempting to stay warm as the dog sniffed every blade of grass before finding the right place to squat.

He turned his attention back to the house. A light was on. Someone was up. Wasting no time, he hurried to the front door and knocked.

He waited only a few seconds before the door swung open.

"What are you doing here?" She looked shocked to see him. That stung and pissed him off at the same time.

"Aren't you going to invite me in?"

She moved to the side, allowing him to enter.

He glanced down at her bare feet and frowned. "You're going to catch a cold."

"Then I'll heal myself." She muttered.

"Right, I forgot. You are invincible."

"I didn't heal myself from death." She glared at him.

"But you . . ."

"Are you crazy? It's not even seven o'clock. Eric, when did you get here?" Andrea Leigh looked between them. She wore a brightly colored robe and rubbed her eyes with the back of her hands.

"I've come to see my son. I've been waiting for two hours in my car."

"Why didn't you just knock?" Andrea Leigh offered.

"I didn't want to wake the baby."

"He's in Celeste's room upstairs. You can't hear anything up there." Andrea Leigh yawned.

Before he could say anything, the baby let out a cry.

He and Celeste moved toward the stairs, then they both stopped. He waved his hand for her to go first. He followed behind her up the stairs and into a bedroom, where she picked up Christian and grabbed a diaper.

"I'll take him." He held out his hands.

She narrowed her eyes at him and cuddled the baby against her chest.

"I'll change him before you nurse him." She seemed to be afraid of him. Didn't she know he would never hurt her or their son?

She handed Christian to him and watched as he changed his diaper.

"Hey, buddy. Did you sleep well last night?" He removed the old diaper and wrapped him in a clean one. Once the baby was changed, Eric snapped the onesie back into place and picked him up.

"Are you ready?"

"Yes." She took Christian to the rocking chair by the bed. She looked self-conscious as she unbuttoned her top and pushed it to the side and put the baby to her breast.

☾

WHILE SHE NURSED, SHE FELT Eric's eyes on her. Her skin grew hot, and she knew she was blushing. She took a deep breath and cleared her throat. Maybe conversation might make things a little less tense between them.

"You got here this morning?" She kept her attention on Christian.

"No. Last night."

She jerked her head up.

"It was late, so I stayed at a hotel." He crossed his arms. "Your mother was under the impression that I knew you were leaving."

She stroked Christian's cheek. "I needed some time away from everything."

"It seems like you are always running, Celeste. Tell me, what are you running away from this time? Is it me?"

Spots flashed before her eyes, stinging. She knew if she said something, she would start crying. So she stayed silent.

"I'll take that as a yes."

She finished nursing Christian and placed him on her shoulder, patting him gently on his back.

"He's almost asleep. Do you want to rock him?"

"Yes." He gently took the baby and held him close, kissing the top of his head.

Celeste grabbed the quilt and headed out the back to sit on the porch without saying a word.

As much as she loved Andrea Leigh, she didn't feel like answering questions.

ERIC WALKED INTO THE KITCHEN and frowned. "Where is she?"

"Coffee?" Andrea Leigh waved him toward the coffee pot.

He scowled as he poured himself a cup and looked out the window. Andrea Leigh's car was still in the driveway, which meant Celeste hadn't left.

"She is sitting out on the porch."

He headed in that direction.

"If it doesn't involve an apology, I wouldn't bother going out there." Andrea Leigh lifted an eyebrow at him.

"What are you talking about?"

"You've got some nerve, busting in, demanding to see your son. After what you did." Andrea Leigh hissed.

He glared. "She can't keep me from seeing my own son."

"Keep your voice down. I won't have you upsetting her again."

"What are you talking about?"

"Look, she told me, so don't act innocent with me."

"Told you what?" He cocked his head. Surely Celeste hadn't told Andrea Leigh about the demons and the fairies and coming back from the dead.

"She told me she saw you sticking your tongue down some slut's throat while she was in labor. How could you do that? It's bad enough that you were unfaithful, but to do that deliberately in front of her face." Andrea Leigh shoved away from the table and turned to leave.

He grabbed her arm. "Wait. Andrea Leigh, wait."

She whirled around on her heel.

"She thinks she saw me kissing someone?" So she hadn't left him because he'd failed her? And why in the hell did she think he'd been unfaithful?

"Don't pretend you didn't do anything. And if you think I'm going to let you drag Celeste and that baby out of here, you've got another thing coming." Andrea Leigh poked her bony finger in his chest.

He frowned, trying to contemplate what she was saying.

"Why would she think she saw me doing something like that?"

It dawned on him. That night in the cave, Donovan had shifted into him to distract the Queen. It was Donovan she saw kissing the Queen.

"Celeste left because she thought I was unfaithful?"

"Of course. Why else would she leave?" Andrea Leigh looked at him suspiciously. "Is there something else I need to know about?"

"Of course not."

"Because sometimes I get the feeling you two are keeping me out of the loop. And you know I don't like to be out of the loop."

He snorted. "I know." His shook his head. "I thought Celeste left because she didn't . . ."

"Didn't love you?" Andrea Leigh rolled her eyes. "Right. That girl is so in love it's crazy."

A boulder lifted off his heart. There was hope. There was a future for them.

"I need to talk to Celeste." He walked toward the porch before Andrea Leigh could stop him. Pushing open the French door, he walked out into the cold air.

She stood, her quilt hanging loosely around her shoulders. Drawing the quilt closer, she lifted her chin. She looked ready for a fight.

"I think there are some things we need to talk about."

She nodded.

"Why don't we talk over dinner tonight? Andrea

Leigh can watch Christian. I'll pick you up." He said.

"No. I'll meet you there." She met his gaze.

He bit his tongue. He wasn't going to argue over something so insignificant when they had bigger issues to focus on. "Okay. I'll call you with the time and place."

"That will be fine." She pulled the quilt around her like a shield. He knew he couldn't push her again, or she would run away without hearing the truth.

"I'll check on Christian before I leave. I'll see you tonight." He turned and walked back into the house.

CHAPTER FORTY-EIGHT

CELESTE HAD NOTHING TO WEAR to the upscale restaurant to meet Eric. Thank God for Andrea Leigh. She knew just the place to go shopping. By the time they were finished she had bought a very expensive red dress with matching heels. All paid for by Eric's credit card, of course.

She had insisted on taking a cab instead of Andrea Leigh's car. She explained to Andrea Leigh that she felt better leaving Christian if they had the car with them just in case anything happened.

She stood on the sidewalk. Cold wind stung her skin and lungs as the cab pulled away. She couldn't back out now.

There was no running this time.

Taking a deep breath of the biting winter air, she opened the door.

She spotted Eric as the hostess led her to her seat. Her stomach dropped to the floor. He was not alone.

Leslie Andrews leaned in and pushed a drink in front of him. She smiled and touched his arm in an intimate display of affection.

She gritted her teeth until she was sure they were going to break. They weren't even trying to hide their affair. Is this why Eric had invited her to dinner? To rub Leslie in her face?

Well, two could play at that game.

☾

ERIC HAD NEVER BEEN MORE irritated by one person than he was right now. No sooner had he arrived at the lavish restaurant than he spotted Leslie heading straight for him. How in the hell had Leslie Andrews ended up here tonight? Did he have bad luck or what?

At first he'd tried pretending he didn't see her, but it was too late. The minute he sat down she was at his side, determined to talk his ear off. She had even brought a drink over to him from the bar.

He hadn't had a chance to touch it.

He didn't want anything Leslie was offering.

Maybe if he excused himself to go to the bathroom, Leslie would be gone by the time he came out.

He looked up and had the breath knocked out of him.

He was hypnotized by the blond bombshell who had just entered the room.

His wife.

She wore a red cocktail dress with a slit up to her thigh. Every time she took a step, a glimpse of those long slim legs teased him, along with every male within a fifty mile radius. The dress hugged every delectable curve, and the plunging neckline revealed her full breasts.

He shifted in his seat, attempting to ease the

growing tightness in his pants. When he lifted his eyes from her breasts to her face, their gazes met. He stared into those emerald pools and envisioned himself taking her right here on the linen-covered table.

"Hello." Her tone was cool as she flicked her eyes in Leslie's direction before fixing a glare on him. She looked mad as hell, though she tried to hide it behind a veneer of indifference.

Leslie's head jerked up. She seemed genuinely shocked to see his wife. "Celeste?"

"She apparently saw me come in and brought me a drink." He didn't need Leslie insinuating anything that wasn't true.

Raising a beautiful eyebrow, she addressed him. "Oh, well, I don't want to interrupt."

"I just brought him a drink to celebrate the birth of his son," Leslie answered.

He winced at her choice of words. She was deliberately trying to bait Celeste and he wasn't having it.

"Our son," Eric corrected, keeping his eyes on Celeste.

"Well, by all means. Let's celebrate Eric's son." Celeste smirked at him and grabbed his drink.

"Wait." Leslie reached for the drink, but it was too late.

Celeste threw back the shot and placed the empty glass in front of him without blinking. "Tell me, Leslie, are you here to try to fuck my husband like you tried to in Atlanta?"

"I just remembered an appointment." Leslie grabbed her purse and scrambled to stand.

"No need to rush off. What Eric and I have to

say to each other won't take long." Celeste narrowed her eyes at him.

Leslie tripped as she rushed past Celeste toward the door.

"I wonder why she left so quickly."

He stood up. "I don't give a shit. I'm just glad she's gone. We need to talk."

He held out her chair. As she gracefully sat down, her scent surrounded him. He closed his eyes, attempting to control himself from the overwhelming desire only she aroused in him. When he opened them, he made the mistake of glancing down, giving him an uninhibited view of her breasts.

"Are you going to stand all night or can we get this little talk out of the way?"

"I prefer standing. It gives me a spectacular view," he said against her ear. She shivered.

"Well, I'm not going to keep talking to you over my shoulder."

After they ordered, she averted her gaze from his and drummed her fingers on the table. Catching her hand in his, he brought her hand to his lips and kissed her knuckles. "Are you nervous?"

"No. Just ready to get this conversation over with. The sooner I can leave, the sooner you can go find Leslie." She smirked.

He frowned. "As I said, she spotted me when I walked in. The minute I sat down, she came over with a drink. I tried ignoring her but she wouldn't take the hint."

☾

SHE TRIED PULLING HER HAND from his, but he tightened his grip. With her free hand, she touched her temple and closed her eyes.

"Are you all right?" He leaned closer.

"I'm fine." Opening her eyes, she waved her hand. "I guess that Leslie has a habit of that."

"Of what?"

"Buying you drinks." She took a deep breath as her eyelids fluttered closed.

"What do you mean?"

"She's the one that sent you that drink at the Cryptic party. She put something in it." She laughed.

"How do you know that? I didn't even see her at the party."

She closed her eyes. "The demon told me. He said he didn't know who it was, but I figured it was her. She drives that red Audi, right?"

"Yeah. How did you know?"

"Because I saw it parked at your uncle's house as I walked up to the door. I saw the same car when you threw her out of our cocktail party. She was trying to spike your drink to get you to sleep with her." She opened her eyes.

"Instead, you slept with me."

He moved closer and slid his hand to her wrist. "You're pupils are dilated. Did you take anything before you got here?"

"Of course not. The only thing I had was your scotch." She wanted to glare at him for insinuating she was high, but she didn't really feel anger. She felt something else instead.

Her body burned like she had a fever. But it was unlike anything she'd experienced. Pleasure arced between her legs, and all she wanted to do was take all her clothes off and straddle him right there.

She inhaled deeply. She'd just been drugged.

CHAPTER FORTY-NINE

ERIC GRABBED THE EMPTY GLASS and held it up to the light. On the very bottom lay a thin layer of crystals.

"Damn it."

"What?" Her eyes were closed and she gripped the seat of her chair.

"Celeste. Look at me." He cupped her face.

She slowly opened her eyes. The green of her eyes seemed darker and her lips curved upward.

He swallowed.

"I think Leslie put something in my drink. I think it's the same stuff that I had that night at the party."

She leaned closer, her lips inches from his ear. "Did it make you incredibly horny?" Her lips brushed his ear as she spoke and he groaned softly.

"Celeste, I think we need to leave." He threw his napkin on the table.

"I'll tell you what I need. I need you inside me." Her hand traveled into his lap and grabbed his cock.

He groaned. "We need to leave. Now."

She slung her leg over his, immobilizing him. She grabbed his napkin and placed it in his lap.

He moaned as she stroked him through his pants. Raising her eyebrow, she smiled. "Do you think you are ready for everything I'm going to do to you?"

He watched helplessly as her pink tongue darted out and followed the curve of her top lip.

Her hand inched up to the top of his zipper. He grabbed her hand. "We can't do anything right here."

"Why not?" She licked his neck. He didn't think he had ever experienced anything so good in his entire life. He didn't care that they were in a public restaurant. It had been too long. He needed to touch her.

He cupped her face and brought it to his. He kissed her deep, tasting the sweetness of her mouth. She kissed him back, clearly just as desperate for him.

The waiter cleared his throat and he broke the kiss. "Sir, I've brought the champagne you asked for. Would you like to taste it?"

The waiter stared at Celeste in fascination and lust as she nibbled at his neck. She either didn't notice or didn't care.

"We'll take it with us." Eric threw a wad of hundred-dollar bills at the surprised waiter and stood.

Her dress got caught on his zipper, exposing more of her leg than she'd likely ever intended. Ignoring the dumbstruck waiter, he straightened her dress and quickly exited the restaurant.

When he got to his car, he reached for her door. She shoved him up against the car and pressed her body against his.

Grabbing him around his neck, she pulled him into the kiss, her mouth demanding and thorough.

His hands were everywhere at once: over her face and down her back to her ass. Holding her tight against him, he kissed her back with all the love and lust in his body. Without warning, she slipped her hand between them and into his pants. Her cool fingers wrapped around his cock.

She was going to make him come in his pants if he didn't make her stop. He gripped her arms and pulled her away.

"Get in the car." He opened the door and put her in. He knew if they stayed there he would end up taking her right there in front of the restaurant.

No sooner had he gotten in than she maneuvered her body over the console and halfway into his seat. Picking her up, he settled her in the passenger's seat and tightened the seatbelt.

She narrowed her eyes at him. When she spoke her voice was low and sexy and feral. "Do you think you are going to stop me from fucking you senseless?"

His throat dried up at her question. He turned his attention back to the road. Picking up his cell phone, he punched in Andrea Leigh's number.

When he finished his conversation, he looked at Celeste, "Andrea Leigh is going to watch the baby overnight. She picked up some baby formula so he should be good until we get back in the morning. I told her that you were with me and that we still needed time to talk."

She unbuckled her seatbelt and began unbuttoning his shirt with one hand while licking his neck.

She went from licking to sucking, causing his balls to tighten painfully.

He was so distracted that he almost rear-ended a car in the parking lot of the hotel.

Quickly killing the engine, he pulled her onto his lap and kissed her. His hands raced over the front of her dress, feeling each curve under the thin, silky material. She wiggled her bottom in his lap. Gripping her hip, his hand made contact with her thigh where the slit of the dress gaped open.

"Touch me," she said against his neck. She grabbed his wrist and pulled his hand under her dress. His fingers found her thin, lacy thong, and he groaned in frustration.

A persistent tap sounded on his window. He squinted against the blinding light being wielded by the hotel's security guard. Rolling down the window, he glared back at the man.

"Sir, this is not public parking."

"I am staying at this hotel," he said impatiently. Celeste gave the security guard only a glance before slipping her hand inside Eric's shirt.

"Then maybe you two should head up to your room."

He rolled up the window and managed to get out of the car with Celeste still attached to him. The man gave him a wink as he got a good look at Celeste. Scooping her up in his arms, Eric strode to the hotel's entrance.

Ignoring the shocked glances of the other guests, Eric marched straight to the elevator. After the longest elevator ride in history, Eric pulled his key out of his pocket and tried to unlock the door. Celeste was busy pulling his shirt off his shoulders and making her way down his body with her mouth. He attempted to open the door three times before he succeeded.

Once inside, he hooked the "do not disturb" sign on the doorknob and locked it. When he turned around, he found Celeste nearly naked. She stood before him in red panties and matching bra.

She was glorious.

Grabbing him by his hand, she led him toward the bed and shoved him backward into the mattress.

Stunned and aroused, he looked up at her as she crawled on top of him. Moving her face to his stomach, she licked him in one long stroke from his stomach to his neck. Catching him off guard, she had his pants unzipped and his dick in her hand before he knew it. Her hand fisted around him and slowly moved up and down. Swiping her thumb across the head of his cock, she lifted it to her mouth and sucked it.

"Baby, you got to stop that or I'm not going to hold out much longer."

"I don't want you to hold out." Celeste gave his cock another tortuous lick.

"I do." Eric pulled her up his body and kissed her.

He pulled at the back of her bra, desperate to have her naked against him. While he slipped her straps off her slender shoulders, his mouth followed, making a trail of hot, wet kisses from her mouth to her shoulder to her breast. When his mouth closed over a hardened nipple, she dug her fingers in his hair and pulled his face closer.

"Don't stop," she moaned.

"I don't plan on it."

He sucked and teased and licked her nipple until she was writhing underneath him and then moved to the other breast. Pressing her back into the bed, he worshiped her bare flesh with his tongue.

He licked past her breast to her flat stomach. She moaned as his tongue found the inside of her thigh. With lightning speed, he ripped her panties off and pressed his face between her thighs.

She arched in pleasure as his tongue licked her soft flesh. She pulled his hair, demanding he give her what she wanted. His tongue flicked her clit before he closed his mouth around her and sucked. It didn't take long for her climax to build and explode. She bucked against him, but he held her against his mouth, making her ride out wave after wave of pleasure.

With his heart echoing in his ears, he moved up her body and brought his mouth down on hers and positioned himself at her entrance. But she pressed her hand against his chest, pushing him back. Confused, he looked down at her.

"I want to be on top," she said huskily.

With his arm around her waist, he flipped their bodies, letting her straddle him. She kissed him hard while sliding her body down his. She impaled herself on his cock. They moaned in each other's mouths.

"You are mine, understand?" He forced her to look at him. "You belong to no one else but me."

She was wet and tight and he didn't think he would last ten seconds. It felt too damn good. Gripping her hips, he stopped her from rocking against him. They locked eyes, desire burning through them both. With his hands, he guided her up along his shaft slowly and brought her down with the same measured rhythm.

She panted heavily with each thrust. Raising his head, he captured a nipple between his lips and sucked.

Impatiently, she began to ride him faster, pushing him back against the bed. Her eyes began to gloss over with pleasure, and he felt the sting of her fingernails digging into his chest. Crying out, she dropped her head back as she once again found her orgasm. Her cry of pleasure set off his own, and he gripped her hips and plunged hard as he came deep inside her.

☾

ERIC WATCHED HER SLEEP. SHE had collapsed, exhausted, onto his chest after they'd made love four more times. Her body curled into his and her hands were tucked underneath her face. All he wanted was to be near her.

He smiled as she shivered in her sleep. He reached down to the foot of the bed and tugged up the sheet, covering them both. His body was exhausted, yet he couldn't sleep. Sighing, he contented himself with lying back and holding her against him until the morning came.

CHAPTER FIFTY

CELESTE ROLLED OVER AND OPENED her eyes. Her breasts ached and her body was sore. She glanced over at Eric. He was sound asleep beside her. His arm, thrown across her waist, tightened and pulled her closer, as if sensing she was awake.

She recalled last night's events and felt the heat rise to her cheeks.

What the hell had she done? The plan had been to make her speech and then leave him high and dry, not to jump him in the restaurant.

Turning, she winced as the sheet dragged across her sensitive breasts, making her all too aware of the fact that she needed to nurse. She wasn't used to her breasts feeling so heavy.

She slid closer to the edge of the bed, trying her best not to wake him. As she sat up, his arm wrapped around her, pulling her up against his hard chest.

"Where are you going?" His mouth moved against her neck. She shivered at his touch.

"I was going to get dressed. I need to get back."

She tried to focus on keeping her voice calm and to ignore the sensations he was causing between her legs.

He let go of her waist only to cup her face and turn her around to him.

"Why did you leave me?"

"I didn't. Andrea Leigh was coming to Boston anyway and wanted some company."

"The truth, Celeste."

Fine. He wanted the truth. He would get it. "I left because it hurt too much to be around you."

"Andrea Leigh told me what you said."

"Then why are we even having this conversation?" She tried to pull out of his grip.

"Because there is something you don't know."

"Look, I know you love Christian. I can see that. But I refuse to be tied to a man who doesn't love me. I think we can agree on shared custody."

"I came here looking for you because I thought you left because you didn't love me anymore. You seemed different since . . . well . . . you know . . . that night. I thought that you were regretting being with me, and so by coming here you were telling me your intention to leave me for good. I thought you left because you hated me because I failed to keep you safe."

"I don't hate you, Eric."

"I know that now. I spoke with Andrea Leigh yesterday and she told me why you left. Celeste, there is something about that night that you don't know."

She blinked back tears.

"You said you saw me kissing the Queen that night."

"That's because I did see you." Celeste glared through her tears.

"No, you didn't."

"Don't try to tell me what I saw. I'm not crazy." She tried to escape, but Eric's grasp was iron. Tears escaped down her cheek.

"No. What you saw was Donovan, who shifted into me. Donovan was the one kissing the Queen."

"Donovan?" She frowned. "But I thought he couldn't shift into humans."

"He didn't say he couldn't, just that he didn't like to."

"It wasn't you?"

He shook his head and grinned. "No, sweetheart, it wasn't me. I would never do that to you."

She wasn't about to give in that easily. Because that certainly didn't explain everything. "Then why was Leslie with you last night?"

"I have no idea. Someone must have told her I was traveling to Boston. The restaurant we met at is one of my favorites when I'm here. She must have called to ask whether I made reservations for that evening, because as soon as I sat down, she came over to my table."

"With another attempt to drug you and get you into bed."

He chuckled. "Yes, well, that didn't go as she planned. You are the one who got me into bed." He traced her cheek with his fingertips. "Celeste, I've not been with another woman since I meet you."

Her eyes widened. "No one?"

"No. I've wanted you, only you. Since that first night with you, I've not been attracted to anyone else."

"What about when you married me? Did you do it because you were still on suspension? Did you marry me because you were afraid of another scandal where you would lose your job?"

His eyes widened.

"Leslie was very eager to share that bit of information with me."

He inhaled and held her gaze. "Honestly?"

"Honestly." She braced herself.

"Yes."

All the air left her lungs.

"I knew that I had tried to convince myself that was the reason I had asked you to marry me. My head reminded me of that daily in order to keep my distance from you. But my heart didn't seem to listen."

Her stomach fluttered in beat with her heart.

"I knew I wanted you to be my wife because I had never loved another like I love you. When you are not with me I can hardly breathe. You own me. I can't live without you. Celeste, I love you."

They were the most heartbreakingly beautiful words she'd ever heard. Tears spilled down her face. She didn't care. Reaching up, she touched his lips with her fingertips.

"You love me."

He smiled down at her. He pressed his lips to her wet cheeks and kissed away her tears. *"I enter this marriage of my own free will. I pledge myself to be faithfully yours and no other's. I pledge to share my body with you and no other. I pledge to give my love to you and no other. I pledge to protect you from danger, both visible and invisible, and I will be a shield for you in difficult times. I shall stand by your side as your mate as long as I draw breath."*

Wrapping her arms around his neck she clung to him, crying and laughing. "You memorized those vows?"

"I found them fascinating, so I asked your father for a copy of them. They stuck in my head." He looked down into her eyes. "Now, you aren't leaving me?"

"No. I'm not leaving you. I'm afraid you are stuck with me for a very long time."

"Promise me." He voice was hoarse against her mouth. "Promise that you'll never leave me."

"I promise that I'll never leave you. And I promise that I'll always love you. I think I loved you from the moment I saw you."

His eyes darkened with desire. She didn't think she'd ever had anyone look at her quite like Eric Nordstrom did.

"I don't think I will ever let you out of my sight or my arms again. In fact, I intend on keeping you in bed a while longer. We've plenty of time before we need to check on the baby."

She pulled him down to the bed, shoving the sheet off their bodies. "We have all the time in the world."

THE END

OTHER BOOKS BY JODI VAUGHN

RISE OF THE ARKANSAS WEREWOLVES
Series

BY THE LIGHT OF THE MOON (BOOK 1)
BENEATH A BLOOD LUST MOON (BOOK 2)
DESIRES OF A FULL MOON (BOOK 3)
DARKSIDE OF THE MOON (BOOK 4)
SHADOWS OF A WOLF MOON (BOOK 5)
SECRETS OF A SILVER MOON (BOOK 6)

CLOVERTON
Series

CHRISTMAS IN CLOVERTON (Novella)
LOST WITHOUT YOU (BOOK 1)
LOST ALL CONTROL (BOOK 2)

SOMEWHERE, TEXAS
Series

SADDLE UP
TROUBLE IN TEXAS
BAD MEDICINE

AUTHOR BIO

JODI WAS BORN AND RAISED in Mississippi. Her deep Southern roots and love of the paranormal led her to write Southern Paranormal novels. She currently lives in Northeast Arkansas with her handsome husband, brilliant son, a temperamental swan, and yellow lab that is fond of retrieving turtles when duck season is over.

Find her on Facebook, Jodi Vaughn, author.
Follow her on Twitter @JodiVaughn1
Sign up for her newsletter and check out her website
http://jodivaughn.com
Find her on Instagram at VaughnJodi

69361126R00239

Made in the USA
Columbia, SC
12 April 2017